Hades raised his head to look into her eyes, which were just now the colour of the ocean, green and mysterious but full of moonlight. 'You will never leave me—say it, Katherine. Say it now!'

'I shall never . . .'

The words were lost as he gave a cry of savage triumph, his mouth devouring hers as he trapped her beneath him in the sand. Once more Katherine was swept away on a tide of passion, her cries of pleasure mingling with the beating of the waves against the reef.

Her surrender was total as she gasped out his name. 'Hades, I love you . . . love you . . .'

And still he did not say, 'I love you, Katherine.'

Anne Herries was born in Wiltshire but spent much of her early life at Hastings, to which she attributes her love of the sea. She now lives in Cambridge and often writes in her garden surrounded by glorious trees and birds which are so tame they come to the kitchen door to be fed. She is happily married and credits much of her success to her husband, who has constantly encouraged her to continue with her earliest dream—writing.

Anne Herries has written three other Masquerade Historical Romances—DEVIL'S KIN, THE WOLF OF ALVAR and BEWARE THE CONQUEROR.

DEMON'S WOMAN

ANNE HERRIES

MILLS & BOON LIMITED
15–16 BROOK'S MEWS
LONDON W1A 1DR

First published in Great Britain 1985
by Mills & Boon Limited

This edition 1985

ISBN 0 263 75273 9

Set in 10 on 11 pt Linotron Times
04–1285–65,200

Photoset by Rowland Phototypesetting Limited
Bury St Edmunds, Suffolk
Made and printed in Great Britain by
Cox & Wyman Limited, Reading

CHAPTER ONE

'YOU CANNOT force me to marry a man I have never met!' Lady Katherine Winters cried, her sea-green eyes flashing with pride as she faced her uncle.

Sir William Morton frowned, his fleshy face dark with anger as he looked at the proud beauty before him, and felt a sharp desire to slap her. He was prevented from doing so not by the presence of his wife, Lady Margaret, Katherine's aunt and sister of the late Earl of Dunline, but because he did not wish to bruise the girl's delicate skin.

'No one is compelling you to do anything at the moment,' he said with forced patience. 'Don Francisco is merely coming to discuss a possible marriage between you and his son.'

'Don Francisco Domingues.' Katherine's lips curled with scorn. 'My father would never have permitted a Spaniard within the castle walls, let alone consider a marriage!'

'Katherine, you should not speak so churlishly to your uncle,' Lady Margaret said, seeing the storm-clouds gathering in her husband's eyes. 'Sir William wants only what is best for you, and this marriage has the Queen's approval. Remember you are Her Majesty's ward, now that both your father and brother are dead.'

'Lewis is not dead,' Katherine replied, tears hovering

on her long, dark lashes at the mention of her twin. 'I know he's not.'

'Katherine, my dear . . .' Lady Margaret's face was anxious. 'His ship was lost at sea more than a year ago; if Lewis were alive we must have heard of him by now. Your uncle has sent out a dozen emissaries to look for him.'

'I know.' Katherine turned away, moving to the window to look out across the sea. The sun was setting in a blaze of glory, turning the water to red-gold as it sank beyond the horizon. Momentarily, the flame of the girl's hair mingled with the sunset and she became almost a part of it.

Katherine blinked away her tears. She would not let them persuade her that Lewis was dead when her heart and mind cried out that he still lived. She had been born only a heartbeat later than her brother, and all their lives they had been inseparable. Even when Lewis ran away to sea against his father's wishes, Katherine had known his joys and his sorrows. She was not aware of him at all times, but only when he felt something very deeply. The awareness of him usually came to her in the lonely hours before dawn: she had experienced it again last night, hearing him call to her with that inner voice.

Turning back to face her uncle, Katherine's eyes glittered. 'Very well, I shall meet Don Francisco, providing . . .' She paused, watching the cunning look creep into Sir William's eyes. 'Providing you send out more emissaries to search for Lewis.'

Her uncle smiled, but his eyes remained cold. 'As you wish—though it will be a waste of money.'

'My money,' Katherine reminded him.

Sir William's mouth tightened with suppressed anger. For too many years he had been made to feel his inferiority by the Earl, and now this chit dared to flaunt her wealth in his face! Not for much longer, he thought, controlling his temper. Don Francisco had promised him a fortune—her fortune—if he could persuade his niece to the marriage, and he meant to have it—one way or another!

'I'm sure you will be pleased with the marriage once you meet Don Francisco,' Lady Margaret said, relieved that the girl had capitulated. 'He is such a charming man, and so handsome . . .'

Katherine regarded her with mingled pity and contempt. She could feel no affection for her aunt, who had never shown any sign of wanting her love. As a child, Katherine had looked to her for comfort when her mother died, but none had been forthcoming.

The Earl's sister, still unmarried when his wife died, might have been expected to devote her life to the two young children, but Lady Margaret had other ideas. Soon after, she had wed a man of small fortune who married her—despite her plain face—for the wealth she brought him, which he soon wasted. Since then she had gone in fear of Sir William's rages, though he had controlled them while the Earl lived; but it was six months now since the death of Katherine's father, and she'd felt the sting of his blows often enough.

The Earl's last act had been to sign a new will leaving everything he owned to Katherine, and making her a ward of Queen Mary I. The Earl did not trust his brother-in-law and had hoped to protect his daughter by this strategy. It was, however, some time since he had visited the Court and he was not aware of the Queen's failing health, or of her desperate wish to please her Spanish husband.

When Don Francisco Domingues arrived at Court bearing a letter from King Philip of Spain, begging his wife to look kindly upon his emissary, the Don's success was assured. Queen Mary would do anything to please her husband, so anxious was she for him to visit her again. The Spaniard's request for a marriage to be arranged between his son, Don Esteban, and the Earl of Dunline's daughter met with her instant approval, which was given without any consultation of Katherine's wishes.

The Don was wealthy, and a friend of the Spanish King—most important in the Queen's eyes!—and the miniature he showed her of his son was charming. The youth was nineteen, handsome in a delicate way, with dreaming eyes. His father said he was a poet and could sing like a bird. What more could any girl want in a husband? Besides, there was nothing against the marriage; the girl's uncle and aunt were eager for it to take place.

Nothing, that is, but Lady Katherine's stubborn refusal to meet Don Francisco, and now that had suddenly ended. Looking at her, Sir William's eyes narrowed in suspicion—why had she changed her mind?

Seeing the wilful line of Katherine's mouth and the haughty pride in her eyes, he knew he was right to doubt her. She was planning some mischief: he would need to watch her carefully if he was not to be thwarted at the end!

Katherine saw the expression on her uncle's face and knew he suspected her. She frowned, annoyed with herself for giving in too quickly. She should have known he would not be easily fooled.

'If I am to meet Don Francisco next week, I must select my gown,' she said. 'But a meeting promises nothing—I shall not marry his son unless it pleases me to do so.'

She curtsied to her aunt, walking swiftly from the room lest Sir William should detain her. She was running up the twisting stone stairs to her apartments before he had collected himself sufficiently to call her back.

Katherine locked the door of her bedchamber behind her. She was taking no chances. Since her father's death, Sir William was becoming more and more domineering. She shuddered to think what he might have done if he had been appointed her guardian! The door safely barred, she made no attempt to look through her gowns, never having intended to do so. Instead, she went to the fireplace, her hand seeking a certain spot in the carved stone above. As she pressed, a section of the wall slid back to reveal a flight of steep steps leading down into the bowels of the castle.

Without hesitation, Katherine stepped into the gloom of the secret passage. It was growing dark, but she had played here so often with Lewis in childhood that she could have found her way blindfolded. Besides, Mathew was waiting for her, and she must hurry or he would think she wasn't coming. She smiled as she thought of Mathew Sommers impatiently pacing the floor of the tiny room which was their meeting-place. They had been driven to such desperate measures by the watchful eyes of Sir William, since they knew he would forbid them to meet if he learned what was afoot.

When the girl reached the hidden room, which could be reached only from her bedchamber and the armoury, Mathew had lighted a taper and she could see his anxious face as he came to take her in his arms. She let him kiss her once before pushing him away impatiently.

'We must talk,' she said. 'The time grows short. They mean to force me to this marriage if they can. What news of the ship, Mathew?'

Mathew sighed, letting her go reluctantly. For some weeks he had secretly been engaged in negotiations to purchase a ship. Katherine had persuaded him into a venture he privately thought a forlorn hope: she intended to go herself in search of her twin. Her plan had been formed over many months, but now it had taken on a new urgency.

'They can't make you marry him . . .' Mathew began, knowing he was deceiving himself. If the Queen held fast to her intent, Katherine would have to yield eventually. Besides, he knew that his own love for the girl was hopeless. It was she who had teased him into confessing it; she who planned their meetings and made him believe in a future for them. 'What's the use? They'll never let you marry me.'

Katherine frowned as she saw the weakness in his face, wondering why she liked him. Perhaps it was his very weakness, she thought. She had always been used to strong-willed men. Both her father and Lewis dominated her, despite her hot temper, but their arguments had always ended in loving reconciliations. Not for the first time Katherine wondered if Mathew's adoration would eventually grow tiresome, but she dismissed the thought as disloyal. Mathew was kind and he loved her—and she needed his help to carry out her daring plan.

'If we succeed in escaping from the castle, my uncle will not be able to stop us,' she said, with a toss of her head. 'So, have you found us a ship?'

'Yes, I think so. But it will cost a great deal of money.'

'What does that matter?' Her eyes glinted dangerously. 'I shall take my jewels with me, and you will steal the chest of gold from my father's strong-room. I have the key here.' She touched the bodice of her gown. 'I shall give it to you now, and you must take a little at a time until we are ready. You will buy the ship and hire a crew. In the meantime I shall pacify my uncle by pretending to agree to this marriage.'

Mathew was appalled by her calm statement that he should steal the Earl's gold. 'But you do not know where to start looking for Lewis . . .' he protested weakly.

'We have been through this before,' Katherine snapped. 'I know where his ship went down. I found some old charts in the armoury, and there are several islands in the vicinity. I think Lewis managed to get to one of them but hasn't been able to send a message. My uncle says his men have visited all the islands, but I don't believe him.'

Mathew stared at her. In her anger she was beautiful beyond belief, setting his mind on fire with her spirit of adventure. Looking at her was a physical pain to him unless he could hold her in his arms.

'You will help me, won't you?' she whispered, moving closer as her lips parted temptingly for his kiss.

He caught her to him, groaning as he felt the desire churning inside him and tasted the sweet honey of her lips. She held him in the palm of her dainty hand and he knew he would risk anything for the faint hope that one day she would be all his.

As their lips met, the fire burned deep inside him, making him shudder with longing. 'Katherine, my darling,' he whispered thickly against the silk of her hair. 'I want you so much, let me love you completely.'

Katherine jerked away from him, a little frightened by the storm of emotion she had aroused in him. Mathew had always been so humble, asking only for the smallest favours. She saw the passion in his eyes and felt a shiver of revulsion: somehow she had never thought beyond the innocent kisses they'd shared.

'No!' she cried, though she was not sure what she was refusing. 'Would you dishonour me before we are wed? We shall be married by the ship's captain. Until then . . .'

Mathew caught her hand, kissing it contritely. 'Forgive me, I forgot myself. It was only that I love you so much.'

He looked so anxious that Katherine forgave him. He was gentle and kind, and she did love him. She did! It would be different when they were married, she assured herself. It was merely modesty which prevented her from feeling the same passion as he did. A maiden was not supposed to have such feelings until her wedding night. Only wicked women thought of the pleasures of the flesh, like the kitchen-maid her aunt had dismissed last year.

The girl had wept bitterly when she was turned out, and Katherine had begged her aunt to be merciful, but Lady Margaret was adamant.

'The wench knew what she was doing. Now she must pay the price,' Lady Margaret said. 'Your father will have no wantonness in this house.'

The Earl had been too ill to concern himself with the problem, so Katherine could only send another maid to the unfortunate girl with a few coins. She had often wondered why the wench had acted so foolishly. Katherine quite enjoyed being kissed, but kissing didn't bring babies, and Anna wouldn't tell her what the kitchen-maid had done to get the child—except that it was something wicked.

Anna was Katherine's nurse. She had fussed over her as a child, doing her best to take the place of the girl's mother, but now she was old and spent all her time in her own little room, dreaming by the fire.

Katherine had once asked her what marriage entailed, but she had answered in riddles.

'You'll know soon enough, child,' she said, shaking her head. 'You'll know soon enough . . .'

But Katherine didn't know, for she had no one to tell

her. She dared not ask her aunt, and when she mentioned it to the maids who waited on her, they only giggled and answered with sly remarks which mystified her more than ever. Ashamed and angry at her ignorance, she did not press for an explanation—but she knew there was something more than kissing. Something that was not permitted for a girl of her station until she was wed.

At seventeen, she was old enough to be wed and with children of her own. Her father had spoken of a marriage when she was but fifteen, but he had been reluctant to part with his beloved child and there seemed to be plenty of time. Then came the terrible quarrel between father and son, resulting in Lewis running off to sea. After that, Katherine's marriage had been spoken of no more.

Happy in her home, which was situated on the north coast of England and close to the Scottish border, Katherine had been content to stay with her adored and adoring father. She was so like the beautiful lady who had given her birth, that it was hardly surprising that the Earl chose to keep her by his side. And she had never thought of taking a husband until her uncle first told her of the arrangements for the match. Until that moment her stolen meetings with Mathew had been a game, and she had merely toyed with her plans for finding her twin. Of late those plans had monopolised her thoughts, and now it was a matter of urgency. Mathew was important to her: she could not manage without him.

'Of course I forgive you,' she said, reaching up to kiss his cheek. 'But you must do as I ask you.'

'You know I will,' he replied. 'I am your slave.'

Katherine laughed, her eyes confident now. How could she have been afraid of Mathew even for a moment? She would always be able to twist him around her finger.

'I must go,' she said, avoiding him when he would have drawn her back into his embrace. 'Meet me here again tomorrow.'

Then she was gone, taking a light from his taper and running back the way she had come.

Dressed in a gown of flowing silk embroidered richly with silver threads and pearls, Katherine walked slowly down the wide stone staircase to the great hall of the castle. It was still called a castle, though of later years, when the need for defence against attack from the north had lessened, much of the old fabric had been replaced with smaller, more comfortable apartments.

It was now no more than a fortified manor house, with walled gardens where the murky waters of the moat had once flowed. Since the establishment of the Tudor dynasty the powerful nobles no longer warred with their neighbours, and though Dunline Castle still boasted a portcullis, it was never used. Attack would now be more likely to come from the sea, which washed the silvery beaches of these northern shores. But, for the moment, England was at peace, and there were no soldiers garrisoned at Dunline.

Yet the castle teemed with life, for it was the heart of the village built around it and the source of the people's livelihood. For several days there had been much coming and going as an army of servants prepared for the visit of Don Francisco and his retinue. It seemed that the Don always travelled with his servants and a small band of armed men.

Katherine asked scornfully if the Don were afraid of being attacked, but Sir William shrugged, saying, 'The roads are full of vagabonds and beggars. Don Francisco is a prudent man.'

Katherine's curiosity was aroused, despite her determination to refuse his suit on his son's behalf. She was not a piece of merchandise to be sold to the highest bidder! But she would greet the Don politely, as befitted a lady of her station, while secretly continuing with her plans to escape.

Pausing midway on the stairs to look down at the vast room, her eyes travelled over the faces of the guests assembled to meet Don Francisco. Everyone of importance in the neighbourhood was gathered beneath the stone arches of the great hall, for the Spaniard was an influential man in his own country and a friend of the English Queen's husband. He must be accorded every respect, despite the loathing most Englishmen felt for the Spanish.

Katherine's gaze came to rest on a tall silver-haired man with a long nose and bright, hooded eyes. He seemed to sense her interest, turning to fasten on her a penetrating stare that made her want to fly back to her apartments. His cold eyes terrified her, and his mouth had a cruel look. She knew at once that this man was her enemy!

Girding her courage about her as a cloak, Katherine forced her stiff lips to a smile. Her head lifted a little higher as she saw him come to the foot of the staircase with Sir William. She walked down to meet them, praying that her face did not betray the wild beating of her heart.

'Lady Katherine—this is Don Francisco.'

'Lady Katherine,' the Don said, his voice like cold steel beneath a velvet sheath. 'I have heard of your beauty, but my informants lied. You are beyond beauty . . .'

'Don Francisco.' Katherine inclined her head regally, ignoring his compliment. 'In my brother's absence, I welcome you to Castle Dunline.'

A glint of amusement flickered in the Don's eyes, but Katherine could not tell what it meant. She sensed a hardness in him which frightened her. If she had ever intended to consider his offer of marriage on Don Esteban's behalf, she would have refused it now. Instinctively she distrusted the Spaniard, and the touch of his hand on her arm sent shivers of fear coursing through her. Yet she gave no sign of it, her lovely eyes glittering as she assumed the mantle of châtelaine of Dunline Castle.

'You must tell me of your country,' she said, smiling into his cold eyes. 'I would hear of your home, sir.'

Don Francisco bared his teeth in a wolfish grin. 'Spain is a land of bright colours and sunshine, Lady Katherine. My home is close to the sea, as is yours, but the winds are soft and warm, scented with the fragrance of flowers, and the water is blue—not grey like the English sea.'

Katherine tilted her chin at him. 'Sometimes the sea is grey, sometimes green or blue—it changes with the seasons.'

The Don laughed. 'As the colour of your eyes changes with your moods.'

Katherine lowered her lashes, veiling her eyes. She must be careful, for this man was clever: she must do nothing to make him suspicious of her.

'And what of Don Esteban?' she asked. 'You tell me nothing of your son, sir.'

'You have seen his likeness?'

'Yes, I have the miniature you sent me. Don Esteban has a pleasant face—but this is not a reason for marriage. I would know more of him before I decide.'

Katherine thought she saw a flash of anger in the

Don's eyes, but then he smiled. 'How sensible you are, Lady Katherine, to realise that a handsome face is not the most important of a young man's attributes. Few girls of your age would agree. Esteban is a poet, a dreamer, a singer of songs. He loves beauty—that is why I know he will love you.'

'But he has never seen me. How can you be sure?'

'I am certain, my lady.' The Don's eyes were like the icy waters of the English sea in winter. 'You are very like your mother, and my son has already fallen in love with her likeness.'

'My mother?' Katherine stared at him, bewildered. 'You have a picture of my mother?'

'Why yes, did you not know?' The Don seemed surprised. 'Your father and I were once good friends.'

'No, I did not know.' Katherine frowned. 'He never spoke of you to me.'

The Don sighed. 'Alas, it was too many years ago. Our lives parted and circumstances prevented my coming to visit—but I knew my old friend had a daughter and I cherished the idea of a union between our two families. Come, my dear, do not disappoint me.'

Katherine gazed up at him, and for a moment she was almost swayed by his persuasive smile; then she remembered her father's hatred of anything Spanish and she knew the Don was lying. Suddenly she felt herself in terrible danger from this man and hardened her determination to escape from him at all costs.

Her eyes were cold as she looked up at him. 'Then I must consider your offer most carefully, Don Francisco. You are to stay with us for a few days, and we shall learn to know each other a little better. But now we must join the others, for the feasting is about to begin.'

Katherine let the Don lead her to the high table, giving him the place of honour and sitting at his right hand. This was the signal for the guests to take their places, and for the banquet to begin. Katherine felt as if she were a prisoner, with the Don on one side of her and her uncle on the other. She cast an agonised glance at Mathew, who was sitting further down the table, below the salt, as befitted his lowly rank. It would be hours before she could speak to him, if she could manage it at all.

Not until the feasting was over, and the jugglers had begun to entertain the company, did Katherine escape from Don Francisco's side. He had kept her close by him throughout the evening, showering her with pretty compliments and telling her stories of his son. The youth seemed to be a fine swordsman and a brilliant horseman, as well as a poet. Indeed, the more the Don praised his son, the less inclined Katherine was to believe him.

Now, at last, he was engaged in conversation with some of the neighbouring gentry, and, ignoring her aunt's signal to go to her, Katherine slipped from the great hall into a small antechamber. Within seconds, Mathew joined her, embracing her swiftly in the dimly-lit room.

Katherine moved away from him impatiently: there were more important matters just now than a few snatched kisses. 'Have you secured the ship?' she asked.

Mathew sighed. 'Yes, the deeds were signed yesterday and are in my hands. She's called *Seabird*, and seems stout enough.'

'What about the crew?' Katherine glanced over her shoulder. 'When can she be ready to sail?'

'The Captain has been taking provisions on board all week; he says she could be ready to put to sea by tomorrow night.'

'Tomorrow!' Katherine's eyes sparkled with excitement. 'So soon? That's wonderful, Mathew. You have done well. Tell the Captain we shall join him after dark tomorrow night. He must anchor out in the bay and send a boat into our cove so that no one will become suspicious.'

'Are you sure you want to leave so quickly?' Mathew asked. His conscience had been greatly troubled of late, and he almost wished he had dissuaded her from the plan. 'Life on board ship is terribly hard: I don't think you realise what it will be like.'

Katherine pulled a face at him. 'You sound like my aunt. Oh, don't spoil it all, now! Besides, I must get away. Don Francisco makes me nervous: he's evil . . .'

Her voice wavered a little and Mathew looked at her in concern; it was not like Katherine to be afraid. He saw she was truly shaken and his doubts were smothered as he gazed into her lovely eyes.

'So be it. I'll arrange for all to be ready by tomorrow night.'

Katherine's brilliant smile was his reward. She kissed his cheek before leaving him to return to her guests.

The next morning Katherine went hawking with the Don, her uncle and Lady Margaret. The Spaniard was in a good humour as they rode leisurely through the pleasant countryside, watching the birds circling after their prey and talking idly to one another as they enjoyed the warm sunshine. Don Francisco leant towards Katherine as he described the mountains at a little village in Spain where he often spent part of the summer.

'The village is built at the foot of the mountains,' he told her. 'But my summer home is higher up; there a cool breeze brings ease to the hottest days. The view from the battlements is something you must see for yourself—nothing but sky, and hills covered with lush greenery.'

'It sounds beautiful,' Katherine said, thinking it sounded like a secure prison and determined never to find herself within its walls.

The day seemed to go on for ever, and the feasting that night was almost more than Katherine could bear; but at last it was over. She bid the Don and her uncle good night, dismayed to find that her aunt seemed set on accompanying her to her chamber.

Lady Margaret followed Katherine inside, closing the door behind her. 'Katherine, my dear,' she began, a false smile on her lips. 'Do you mean to give Don Francisco a favourable answer?'

Katherine looked at her hard. 'Did my uncle tell you to ask me that?'

Lady Margaret turned her face away, ashamed to meet the girl's clear eyes. 'Yes. He is determined on this marriage. You would be wiser to agree and save yourself pain, Katherine.'

'Then perhaps I will,' Katherine replied lightly.

Her aunt gave a sigh of relief. 'I do hope so, my dear, for your own sake. Sir William can be . . . unkind at times.'

Katherine shivered as she saw the look of fear in her eyes. She was convinced that unless she departed tonight, she would be forced into this marriage. She had always distrusted her uncle, but he had been afraid of her father. Now there was no one to protect her from him, and he would do with her as he pleased.

'I am very tired, aunt,' Katherine yawned, 'and I should like to be alone. You may tell Sir William I shall give him my answer tomorrow.'

'Think carefully before you decide.' Lady Margaret kissed the girl's cheek and went to the door. 'Good night.'

As soon as the sound of her aunt's footsteps had died

away, Katherine locked the door. From an oak hutch at the foot of her bed she selected various items of men's clothing. The hose and doublet had once belonged to her brother, but Katherine had worn them before when they took fencing lessons together.

Fencing was not a ladylike pursuit, and if Katherine's mother had lived, it was doubtful if she would have allowed the practice with Lewis. However, the Earl had indulged his beautiful daughter's whims, secretly amused because her quicksilver reactions could outwit both him and Lewis. Naturally, they could have won every time had they used brute force against her, but neither was willing to do so and Katherine's skill was a source of pride to them both.

She tore off her silken gown and petticoats, happy to be free of them for a while. It had always pleased her to dress as a youth, and she often wished she had been born a boy rather than a girl. She pinned her long hair into a tight knot on top of her head and pulled on a flattish cap with a little feather. Glancing into her handmirror, she smiled at her reflection. She could easily be mistaken for a delicate youth.

In planning the venture, Katherine had decided to take nothing with her except her jewels. She could buy what she needed with the gold that Mathew had secreted from her father's strong-room. Opening her jewel casket, she saw the miniature of Don Esteban lying on top. For a moment her hand hovered over it hesitantly. It was not really hers, even though the Don had given it to her as a token of his son's faith. However, it was set in heavy gold and surrounded by diamonds, rubies and pearls; on the back, the Don's family crest was delicately engraved. She added it to the little pile she was tying into her kerchief: she would need all her jewels to sell if the search for Lewis took longer than she hoped.

Letting her eyes travel round the familiar room one last time, Katherine stepped into the secret passage, carrying a lighted taper with her. When she reached the secret room, she found it empty. Mathew had not arrived. She frowned, wondering what had gone wrong, then she saw a piece of parchment lying on the table. Opening it, she scanned the words Mathew had hastily penned.

My dearest.
If I am not here at the appointed time, go to the cove without me. The ship will be waiting as agreed, but I may not be able to join you. I believe our plans have been discovered and that you are in grave danger. I shall come to the cove if I can, but do not wait for me. I love you.

Mathew.

Katherine stared at the letter in dismay, her hand shaking. Go to the cove alone! Suddenly the great adventure seemed much more frightening. She had relied on Mathew's company. For a moment she hesitated, reading his letter uncertainly. How could she sail a ship half-way round the world without Mathew by her side? She was on the point of returning to her chamber when she noticed that the words 'you are in grave danger' had been underlined.

If Mathew was telling her she must escape tonight, then the danger was imminent. Katherine folded his letter and held it to the taper, watching as it was consumed by the flames. Her face was pale but determined. She would go to the cove, but she would not sail without Mathew. The ship must stand out in the bay every night until he could slip away to join them. She would get word to him somehow!

Letting herself into the armoury, Katherine half expected her uncle to be waiting with the Don to pounce on her, but everything was quiet. She crept silently past the stacked weapons, pausing to pick up a small dagger and hide it in her jerkin. Then she went out into the courtyard, moving through the darkness like a shadow, glancing uneasily over her shoulder from time to time to see if she was watched.

No one was stirring in the castle. A crescent moon hung in the dark velvet sky, giving enough light to make her journey to the cove a simple matter. She clambered down the steep face of the cliffs, scraping her hands on the jagged rocks. How much easier it would have been with Mathew to help her!

Reaching the sandy beach at last, she looked about her, hoping that Mathew might be waiting after all. She called his name softly. 'Mathew! Mathew!'

No answer came. She was alone in the stillness of the night, the only sound the gentle lapping of calm waters on the shore. At first Katherine thought the ship was not there either, then she saw a dark shape gliding through the foam-crested waves. She watched as it pulled close to the shore and a man got out, wading through the shallow water.

Katherine ran to him. 'We must get back to the ship at once,' she said. 'Mathew hasn't come—I think our plans may have been discovered.'

'Get in, then,' the man growled, jerking his head towards the boat. 'If someone's betrayed us there'll be hell to pay.'

His words were greeted by a harsh laugh from the other man in the boat. 'We'll all be in Hades tonight,' he said. 'I wouldn't like to be the one to tell the Cap'n.'

Katherine sat crouched in the bottom of the boat, hugging her knees and shivering. She was suddenly very frightened of these rough men and almost wished herself back in her room at the castle. Only her pride and her fear of Don Francisco kept her from begging them to turn back.

Then it was too late. The rowing-boat scraped against the ship's timbers; calloused hands were pulling her to her feet and thrusting her up the rope ladder hanging over the side.

She climbed unsteadily, her heart thumping in her breast. The next moment she was standing on deck, and the boat crew were behind her.

'What's going on? Why are you back so soon? And who is this?'

A large man came towards them through the darkness, towering over them as Katherine raised her scared eyes to his face.

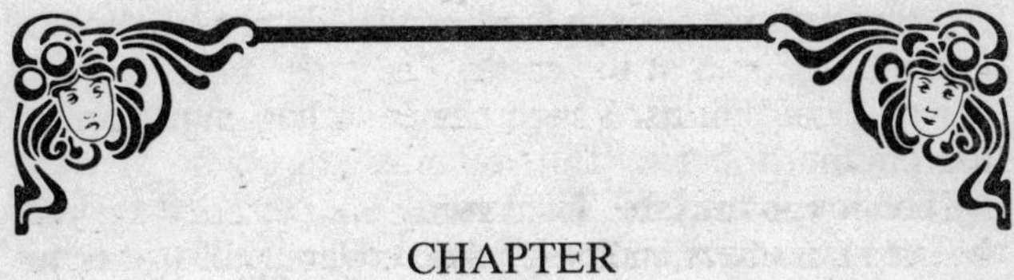

CHAPTER TWO

THE MOONLIGHT showed the man's face clearly, making Katherine draw a sharp breath. His features seemed to be sculptured from stone; his eyes shining like yellow topaz in the moon's glow. Hair the colour of molten gold framed a face tanned by wind and sun to a pale copper, its masculine beauty marred only by a tiny scar above his right brow. In one ear he wore a large gold ring, which glittered as he moved his head to one side, looking at Katherine.

He grinned, his teeth white against the bronze of his skin. 'What have we here?'

The sailor pushed her forward. 'Tell him, then. Tell Captain Hades what you told us.'

Katherine stared up into the Captain's face, her knees shaking. She had been frightened of Don Francisco, but the look in this man's eyes terrified her! She had never in her life seen any man so intensely male. Nowhere in his face could she see a trace of feeling; he had the fierce look of a warrior prince—lord of all he surveyed!

Swallowing hard, Katherine summoned every ounce of her courage. 'Mathew—Mr Sommers—isn't with me. He thinks our plans may have been discovered. He told me to come alone, but I won't sail without him—we must wait in the bay every night until he can join us . . .' Katherine's voice trailed away as she saw the Captain's grin turn to a frown.

'Oh, must we? And who the devil is Mathew Sommers?'

Katherine felt as though someone had punched her hard in the stomach. 'But you must know who Mathew is? He bought the ship from you.'

The man threw back his head and laughed. It was not an unpleasant sound, but it made Katherine tremble.

'So he bought my ship, did he? And you were to meet him here tonight. Well, young sir, it seems you've been tricked.'

Katherine bit her lip. 'Isn't this the *Seabird*?'

'That old bucket?' The Captain's eyes glittered with pride. 'If your friend bought her he's a fool; she'd sink if she ever left harbour. No, this is my ship, the *Golden Eagle*.'

'Oh . . .' Katherine felt as if the world were collapsing around her. Everything had gone wrong. She closed her eyes, fighting her urge to weep. She would have to return to the castle. Opening her eyes again, she looked up at the blond giant. 'I am sorry to have troubled you, sir. Could your men please take me back to the beach?'

But the Captain was no longer listening to her. He had gone to the ship's side and was staring intently at the shore. Suddenly, he gave a loud curse. 'God's body! That's the danger signal—we've been spotted. Up anchor! Bring her round hard, Bos'n, we'll make for the open sea.'

Katherine ran to him, clutching at his arm. 'I must get back!' she cried, her eyes wide with fright. 'Please let your men take me to the shore.'

Captain Hades scarcely glanced at her. 'We've no time to waste now,' he said harshly, his eyes straining into the darkness. 'We must either fight or run—and tonight we run.'

His face was stern as he spoke, but Katherine neither

saw nor heeded the warning signals. Stamping her foot, she raised her head imperiously.

'You will have me taken back this instant, sir. I command you to obey me!'

Hades turned to look at her then, a look of astonishment in his yellow eyes. Eyes which reminded her of a cat's—not the castle tabby, but the wild cats she had sometimes seen on the cliffs when out riding with her brother. Then his mouth tightened, and the snarl which issued from him terrified Katherine.

'You command me?' The words sent shivers down her spine and she sensed the menace in him. 'You little vagabond! Jake, haul this boy below and lock him in my cabin. I'll deal with him later.'

'No! Please take me back. You must!'

Without thinking what she was doing, Katherine flew at the Captain, beating at him with her fists and kicking his shins.

Hades' startled expression turned to one of mild annoyance, and he grabbed hold of her, lifting her from the deck and shaking her as though she were a rag doll. Then something happened: his eyes narrowed and little flames of anger glowed in their topaz depths.

'Behave yourself or I'll thrash you,' he warned, setting her down and thrusting her towards the sailor he had summoned. 'If the boy gives you any trouble, Jake, you have my permission to put him in irons.'

Katherine's face paled as she heard the icy note in Hades' voice. Until a moment ago he had seemed to regard her merely as a nuisance, but now she sensed that he was angry with her. It was her own fault, she knew, but she was confused and frightened at finding herself on board the ship of a man they called Hades. Hades was the god of the underworld, and what kind of man would answer to such a name?

'Come on, matey, behave yourself, or I'll do like the Cap'n says.'

Katherine looked at the man who had been put in charge of her, feeling slightly relieved. He had a wrinkled brown face and button black eyes, which twinkled at her with good humour. Somehow she was not in the least afraid of him. As she went with him, he lowered one eyelid conspiringly at her. When they had moved out of Hades' hearing, he gave her a friendly grin.

'Don't worry, matey. Hades is in a bad mood at the moment. He don't like running away without a fight, but we've got no choice. Look over there.'

Katherine glanced in the direction Jake pointed and saw three ships bearing down on them. She turned to him, puzzled. 'Why is he running from those ships?'

Jake grinned. 'If he don't, they'll blow us right out of the water. We're trapped in this bay, see, unless we can reach the open sea.'

Katherine's eyes widened in horror. 'But we'll never escape from three ships—they're spreading out to head us off.'

Jake grinned. 'The Cap'n will outrun 'em, you'll see. The *Golden Eagle*'s a trim craft; there ain't a Spaniard as can catch her when she runs afore the wind. Mind you, it's mostly them as does the running. That's why Hades is as mad as fire. He'd like to sink 'em, but he's got his orders, see.'

Katherine didn't see, neither was she to be allowed to watch the *Golden Eagle* outmanoeuvring the clumsy Spanish ships, for at a roar from Captain Hades, Jake hurried her below deck. He opened a door, pushed her inside and departed hurriedly. She hoped he might have forgotten to lock the door in his haste, but her hopes were dashed as she heard the scrape of a key. Not that she had much chance of escaping, she thought gloomily, for she could feel the ship cutting through the water as more topsail was crowded on the masts.

A lanthorn swung from the ceiling of Hades' cabin, its pale yellow light enabling Katherine to look around her. She was surprised to find he lived in comparative luxury, having expected something much starker from Mathew's description of life on board ship. There was a rich carpet in the middle of the floor, which made her open her eyes wider: at the castle such a fine carpet would have been hung on the wall or used to cover one of the long tables in the hall. It was another instance of the man's conceit, she thought, as her eyes noted the solid chair and table, the top of which was littered with charts and various instruments of navigation. Beneath the small window was a large comfortable bed, and two sea-chests stood at either side of the door. One was open and appeared to contain the Captain's clothes, the other, with a stout lock, was securely closed.

Katherine went to the window and looked out. She could see one of the ships they were trying to outrun, and as she watched, a puff of smoke issued from the Spanish gun-port. She gasped, but the Spaniard's fire fell short, merely sending up a fountain of spray.

The *Golden Eagle* seemed to be tacking to avoid her pursuers. Katherine saw the cumbersome galleon outmanoeuvred time and time again, her cannon useless against the faster ship. She had no idea what had happened to the other vessels, for her view was limited, but she heard the sound of guns firing from more than one direction, though it seemed to be gradually growing fainter.

Suddenly the lanthorn spluttered and went out, leaving the cabin in semi-darkness. It was a moment or two before Katherine could accustom herself to the gloom sufficiently to find her way back to the table and chair.

She sat down, thinking longingly of the comfortable bed, but afraid to lie on it lest she fall asleep.

She sat stiffly to attention for some time, planning what she would say to Captain Hades when he came. He had been forced to put to sea in a hurry tonight, but perhaps he would take her back to the cove tomorrow if she offered him money. She could send a message to Mathew, and perhaps the Captain would tell them where they could find a seaworthy vessel.

The thoughts went round and round in Katherine's head. Her eyes grew heavy from sitting alone in the darkness for hours on end: still no one came. Her chin dropped forward, and almost without knowing it, she rested her arms on the table and laid her head on them.

The sound of cannon-fire had long since ceased, and Katherine was asleep when the door opened and Hades came in. Her hat had fallen off and the flaming hair was beginning to work loose, silken strands straggling across her cheeks. He frowned and bent down to pick her up, carrying her to the bed and laying her down gently so as not to wake her.

She moaned, and her eyelids flickered as she murmured a name. 'Lewis . . . Lewis . . .' she cried aloud. Hades ran a finger lightly along the soft curve of her cheeks, and she quietened. For a moment he smiled, then his mouth hardened. He turned away abruptly and went out.

It was morning. Katherine awoke as the cabin door opened and a man came in. She sat up hastily, glancing about her in bewilderment until she remembered where she was. Her smooth brow wrinkled in a puzzled frown—how came she to be lying on the bed?'

'Here's your breakfast, matey,' Jake said cheerfully, and then his mouth dropped open as he saw Katherine clearly for the first time. 'Here—you ain't a wench, are you?'

Katherine felt her cheeks grow warm. Her hair had all come tumbling down while she slept, and she knew there was no point in lying. Suddenly the hopelessness of her situation swept over her, and a single tear slid down her creamy-toned cheek.

'Yes,' she said in a low voice. Then she brought her lovely eyes up to his appealingly. 'You won't tell anyone, will you? Please . . .'

Jake looked into the girl's eyes, and was lost. A rough sailor, who had never known the love of a family, he immediately felt the protective affection of a father for his daughter. The girl was very young; he was old and no longer felt the desires of the flesh very strongly. He could look on Katherine's face and love her without wanting to ravish her, but he knew there were many others on board who would do so, given half a chance.

'Well, now, this is a rare mess,' he said, pulling at his chin. 'What are we going to do?'

Katherine smiled, realising at once that he was on her side. 'Thank you,' she said, walking to the table and picking up a piece of bread. 'I'm hungry! It must be the sea air. Where are we now?'

'On our way to the islands of the West Indies.'

Katherine's eyes widened in horror. 'But we can't be! I must get home.'

Jake shrugged his shoulders. 'We went close in just after dawn and the Cap'n slipped ashore to meet someone; then he came back and gave his orders.'

'What am I going to do?' Katherine asked.

Jake shook his head. 'I'm blessed if I know, matey—miss . . .'

'You had better go on calling me matey, or you will betray me. Besides, I rather like it.'

Jake grinned, his old heart swelling with love and a fierce determination to protect her from his shipmates. 'Reckon you're right, matey. Don't you go worrying your pretty head—old Jake will look after you. First thing is to get rid of all that hair.'

'No!' Katherine cried, her hands going to the long, silky tresses protectively. She gazed into Jake's eyes stubbornly for a moment, then she acknowledged he was right. Sighing, she gave him a wan smile. 'If I must . . . Do it quickly, please!'

Jake nodded. Locking the door first as a precaution, he took out his sharp knife and began to cut off the lustrous red curls. He was as gentle as he could be, but still Katherine's cheeks were wet with tears when he'd finished. She ran her hand over the shorn locks, shuddering.

'I must look so ugly.'

Jake grinned. 'You don't look quite so pretty as you did, matey, and that's a good thing. We shan't have every man jack aboard fighting for the privilege of bedding you . . .' He broke off as he saw Katherine's expression. 'It will grow again, matey—and 'tis for your own good.'

Katherine nodded, watching as Jake gathered up her hair and stuffed it inside his jerkin. 'I'll get rid of this when it's safe. Now we must . . .' He was interrupted by a loud hammering on the door.

'Open up this instant!' Hades' voice terrified them both.

'Be careful with him,' Jake warned hastily. 'He's a demon—he hates women . . .'

He had no time to say more, for the hammering was getting louder. He rushed to unlock the door and was knocked backwards as it flew open. Hades stood on the threshold, his face cold with anger.

'Who locked this door?' he thundered, sending shivers through the pair of them.

Jake straightened himself up and looked at Hades. 'It were me, Cap'n. This young rascal tried to escape—kicked me, so he did. I locked the door while he ate his victuals.'

Hades' eyes went to Katherine's shorn hair, his eyes narrowing. Jake had done his job well, and the flaming tresses were mutilated beyond recognition. The girl's oval face was pale, tear-streaked and dirty. She could now pass reasonably well for a delicate youth.

Hades grinned suddenly, his eyes alight with mockery. 'I'd forgotten our unexpected guest—what are we going to do with him?'

Jake drew a sigh of relief. 'I was wondering if you'd let me have him in the galley? I could do with a boy to help me.'

Hades appeared to consider his request, then shook his head. 'No, I don't think so, Jake. I need a cabin-boy, and he will do well enough.' His bright gaze came to rest on Katherine's face. 'What is your name, boy?'

Katherine shivered, her heart thumping wildly in her breast as she met the challenge of those lionlike eyes. 'K-Kit, sir.'

'Kit . . .' Hades repeated, frowning. 'Well, Kit, I've decided to try you out as my cabin-boy. I shall expect instant obedience—none of this kicking and screaming. Do you hear me?'

'Yes, sir.'

Katherine lowered her eyelids to conceal her mounting fury. How dare this common sailor speak to her so? Yet she knew it would be foolish to defy him for the moment. She must wait for her chance to escape. Besides, they were sailing towards the area where her brother's ship had gone down—at least she thought they were. Katherine's knowledge of charts was hazy and she could not be certain, but she believed they would pass the islands she'd intended to visit. Perhaps she could persuade Hades to look for her brother if she won his confidence first.

She smiled at him, her eyes wide and clear. 'I'll try to behave, sir, but I don't know much about ships.'

Hades frowned, his mouth suddenly hardening. 'Jake will show you how to find your way about,' he said, his voice cold again as he turned his gaze on the sailor. 'The boy is mine—make sure the crew know it, and you remember, too.'

'Yes, sir.' Jake's face paled as he met the jewel-hard look in Hades' eyes. 'Come on, matey. You can trot along o' me and bring the Captain's grub back.'

Katherine followed Jake out of the cabin, glad to be escaping Hades' penetrating eyes. They were in the stern of the ship and had to descend two levels by means of wooden ladders, walking the length of the gun-deck to reach the galley, which was midships and on the same level as the holds. It was very warm there; a fire was burning in the brick-lined stove, over which hung a large black pot full of an aromatic mess of meat and vegetables.

Another man, with greasy hair and narrow-set eyes, was ladling some of the stew on to a pewter plate, which he placed on the table with a chunk of coarse bread and a mug of ale.

'Them the Cap'n's?' Jake asked, jerking his head towards Katherine. 'This 'ere's Kit, Hades' new cabin-boy. He'll be taking the Cap'n his food from now on. Kit, this is Ram. He helps out in the galley when he feels like it.' A sour note in his voice told Katherine that he did not much like the other sailor.

Ram turned his little eyes on her, wiping a filthy sleeve

across his sweating brow. 'You'd best get on, then,' he grunted. 'Hades don't like to be kept waiting, and he likes his grub hot.'

Katherine stared at him haughtily. She had never been addressed by a menial in that fashion before. It was on the tip of her tongue to rebuke him, but a warning glance from Jake stopped her just in time. She picked up the plate, balancing the bread on top, taking the tankard in her other hand.

Retracing her steps through the length of the ship, Katherine wondered how food ever arrived hot at the Captain's table. She found it difficult to climb through the hatches carrying a plate and tankard, and she spilt some of the ale. However, at last she reached Hades' door, putting the tankard down while she knocked.

'Come in,' Hades commanded, and Katherine did as she was told, setting the food in a space on the table before him.

'I'm sorry if it's cold,' she said, retreating several feet to watch him in respectful silence. 'It was a long way to come.'

Hades dipped the bread in the gravy and began to eat. 'It's no colder than usual,' he said, frowning.

Katherine waited as he cleared the plate and drained his tankard, uncertain of what she ought to do now. Just what were the duties of a cabin-boy? she wondered. Hades seemed to be considering the matter too, for he suddenly fixed his topaz gaze on her face.

'Can you wash clothes?' he asked.

'No,' Katherine said, adding quickly as he scowled, 'but I can learn.'

Hades nodded. 'Yes, you can learn.' He got up and went to one of his sea-chests, dumping an armful of clothes on the floor. 'Jake will give you water when you return the dishes. Bring it back to the cabin. You can wash these; then you can scrub the floor in here and after that you can polish my boots—then we'll see.'

Katherine stared at him in horror. Used to being waited on all her life, the only work she had ever done was her embroidery—and she neglected that whenever she could. The Earl had spoiled and petted her from childhood, allowing her to do almost as she pleased.

'Well, what are you waiting for?' Hades barked, and Katherine jumped guiltily.

Hastily gathering the plate and tankard, she began the long scramble back to the galley. The sailors she passed called to her; some friendly, some jeering, but none of them tried to molest her, and she realised they all regarded her as Hades' property.

When she told Jake the list of chores the Captain had set her, he frowned and tutted. 'You're sure he told you to take the water to his cabin?'

'Yes—why?'

Jake shook his head. 'No matter. The devil's in him today, and no mistake. Never you fret, matey, old Jake will help you out.'

He poured water into two large wooden buckets, giving one to Katherine, but she could hardly lift it from the ground, so he signalled to Ram.

'Bring this along o' us,' he said. 'Cap'n wants his clothes washed.'

Ram eyed him sourly. 'Clothes washed in fresh water,' he muttered bitterly. 'This'll mean a stop to take on more water, mark my words.'

Privately, Jake was of the same opinion. Water was scarce enough on board ship as it was, but they habitually carried more than enough for the first stage of their voyage. Besides, Hades was a law unto himself, and Jake wasn't the man to question his orders.

'Hush your mouth—and bring that bucket if you know

what's good for you. A stop for water's better than Hades in a temper, matey.'

Ram grumbled that he had better things to do with his time, but he picked up the brass-bound bucket and followed behind them, leaving Katherine to bring the tub of soap. Trailing in the rear, she was already beginning to feel tired. She had slept little the night before, and her neck ached from lying awkwardly—and it was a long way from the Captain's cabin to the galley.

When Jake knocked and entered Hades' cabin, he was still at his table, working on the charts. He stared in surprise as the two men trooped in, followed by Katherine.

'What's this?' he asked. 'I told Kit to wash the clothes.'

Jake set the bucket down, motioning to Ram to do the same. 'Beggin' your pardon, sir, but the boy couldn't carry the water all this way.'

'Then he'll have to learn, won't he?' Hades' nostrils flared, and his eyes flashed little gold flames. 'He's not to be coddled—that's an order.'

'Yes, sir. Won't happen again.'

Jake and Ram went out. Katherine picked up a pair of breeches, dumping them in one bucket and rubbing in a handful of soft soap. The breeches seemed very dirty, so she took another handful and rubbed that in too, swishing them round and spilling water on the floor. Then she pulled them out, transferring them to the other bucket without wringing them out. Immediately the fresh water turned cloudy with soap. She swished the smallclothes round, dumping them on the floor soaking wet.

Next she selected a shirt and put that in the first bucket, rubbing in more soap. The water was running out of the sopping breeches, making a puddle on the floor. She became aware that Hades was standing over her, an incredulous look on his face.

'I said I wanted the floor scrubbed after you'd done the washing—don't you know you have to wring the clothes to get the water out?' He frowned as he watched her transfer the shirt to the second bucket. 'That water is no good for rinsing now. You'll have to throw it out and fetch more.'

Katherine glared at him, opening her mouth to reply indignantly, then she closed it again as she saw the challenge in his eyes. Picking up the bucket, which was now half empty, and considerably lighter, she staggered out and climbed the ladder to the deck above. It was the first time she'd been on deck since her arrival, and the sun felt good on her face. She saw some sailors scrubbing the decks; others were coiling ropes or climbing the rigging. One of them called out to her as she walked to the ship's side, but she didn't hear what he said. Lifting the bucket, she threw the dirty water overboard, gasping with shock as it came back into her face, soaking her to the waist.

Hearing the laughter of the sailors, she turned in a fury. 'Why didn't you tell me?' she demanded. Her protest was greeted with a chorus of raucous laughter and coarse jests.

'You didn't ask.'

'Anyways, we thought you could do with a bath!'

'Scruffy little devil, ain't he?'

'Remember to watch for the wind in future.'

Katherine pushed past them, their laughter following her as she disappeared down the hatch. Once more she returned to the galley, where Jake gave her a towel to dry herself. This time he half filled her bucket, leaving her to struggle back to Hades' cabin with it.

She was forced to make the same journey several times during the day, and the distance to the galley seemed to grow longer and longer. Her back and shoulders ached, and her hands were sore from rubbing. All the time she was working, Hades sat at his desk watching her. She finished the washing at last, and hung it on a line Jake fixed for her from the mizen-mast. Then she returned to the cabin with fresh water and began to scrub the floor. Hades had gone up on deck, and she was alone.

'He's a vindictive, loathsome beast!' Katherine muttered to herself as she worked, brushing away the tears of self-pity which started to her eyes. She wasn't going to cry! She'd die before he broke her spirit. 'I'd like to boil him in oil, cut his heart out and feed it to the dogs!' Hearing a deep laugh behind her, she looked round and frowned as she saw Hades standing grinning at her, getting to her feet, she wiped her hands on her breeches.

'I've finished the floor. I'll clean your boots when I've got rid of this water.'

Hades nodded, his eyes bright with mockery. 'Good. While you're about it, you can ask Jake to bring the tub to my cabin. I think I'll have a bath. Jake can help you carry the water to fill it.'

'A tub? You mean there's a big tub? I could have taken your clothes to the galley and washed them all in a big tub?'

Hades' eyes narrowed. 'Yes. Why?'

Katherine's eyes suddenly flashed with anger. 'You made me carry water all that way for nothing! Oh, I could kill you!'

Hades grinned. 'You could try—but if you did I'd break your neck. Tell Jake to bring that tub, and look sharp about it!'

Katherine bit her lip. She thought longingly of the knife hidden in her jerkin: how she would have loved to plunge it into his black heart! However, she fought down the temptation to try. He had promised to break her neck, and she did not doubt he would do it if provoked. Picking up her buckets with a sigh, she went out.

It took Jake all his time to carry the big tub to Hades' cabin, and several buckets of water to fill it. By the time they had finished, Jake was muttering and cursing beneath his breath, though he dare not say anything in Hades' hearing. When Katherine had emptied her last load into the tub, she turned to leave.

'Where do you think you're going?' Hades' cold voice stopped her.

Katherine did not look round. 'Jake said my supper would be waiting in the galley.'

'You haven't earned it yet. You can eat when you've finished your work.'

Turning slowly to face him, her cheeks grew warm as she saw he had removed his doublet and was unbuttoning his shirt. 'Couldn't I clean your boots after supper?' she asked, averting her eyes from his bare chest.

'The boots can wait—I want you to wash my back.'

Katherine's eyes flew wide open. 'W-Wash your back?' she gasped.

'Yes. And mind you scrub it well. It's a month since I took a bath; I've been too busy to bother.'

Katherine swallowed hard as he sat down and pulled off his long leather boots. She turned her back quickly, pretending to be busy gathering up his clothes as he began to strip off his breeches. She spent a long time folding his shirt and laying it neatly on the bed. Then she heard a small splash and knew he was in the tub.

'Come on, then—What are you waiting for?'

Katherine turned round slowly. He had his back to her, and she could see only a pair of wide shoulders and the sinewy muscles rippling beneath his tanned flesh to his waist. She walked towards him, drawing a deep breath.

Taking a handful of the soap she had used earlier for washing his clothes, she began to rub it into his skin. Concentrating on one small patch at a time so that she need not look at him as a whole, Katherine rubbed as hard as she could, deliberately making her mind go blank.

Hades made a purring sound of satisfaction, twisting his arm to indicate a spot further down his back. Katherine obeyed his unspoken order. Despite herself, she found she was beginning to enjoy the combination of smooth, firm flesh and soap beneath her fingers. As she worked, something odd happened to her: she felt a warmth spreading slowly through her body, and her hands began to stroke his back with long, sensuous movements without her volition.

Suddenly Hades made a sound half-way between a snarl and a groan. He stood up, waking Katherine from her trance as he turned round to face her, his golden eyes blazing with an emotion she did not recognise as passion, but instinctively knew spelt danger. Her eyes travelled haltingly, reluctantly down the length of his lean, muscled body.

Katherine was aware that men and women were made differently: she had gone bathing in the sea with Lewis when they were still children. She had been whipped for her wickedness—the only time in her life—and forbidden to do such a thing again. But in her innocence she had thought she was being punished for going into the sea, not for what she had seen.

Her brother's body had been pale and thin, nothing like this giant's bronze torso. There was altogether much more of him, and even as Katherine stared in spellbound admiration of his male beauty, something was happening to him. Something which made her eyes widen with shock and gave her a sudden awareness of much that had hitherto puzzled her.

Hades laughed as he saw the look in her eyes. Reaching for a coarse towel, he stepped out of the tub and began to dry himself.

'Your turn now,' he said, jerking his head towards the water.

Katherine gasped, her eyes dark with horror. She backed away from him, shaking her head. 'No—I'm quite clean. I bathed only yesterday.'

Hades' eyes glittered and his mouth hardened. 'I said into that tub with you, and I meant it. Take your things off, or I'll do it myself.'

Tears gathered on Katherine's lashes and her lip trembled. She gazed up at him with a desperate appeal in her green eyes, but his stern face showed no sign of softening.

'Please . . .' she whispered. 'Don't make me . . .'

Hades' nostrils flared, and he made a threatening move towards her.

Katherine gave a little squeal of fright, realising that she had no choice but to tell him the truth. She bit her lip, her voice shaking as she said, 'Y-You don't understand. I'm a—girl . . .'

Hades' face remained impassive. 'Prove it.'

Katherine gasped as she looked up into the topaz eyes. 'You—You knew all the time!'

Hades smiled, a mocking triumph in his face. 'Did I? Well, Kit—or is it Kitty? Are you going to obey me, or shall I undress you myself?'

In stunned silence she stared at him knowing he meant what he said. Her mind twisted and turned, seeking escape from the humiliation he was forcing on her, but there was none. If she did not obey him he would be angry—and Katherine was afraid of him when his eyes went cold.

She began to undo the fastenings of her doublet, feeling the bulky pouch of jewels hidden inside. For a moment she considered offering them as a bribe to him to let her go, but she thought he would simply take them anyway. She did not trust him. Taking off her velvet jerkin, she laid it down carefully so that the pouch should not fall out. Then her hand touched the small dagger she had picked up on her way through the armoury. Her fingers curled round it as the humiliation and pain turned to anger.

Suddenly she whirled round, her eyes glittering blue-green, like the sea on a bright spring morning. Springing towards him in a rush of fury, she struck wildly at his chest. The dagger's blade scraped across Hades' upper arm as he fended her blow and sent the weapon flying, leaving a thin trail of blood. The next moment he had gripped her wrist in a punishing hold, twisting it behind her and pulling her against him. She looked up into his golden eyes and shivered with fear.

'You little bitch!' he snarled. 'If you ever try anything like that again I'll break your neck! I ought to do it this minute.'

One hand circled Katherine's slender throat, while the other held her pressed against his naked chest. She trembled, closing her eyes in fear. Then his mouth came down on hers in a grinding kiss that bruised her lips and left her gasping for breath.

The warm glow she had earlier felt spreading through her body suddenly became a raging fire which threatened to consume her. She felt her head reeling wildly, her heart hammering in her breast so loudly that she thought it would burst. Even her fingertips tingled with this strange sensation that was like a fever in her blood. She hung limply when he released her at last, shaken and trembling. Gazing into his eyes, she felt as a mouse might before the cat's sharp claws delivered the final blow, frightened but mesmerised by the golden glow which held her. She parted her lips, drawing a ragged breath, waiting.

Hades grinned, triumph blazing in every line of his carved face. He undid the fastening of her shirt, pushing it roughly back from her shoulders to reveal her naked breasts. Her skin, creamy and silky in the lanthorn's pale light, seemed to please him. Katherine shivered as he began to caress her, a token denial issuing from between stiff lips.

'No—please don't!'

He laughed softly. 'Your words deny me, but your body speaks more truly. Soon your lips will beg me to love you. Don't be afraid, Kitty, I shan't hurt you—if you behave yourself.'

Tears welled up in Katherine's eyes as she heard the softness in his voice, but before she could answer, a loud hammering came at the door.

'Cap'n! . . . Cap'n Hades, sir!'

His mouth tightened with annoyance. 'What do you want?'

'It's the Bos'n, sir. He says for you to come on deck at once. There's a ship closing in on us fast.'

Hades cursed loudly, then said, 'Tell him I'm coming.'

'Ay, ay, sir.'

The Captain began to pull on his breeches and boots, his face turned from Katherine. But as she reached for his shirt, he swung her round and gripped her wrist, his fingers bruising her delicate skin.

'I'll be back,' he snarled. 'So get in that tub and scrub yourself. I like my women sweet.'

She gasped, her eyes flaring with anger as she watched him snatch up his shirt and disappear through the door before she could think of a suitable reply.

* * *

For several minutes Katherine stared at the door, her cheeks hot as his last words sank in. He was treating her as if she were a tavern wench who never took a bath! Anger made her eyes bright, banishing the tears. No one had ever spoken so to her in the whole of her life—no one!

She started to pull on her shirt, then hesitated. The water was still warm, and she knew the chance to bathe in fresh water would not come often on board ship. Jake had already grumbled several times about the waste of precious drinking water. He'd told her the crew mostly settled for dousing themselves in sea-water unless they were in port.

Running to the door, Katherine turned the heavy key in the lock. That should keep him out, she thought, eyeing the door hopefully. It was stoutly made, and she doubted Hades would go to the trouble of breaking it down. He would know she must unlock it at some time, and no doubt retribution would follow. She shut all thoughts of the future out of her mind as she stripped off her breeches and hose and slipped into the tub. She sighed with pleasure, the warmth of the water easing her aching limbs as she closed her eyes and relaxed.

If only Mathew had been here, she thought dreamily, that demon would not have dared to insult the daughter of the Earl of Dunline! Then she sighed, knowing that Mathew would have been of little help to her. The Captain would kill him as easily as other men swatted a fly. She was his prisoner—his to do with exactly as he pleased. What were his intentions? She was sure only that they involved something terrible—something that would cause her dishonour in some way.

This thought made her sit bolt upright, her sense of peace vanishing. She was the daughter of a proud family—she must not let him force her to his will! Yet what could she do? He was too strong for her to fight him. Then the answer came clearly to her mind. She must die before she allowed herself to be shamed by this brute. But how? The idea of taking her own life appalled her. She got slowly out of the bath, rubbing herself with the towel Hades had abandoned; then she picked up her knife, staring at it in dismay. She tested its sharpness with her thumb, crying out as a tiny point of blood appeared on her skin. Holding it in front of her, she practised bringing it towards her heart, wondering if it would hurt very much. She did not mind dying for her honour—at least, she knew it must be done—but she could not bear the thought of terrible pain.

Suddenly Katherine heard the sound of running footsteps on deck, and loud voices shouting. She came to a quick decision. Bringing back her arm, she prepared to plunge it into her heart before Hades could return. But even as she did so, there was a tremendous roar of cannon-fire, and seconds later the ship shuddered from bows to stern. They had been hit! Dropping the knife, she ran to the window, kneeling on the bed to look out.

What she saw was utter confusion. The two ships seemed to be locked together, and she realised the shock she had felt was not the thud of a cannonball but the sides of the two ships coming together with a crash. Grappling-irons were holding the two vessels fast to one another, and the crew of the *Golden Eagle* were swarming up the rigging and over it on to the other ship. She could hear the ring of steel against steel, and the cries of men wounded in the fighting.

She began to pull her clothes on feverishly. She had no idea who the other ship belonged to, or why they had attacked Hades, but perhaps they would be honourable men. Perhaps she could find a way to escape from this demon who meant to make her his slave!

Unlocking the door, Katherine climbed the ladder on to the deck, which was almost empty apart from a few sailors attending to the sails. Most of the fighting seemed to be taking part on board the other ship. She stood watching the contest, and listening to the shouts and screams. It looked as if Hades' men were winning, and her heart sank. If he won, there would be no chance for her to escape. She began to walk towards the rigging, waiting her opportunity to climb over the side when someone touched her arm, making her whirl round in a panic.

'I was just coming to find you, matey,' Jake said. 'I've got a wounded man here: I want you to help me.'

Katherine hesitated, poised for flight. This was her chance to run: she might never have another if she let it slip away. Then she looked into Jake's eyes and knew she could not leave. Sighing, she followed him to a sheltered part of the deck, away from the fighting.

The wounded man was lying on his back, groaning, and she was amazed to see that his skin was the colour of ebony. Even as she stared in astonishment, the man opened his eyes and stared right at her, lifting his hand as if to appeal for help.

'Rest easy, matey,' Jake was saying. 'Just you lie still while we patch you up.'

Katherine knelt by the sailor, her face ashen as she saw the blood pouring from a gash in his side. All thought of escaping left her; she turned to Jake with tears in her eyes, waiting for his instructions.

'We've got to pack the wound to stop it bleeding, see. I want you to tear this sheet into strips and fold it like I'm doing. Then we'll bind him up—there'll be more in a minute.'

She nodded, obeying him immediately. As they worked on the big black man, another sailor came hobbling towards them, blood gushing from a slash in his leg. She recognised one of the men who had laughed at her when the water blew back into her face, but he wasn't laughing now. He was so white that she thought he was about to faint, but he managed to grin at her as she bent to slit his hose and wash away some of the blood. He was lucky; the wound was only slight, and Jake soon had it bound up for him. He leant against a coil of ropes, watching as Jake and Katherine attended to the injured men who followed him, some managing to drag themselves, others carried by their friends.

The sound of fighting was growing less fierce, and the screams of dying men could be heard above the clash of the swords. Then the noises changed to moans and the tramp of returning feet, and occasionally a shout of triumph. Mindful now only of the injured sailors she was tending, Katherine worked on, oblivious of being watched. She was startled when Hades spoke to her.

'Go to bed now, Kit. You've done your share for today.'

Her eyes widened in surprise, and then she frowned. He was not concerned for her: he wanted only to continue with his evil purpose of humiliating her. Hades saw her expression and shook his head, a half-smile on his lips.

'No, I'm not coming. I shall be needed on deck for the rest of the night. You can sleep in peace—this time.'

Most of the injured men had been tended now. Katherine stood up, wincing as she felt the ache in her back for the first time. She gazed up into his eyes, her face pale but proud.

'Did you win?' she asked.

The golden flames burned fiercely in his eyes for a moment, then he grinned. 'I always win,' he replied softly.

CHAPTER THREE

KATHERINE STUMBLED wearily back to Hades' cabin. Every muscle in her body was making itself felt after the strenuous day. Sighing, she lay down on the bed, not bothering to take off her clothes or lock the door. Somehow she believed the Captain when he had said he would not trouble her again tonight. Besides, she was almost too tired to care. Very soon her eyes closed, and she slept.

The sun had risen high in the sky when she awoke to find Hades standing over her. Gazing into his golden eyes, she shivered with fear, jerking up to a sitting position as if she thought he meant to attack her. But this morning his eyes were clear and cool, with no trace of the simmering passion which had frightened her the previous night. Suddenly his carved features relaxed into a smile with little or no mockery in it.

'Well, Kit, what are we going to do with you today?' he asked, more of himself than her.

Avoiding his gaze, Katherine rose to her feet. 'I haven't cleaned your boots yet.'

'No, you haven't, have you?' he laughed. 'You can do them after you fetch me something to eat—and after you've eaten, too.'

Katherine nodded, and looked at the tub, which was still full of soapy water. 'It will take me a while to empty that. Is there anything else you want me to do first?'

He hesitated, an odd expression in his eyes. 'No, not today . . .' Then, as she turned to leave, 'Show me your hands.'

Katherine stood with her hands behind her back, unwilling to let him see the red weals and blisters caused by carrying buckets the previous day. But he frowned, making an imperious movement towards her, and took both hands in his own, to turn them upwards.

His eyes narrowed as he saw the marks. 'I'll have some of my men empty that,' he said, jerking his head at the tub. 'Jake tells me you were good with the wounded last night, so you can help him to tend them today.'

'Thank you,' she muttered stiffly. 'You are kind.'

Hades' mouth twisted wryly. 'No, Kitty, I am not kind. Sometimes I'm a demon—at others I can be a reasonable man. You've earned a rest for what you did last night.'

Katherine felt a queer little pain in her breast. At this moment she had a foolish desire to rest her head against his broad chest and feel his strong arms close around her. Dismissing the idea at once, she sighed. It would be most unwise to trust this new, softer Hades, for she had seen the demon which lived within him.

'I'll fetch your food,' she said, turning away quickly so that he should not see her face.

He did not call her back as she left the cabin.

Surprisingly, Katherine did not feel tired as the day progressed. She was growing used to climbing the steep ladders between decks, and the roll of the ship did not bother her though the wind had risen and the waves were quite rough. In fact she liked the feel of the spray on her face as she made her way about the deck, and the sight of the big waves crashing against the ship's sides excited her. Jake told her she was a born sailor and seemed to take pride in his protégée.

She was aware of a new attitude towards her from the rest of the crew. She was one of them now. They called to her as she went about her duties, but their jests were not unkind. Many of those only slightly injured in the fighting were lounging on deck, or tackling their normal tasks. There was an atmosphere of peace, as if the calm of the day after the turmoil of last night had affected everyone. The sailors smiled at her as she passed them, some of them ruffling her hair and teasing her good-naturedly.

The ship they had captured was sailing a little to the leeward, manned by a skeleton crew. Katherine thought it must be one of the Spanish galleons that had attacked Hades in the bay. It must have followed at a safe distance all day, hoping to surprise him by a night attack. The element of surprise had done its crew little good, however, and Katherine dared not think what had become of them.

Some of Hades' crew had been badly hurt and were lying on a sheltered part of the deck. Katherine asked Jake if they could be moved to somewhere more comfortable, but he shook his head.

'They're better up here for a time, where the air's fresh. Less chance of fever. Leastways, that's what I reckon.'

Katherine nodded. Jake seemed to know what he was doing, and she watched with admiration as he skilfully changed bandages with deft, sure hands. She was kept busy bringing drinking water to the injured and assisting Jake. Ashamed of being able to do so little, she wished she knew more of nursing as she witnessed the men's pain; but they were grateful for what she did, the sight of her elfin face bringing a smile to their faces. They thought her a delicate youth, and her fierce spirit amused them.

When they had all been made as comfortable as possible, Katherine returned to Hades' cabin. He was lying on the bed, his eyes closed. Creeping closer to peer at his face, she saw that he was sleeping soundly. With a sigh of relief, she picked up his boots and began to clean them, taking care not to disturb him.

Her task finished, she sat and watched him for a while, thinking his face looked less harsh when he slept. Since he showed no sign of waking, she considered returning to the galley to help Jake with the crew's evening meal; then her eyes fell on the chart Hades had been working on the previous night, and she began to study it.

It was drawn in a fine hand with neat, precise markings, and had none of the drawings of seabirds and fish she'd seen on those in her father's armoury. Katherine found some of the islands she had noticed on the Earl's maps, but they seemed to be in different places, and there were more of them. Whoever had cast this chart was an experienced sailor, for he had written in many details of distance and winds which had not been on the old maps at Dunline Castle.

She picked up the two-legged instrument she had seen Hades using, experimenting with it on the chart, but the strange markings confused her. Lewis had taught her a little about charts, explaining how to read them and plot a course between two landfalls, but she knew that the winds could make much difference to the timing of a voyage. She sighed, laying down the instrument with a little frown. Without help from someone who understood the sea, she had little chance of ever finding her brother, even if she could improve her knowledge and learn how to plot a course on these maps. First, she would have to escape from Hades!

Suddenly the hopelessness of her situation overcame her, and tears welled up in her eyes. Burying her face in her hands, she began to weep silently, her shoulders shaking. She was startled by the deep voice from the bed, unaware that the Captain had been watching her for some time.

'Don't cry all over the charts—you'll wash out Hispaniola!'

There was an oddly gentle tone beneath the mocking words, and Katherine gulped, brushing away her tears. Looking at him through misty eyes, she thought it might have been her father or Lewis talking to her—or was she imagining that look in his eyes? Perhaps it was a trick to deceive her?

'Why are you crying?' he asked. 'Are you still tired from yesterday?'

Katherine shook her head, wiping her wet cheeks with the sleeve of her shirt. 'No, I'm not tired.'

'What, then?' Hades got up and came to stare down at her, his expression unreadable. 'Are you afraid of me?'

She tilted her chin at him defiantly. 'No.'

Hades grinned. 'You've got spirit, Kitty! I like that. We should deal well together, you and I.' He looked at her thoughtfully. 'It's a pity about your hair—I suppose Jake cut it?'

'Yes. He hoped I would be safe with the crew if they thought I was a youth.'

Hades nodded. 'The men would fight over you, given half a chance, but you're safe enough now. They won't touch my woman.'

'I'm not your woman!' Katherine's eyes flashed fire.

'No?' His brows rose. He reached out and drew her to her feet, his hand caressing the short hair, which had begun to curl since her bath the previous evening; then his fingers slid slowly down the slender curve of her throat, stroking persuasively. He tipped her chin upwards, bending his head to brush his lips lightly over hers. 'Are you sure about that, Kitty?'

Katherine's heart began to thump madly. Biting her lower lip to keep it from trembling, she flicked her lashes down, refusing to meet his teasing gaze as she felt strange sensations flooding through her body, and wondered why this man should have such an impact on her. The sweet, heady pulsing of her blood made it difficult for her to think clearly, and her breath was coming in little gasps.

Was this what it meant to be a woman? she wondered. Certainly she had never felt like this when Mathew kissed her, and yet Mathew had been kind and gentle, whereas this man was a brute who wanted only to humiliate her.

Hades laughed softly in his throat, and Katherine brought her unwilling eyes up to his, mesmerised for a moment by the golden promise she read there. She felt a strange longing to melt into his arms, and of their own accord, her lips parted for his kiss.

The moment passed swiftly, for as he slid his hand beneath her shirt and began to stroke her firm young breasts, she felt a thrill of fear run through her. What was she doing? This must not be! She was beginning to understand what the intimacy of love between a man and a woman might be, and she suspected it might be very pleasant—but this man did not love her. He had treated her with a mixture of contempt and cruelty, and now he meant to dishonour her!

Hades' hands were unfastening her shirt, slipping it back from her shoulders. His lips moved down her throat, his tongue flicking between the sweet valley of her breasts. She gave a cry of terror as she broke away from him, her hands trying vainly to cover her nakedness as she saw the hot flame in his golden eyes.

'Sweet, lovely, Kitty,' he breathed. 'So beautiful—so full of fire. How much I want you . . .'

'No!' Katherine cried fearfully. 'Please don't touch me! If you dishonour me, I must take my own life.'

His eyes narrowed, and she saw a flicker of anger deep within them. 'You're very innocent for a girl who had arranged to meet her lover in a lonely cove at midnight,' he said coldly. 'Who are you, that you talk of dishonour? I thought you a serving woman to a lady of high quality who had learned to ape her betters. Now I wonder if I was wrong.'

Katherine hung her head, frightened to confess the truth. There was no telling what he might do if he knew she was the daughter of an earl.

Hades reached out, his fingers curling round her wrist. 'Well, will you answer me—or shall I continue where I left off?'

'Mathew loved me! He wanted to marry me,' she cried, angry tears starting to her eyes.

'And you loved him, I suppose?' Hades' eyes were cold. 'So why did you cry another man's name in your sleep? You are nothing more than a common little wanton—and I'll not be denied what you give so willingly to others.'

So saying, he pulled her roughly into his arms, his mouth bruising hers in a kiss unlike those which had gone before. There was a raw savagery in him now, and it terrified her. With a gasp of desperation, she tore herself from his embrace and ran to where her doublet lay on the table, knowing that she no longer had a choice. She must kill him, or die in the attempt!

As her hand reached towards the little knife beneath her jerkin, Hades' strong fingers closed round her wrist.

She gave a squeal of dismay, wrenching away from him and sending her doublet flying with a little shower of Hades' papers. There was a dull thud as her pouch fell to the floor, spilling its contents.

'I'll take that knife of yours . . .' he began, his eyes narrowing as he saw the glitter of jewels spread on the floor. 'What the . . .!'

As he let her go, Katherine bent swiftly to retrieve her property. 'They are mine,' she cried defiantly.

'Where did you get them?' He stared at her hard, his nostrils flaring as she set her mouth stubbornly.

'That's none of your affair!' Katherine's eyes were blazing.

'I asked where they came from. Answer me, Kitty, or you'll be sorry. You haven't seen the worst of me yet, I promise you that.'

She swallowed nervously. If she hadn't seen the worst of his temper yet, then God save her! She held out against him for a moment more, her defences crumbling as she saw a dart of golden fire spark from his eyes and a tiny pulse begin to drum in his temples.

'I told you that they belong to me. I am Lady Katherine Winters, daughter of the late Earl of Dunline.' She raised her head, her lovely face haughty with pride.

'Let me see them.' Hades held out his fist commandingly, and Katherine reluctantly handed the jewels over. 'That was wise of you,' he murmured. 'I've had enough of your temper.'

Hades turned the jewels over in his hand, his brow furrowed as he appreciated the worth of some of the pieces; then he stiffened as his eyes fell on the miniature of Don Esteban, and he traced the elaborate crest with the tip of his finger. Suddenly his face became a block of stone. 'Who gave you this?' he growled harshly, his lips white with anger. 'I want the truth, so don't lie to me, Kitty. I'm warning you.'

She gazed into the hell of his eyes, and shivered. She saw at once that there was something significant about the Domingues crest, and her knees felt as though they would give way beneath her.

'Don Francisco Domingues sent me the miniature as a betrothal gift from his son,' she whispered, trying not to show how nervous she felt. 'He came to the castle to arrange a marriage between us.'

'Don Francisco Domingues . . .' Hades breathed the name with a savage quiet that was more dangerous than all his raging. 'You are betrothed to that man's son? Answer me! Are you promised to Don Franciso's whelp?'

Katherine hesitated, not knowing how best to reply. If she told him she was not betrothed to the Spaniard, Hades might think she had stolen the jewels, and then he would call her a wanton again and renew his assault on her virtue. But if he believed she was promised to a man of importance, he might agree to ransom her—and even a return to the castle and Don Francisco would be easier to bear than her present situation.

Raising her eyes to his, her mouth curved in scorn. 'Yes, I am betrothed to Don Esteban. And when his father learns you have abducted me, he will take a terrible revenge . . .' Katherine broke off as she saw the murderous expression in his eyes. Suddenly he smashed his fist on the table, scattering the jewels on the floor once more. Then he began to laugh, a harsh, bitter laugh which made Katherine's blood turn to ice.

'By God I did not know what a prize I had captured!' he cried, his tawny eyes blazing with hatred. 'No wonder Don Francisco sent the *Santa Maria* after us with orders to fire only a warning shot across our stern, and then board us. I thought her Captain had run mad when he did not fire on us!'

'You mean—that ship last night . . .' Katherine stared at him, feeling sick. 'They were coming for *me*?'

All at once she understood what had happened. Somehow the Don had discovered Mathew's plans and prevented the *Seabird* from reaching the cove, hoping to thwart her escape. When he learned that Katherine had been taken on board the *Golden Eagle*, he must have sent his ship after her to fetch her back. That explained why the Spanish vessel had kept out of sight all day and hoped to take them by surprise. But why had Hades' ship been in the cove, and why had Don Francisco's ships attacked him that night, before it was known that she had been abducted?

Hades was watching her closely. 'Why were you in the cove that night?' he barked. 'And who is Mathew Sommers? I thought he was your lover.'

'Mr Sommers is my uncle's secretary—and we are in love. I persuaded him to help me find a ship so that we could look for my twin brother.' Katherine's eyes clouded with tears, making her blink rapidly. 'He was lost at sea some months ago, but I know Lewis is still alive. I know it.'

'Lewis . . .' the Captain breathed, his face thoughtful as he studied her. 'So you decided to run away. Why? Did you not want this marriage with Don Francisco's son? Tell me the truth, Kitty.'

For some reason the anger had died out of him, and his voice was soft, almost gentle. His change of mood made her vulnerable, and she turned her face aside so that he should not see how close to tears she really was. 'I told you. I'm in love with Mathew. My—My father's will made me Queen Mary's ward; she has consented to the match. I—I have no choice . . .'

'Bloody Mary!' Hades muttered, his face darkening with anger again. 'She who burned so many good Englishmen to satisfy the craving of her evil soul. She is nothing less than a murderess, and the sooner she lies in her grave, and Elizabeth sits on the throne of England, the better!'

Even though she secretly agreed with him, Katherine was disturbed by his words. 'That is a traitor's talk, sir.' Her chin went up and she was once more the proud daughter of an earl.

Hades' eyes narrowed to thin slits. 'You may think me a traitor, but you are the ward of a woman I despise and betrothed to the son of a man I have sworn to kill.' Katherine trembled at his scowl, fearing that he meant to kill her. For a moment she wondered why her association with the Spaniard should arouse such fury in him, but her thoughts were scattered as she backed away from him, her mood defiant but scared. His lips twisted cruelly. 'No, I shall not kill you, my lady, though I am tempted to break your beautiful neck. But dead, you would be of no more use to me . . .'

Katherine drew a deep breath. 'Then you will return me to my home? You have my jewels; and there will be gold if you do as I ask.'

Hades' harsh laughter sent shivers down her spine. 'Do you think me a witless fool? I have the jewels, and I have you. Why should I let you go? No, Kitty, I have you, and I shall keep you until I decide what to do with you. Perhaps I shall sell you to the Don, or perhaps I shall use you as my whore and then, when you no longer please me, I shall send you to him as a gift. I think he would appreciate the jest, don't you?'

'He would not want me as his son's bride if you dishonoured me . . .' Katherine's face drained of colour, and she broke off as her voice failed. 'Kill me, I beg you,' she cried desperately. 'I would rather die than suffer the fate you plan for me!'

'Then I shall have to make sure you cannot cheat me of my prize, shan't I, Kitty?' He tucked her knife into his belt. 'It would be a sweet revenge . . . and yct perhaps the Don's gold will suffice. It would in truth give me little satisfaction to bed you. I prefer my women more comely.'

Hades grinned as he saw the anger in her eyes. Picking up the scattered jewels, he stuffed them back in the pouch; then he went to the chest, and taking a key from inside his doublet, unlocked it. As he lifted the lid, Katherine caught a glimpse of rich velvets, silks and jewels. He added her pouch to the precious hoard, closed the lid firmly and locked it, returning the key to its place of safety.

She gazed at him in horror as he turned to look at her. 'You—You are a pirate,' she whispered, her hand flying to her throat.

He grinned, his teeth gleaming against the bronze of his skin. 'Some might call me that,' he agreed. 'I consider that every Spanish ship I sink is a blow for England —a small revenge for those poor fools who died to please the King of Spain and those murdering devils of the Inquisition!' She saw the flames dancing in his eyes, and then, before she could think of a reply, he walked to the door and went out.

Katherine remained motionless, staring after him in stunned dismay. A pirate ship! She was on board a pirate ship—why hadn't she realised it at once? No matter what Hades said about striking a blow for England, he had not denied the main purpose of his life. She should not have trusted him for a moment. She ought to have known that no honest captain would send his men ashore in a lonely cove at the dead of night, and that there was good reason for Spanish ships to attack the *Golden Eagle*.

Suddenly the tears began to course down her pale cheeks. Any faint hope she might have harboured of persuading the Captain to help her to find Lewis was finally crushed. She was the prisoner of a pirate captain, and the best she could hope for was that he would carry out his threat to sell her to Don Francisco.

They had been at sea for so long that Katherine had almost lost count of the days and weeks—weeks she had spent helping Jake in the galley or with the wounded. The men hurt on their second night at sea were fit enough to return to their duties, except for one who had died despite all their efforts to save him. She had wept when the sailor died, but now she was growing used to seeing men wounded or dying.

Towards the end of her fourth week on board, they had sighted a Spanish vessel returning home with a cargo of silver from the New World. Hades had ordered his men to run up a flag bearing the skull and crossbones to fly beside his own emblem—a black banner with a golden eagle in flight stamped boldly on it—then they had moved into the attack. Jake told Katherine that Hades always gave his victims fair warning, unlike some of the corsairs who plundered the Mediterranean coastline.

'Many of the Barbary pirates are Moors,' he said, as they worked in the galley one day. 'They attack any vessel—and they often fly the flag of their victim's country to deceive them deliberately. Hades only attacks Spanish ships.'

'That doesn't make him any less of a pirate,' Katherine replied sharply. 'The Queen would have him hanged if he were captured.'

Jake tipped his head to one side, his little eyes bright.

'Ay, that she would—or burnt as a heretic. She'd burn me, too, most like.'

Katherine's mouth opened slightly. 'Oh, Jake, I didn't mean . . . I wouldn't want anything to happen to you— You've been so kind to me.'

He grinned at her. 'I know that, matey.' Then his smile faded and his face grew anxious. 'You've no cause to love Hades: he's been hard on you the whole voyage. I've never seen him in quite this mood afore—the demon's roused in him this time, sure enough.'

Jake did not know how rough the Captain had been with her, Katherine thought. She had never forgotten the night he discovered who she was, and she never would! 'I know—he terrifies me sometimes when he's in a rage. I think he hates me.'

Jake scowled. 'He hates all women—allus has, as far as I know. Uses 'em for his pleasure, then throws 'em aside. Some say as he was crossed in love once.' He shrugged. 'Hades is a hard man, matey. No heart in him.'

Katherine nodded thoughtfully. There was certainly some mystery about Hades: he was a man possessed—driven by some inner urge that she could not fathom. She had not told Jake about the night Hades had started to make love to her, or of their ensuing quarrel. Since that night he had shown no interest in her as a woman at all, treating her with a cool indifference as if she really were his cabin-boy—though sometimes she caught him watching her with a strange, brooding expression. He had given her blankets to make a bed for herself on the floor at the far side of the cabin, and he spoke to her only when he needed to. The memory of those passionate kisses which had seared her seemed almost a dream now, and sometimes she wondered if she had imagined the tenderness she had glimpsed so briefly in his face.

These days it was carved from stone, his eyes as cold and bleak as the northern sea in winter.

She was roused from her day-dreaming by the sound of shouts and running feet on deck, and looked at Jake, startled. 'Do you think they've sighted another Spanish ship?'

Jake frowned. 'Dunno, matey, ain't heard no firing . . .' He broke off as Ram came into the galley. 'What's up, then?'

'Everyone on deck—Cap'n's orders.'

Jake and Katherine looked at each other. There was an odd air of excitement about Ram. Abandoning their task, they followed him up on deck, looking curiously at the assembled crew. Then a low, rumbling sound went through the men as Hades appeared on the poop. Katherine glanced around her, sensing the charged atmosphere, her nerve-ends tingling. She waited expectantly for Hades to speak.

'You have been called here to witness justice done,' he said, his voice harsh. 'You all know the rules by which we sail. You have all sworn to obey them, and you know the punishment for breaking them.'

Katherine turned her anxious gaze on Jake. 'What does he mean?'

The man's face was grim. 'You'll see soon enough,' he grunted, jerking his head towards the hatches.

She saw that a man was being brought up by two of his comrades. His hands were tied behind his back, and his ankles were shackled by cruel iron manacles fastened together by a chain. She gasped as she recognised the huge black man she had helped to tend when he was wounded.

'Oh no!' she cried involuntarily. 'Not Fabius!'

Jake motioned her to be quiet, and she watched as the prisoner was dragged to the mainmast, struggling and cursing in a tongue that was foreign to her. Then his hands were tied spread-eagled around the mast so that he could scarcely move.

As she realised what was about to happen, Katherine's face paled. 'I can't watch this,' she whispered to Jake, turning to leave.

He grabbed her wrist, restraining her. 'You must,' he grunted. 'Else he'll likely punish you, too.'

She looked at him, feeling sick and faint as she acknowledged the truth. Shuddering, she stared as the Bos'n stepped forward, flexing his burly arms as he prepared to lash the wretched Fabius. The whip snaked out, making a high-pitched whine as it curled through the air and landed with a sickening thud, biting into the ebony flesh. She gasped with horror as she saw the trickle of fresh blood on the sailor's back, but hardly had she drawn breath when the next blow landed, and the next. For a moment she swayed on her feet as the sickness built up inside her; then, hearing the whine of the whip again, her faintness was swept away by a surge of anger. Without thinking what she was doing, she pushed her way through the ranks of silent sailors and ran to the burly Bos'n.

'Stop it!' she cried angrily, kicking his shins to make sure she had his full attention. 'I command you to cease this instant!'

The Bos'n stared at her, his mouth dropping open in surprise, and the whip hanging loosely in his hand. Acting on blind impulse, Katherine snatched it from him and dashed to the ship's side, casting it as far as she could into the foaming water. Then she turned round to face the astonished crew, her eyes blazing defiantly, her breast heaving. For a long, tense moment no one moved. It was as if her actions had stunned them all. Then, drawn by a force stronger than her will, she lifted her eyes to Hades' face, shivering as she saw the golden fury in his eyes.

'Take Kit to my cabin and lock him in,' he said, his voice dangerously soft. 'I'll deal with him later. Bos'n, continue with the punishment.' He threw a knotted rope down to the deck.

'No!' Katherine screamed, avoiding the sailor who tried to grasp her, and stepping on to the rigging. 'Listen to me, all of you! He can't make you obey him. I am the child of an English earl: if you take me back to my home, I shall give you gold . . .'

Jake came to the foot of the rigging, looking up at her anxiously. 'Now you've done it, matey! For Chrissakes, come down or he'll murder you—and me, too.'

None of the crew had made a move, and the Bos'n had picked up the rope to finish his work. Katherine realised that she had done no good at all by her intervention: she might not have spoken. The men were too frightened of Hades to disobey him, she thought. Climbing down the rigging with a feeling of dull resignation, she went quietly to Jake, letting him lead her away without protest, the sound of the prisoner's cries ringing in her ears. One of the sailors grinned at her as she passed.

'A brave effort, Kit . . .' He laughed mockingly. 'Son of an earl!'

Katherine's eyes were dull with anger as she heard the note of disbelief in his voice, but she made no reply. He would not believe her, whatever she said—none of them would. Tears were building behind her lashes as she disappeared down the hatch, closely followed by Jake. She brushed them away angrily, knowing this was not the time to show weakness. Let Hades do his worst, she thought, trying not to remember the prisoner's moans as the whip cut into his back. He would not do that to her—or would he? She realised that she had no idea of his true nature. He was a man who walked alone, allowing no one to come close. She clenched her hands into tight balls, determined not to let her fear of him show. For it was certain that some form of retribution would follow, and swiftly!

Jake shook his head at her, his anxiety showing as he prepared to lock her in the Captain's cabin. 'What made you do it, matey?'

Katherine swallowed hard. 'I couldn't watch, Jake. It was too cruel.'

Jake sighed. 'You don't understand, Kit. It were justice. Hades didn't do it for fun. When you've got a crew like this—some of 'em the worst scum from the dockside—you've got to have rules. Fabius knew that: he expected to be punished.'

'Oh . . .' Katherine stared at him in bewilderment. 'You mean—you think Hades was right to do it?'

Jake shrugged. 'I dunno, matey. All I knows is that Hades is the Cap'n, and he gives the orders. Besides, it looked a lot worse than it was—Hades ain't never had a man flogged to death—lots of 'em do. As a lad, I were pressed for the King's navy: it were a hundred times worse than serving under Hades, I can tell you.'

Katherine bit her lip. 'I didn't know. I hardly thought what I was doing . . .'

'I reckon you ain't been used to this sort o' life, matey. I'll have a word with him. Mebbe I can cool him down a bit.'

Brushing away the tears his kindness had brought to her eyes, Katherine smiled at him. 'Thank you, Jake. I don't know how I should have managed these past weeks without you. You've taught me so much about the sea: how to navigate by the stars, the names of all the different parts of the ship—I could almost sail her myself . . .'

Jake grinned. 'I've enjoyed having a young'un about me. Never did have no family, see.' He ruffled her hair, which had begun to curl on the collar of her shirt. 'We'll have to cut this again soon. For now, I'd best get back to Hades afore he gets hisself in a worse temper.'

Katherine nodded, saying nothing as he went out, closing the door behind him. She trembled as she heard the scrape of a key in the lock. The next person to come through that door would be Captain Hades, and he was very, very angry with her!

Katherine perched on the edge of the bed. All at once she was shaking from head to toe as she realised what she had done. Since their last quarrel, Hades had treated her with a cold indifference, taking little notice of her even when she stood watching as he worked over his charts, though he had once unbent enough to show her how to measure distance with the two-pronged instrument he called a compass. By watching him and listening to Jake, she had begun to understand what some of the markings on the maps meant, and she was memorising the details as best she could in the hope that it would prove of use in the future. But the Captain's careless attitude would be bound to change after what she had done, she realised. He would have to punish her, because she had openly disobeyed him.

Before very long the sound of heavy footsteps and a key turning heralded his arrival. Standing up, she brushed the tears from her eyes impatiently, lifting her head in a show of defiance as he came in. For a moment he stood on the threshold, glaring at her, his very maleness a threat. She saw the pulse pounding in his temple and the smouldering haze of gold in his eyes, and her knees shook. She ran the tip of her tongue over dry lips as he stepped inside, locking the door behind him.

Katherine swallowed nervously at this ominous sign, her heart thudding against her ribs like a bird in a cage fluttering vainly against the bars. What was he going to do to her?

'Well?' Hades' mouth curled in a snarl, his carved features giving no indication of the feelings aroused in him by that lovely, proud face and lithe young body—feelings he had believed long dead. 'What have you to say to me, Kit?'

'Nothing.' Katherine tilted her chin at him. She wasn't sorry for what she'd done, despite Jake's explanation. She still thought the beating cruel and bestial—and no one was going to make her change her opinion!

Hades frowned. 'So you are unrepentant? You mean to defy me, even now? Don't you know I'm bound to punish you?'

'Yes.' Katherine's eyes sparkled with the tears she was too proud to shed.

The Captain's lips twitched, and she saw to her surprise that he was trying not to laugh. 'By God!' he cried. 'If I had a dozen men like you, Kit, I'd storm Cadiz itself.' Then the light died out of his eyes, and he sighed. 'Come on then, Kitty, justice must be done—however much it hurts both of us.'

She moved back nervously, not understanding the new tone in his voice. What did he mean by 'hurt both of us'? He could not mean that it would grieve him to punish her? He caught her wrist, holding her firmly but without pressure.

'W-Where are you taking me?'

'You'll see.' Hades' voice reflected none of the anger she had expected when he walked in.

Arriving on deck in a state of nervous uncertainty, Katherine saw that the crew were all still assembled as before, and that a stool had been placed before the mast.

She shivered, her frightened eyes flying to Hades' stern face. He was going to have her whipped like Fabius! She faltered as her heart stopped for one terrible moment and then raced on wildly. He was going to teach her a lesson she would never forget . . . if she survived it!

However, when they reached the stool, Hades paused for a moment, his golden gaze travelling slowly over the crew's faces. 'As I said earlier, justice must be done.' He paused, to let his words sink in. 'Kit has broken the laws by which we sail, and he must be punished.' He grinned suddenly, an imp of pure mischief dancing in his eyes. 'But I think you'll agree that the punishment should fit the crime.'

Sitting down on the stool, he had pulled Katherine face downwards across his lap before she realised what he intended. Then, very deliberately, he began to administer hard, regular slaps with the palm of his hand. After a moment's stunned silence, the crew started to laugh, calling out encouragement to him as his hand came soundly in contact with her rear.

Katherine shrieked in fury as she realised what he was doing. He was treating her like a spoiled child, ridiculing her before his crew! She struggled and kicked indignantly, beating at his thigh with her fists and letting loose a stream of abuse in language she had picked up from the crew. Her outburst brought more laughter from the men, while doing nothing to stop Hades' determined assault on her dignity. He merely held her still with one hand, while continuing to smack her with the other. Hearing his laughter, she twisted her head to peer angrily at his amused face. So he thought it was funny, did he? Suddenly she sank her sharp teeth into his thigh.

Hades gave a yell of surprise. 'You little wretch!' he cried. 'It's time you were taught a lesson.' His hand came down even harder on Katherine's bottom, and she felt its sting for the first time, bringing tears to her eyes. Until now he had only been patting her, she realised. Then, as she prepared to scream another salty torrent of abuse at him, she found herself set on her feet once more, though he retained his grip on her wrist as he looked at her, a faint smile playing about his mouth. 'Had enough?' he asked mildly.

Katherine rubbed her breeches, feeling the sting of that last blow. She nodded, her eyes smouldering with suppressed rage. She wanted to scream her defiance at him, but she knew it was pointless. He had demonstrated her inability to make him take her threats seriously only too well. He was too strong for her, both physically and mentally. She couldn't fight him. Besides, she could hear the crew's laughter, and her humiliation was complete.

'You are a tyrant—but I'll pay you back for this!' she cried, wrenching away from her captor and racing across the deck to clamber down the hatch before anyone could stop her.

CHAPTER FOUR

HER PRIDE smarting as much as her posterior, Katherine brushed away the angry tears that trickled down her cheeks as she made her way towards Hades' cabin. She was not going to cry; he was a brute and a tyrant, and she hated him! She did! Suddenly she remembered that someone else had suffered far more than she at the Captain's hands. Fabius had been badly beaten, and his back would need attention. Stopping in her tracks, she turned in the direction of the galley, collecting water, bandages and salves before hurrying to the crew's sleeping quarters.

Fabius was lying face downwards on his bunk when she found him. He lifted his head apprehensively as she approached, obviously wondering who was coming, but when he saw her, a faint smile spread across his face.

'It's only me,' Katherine said, wincing as she saw the bloody lacerations on his back. 'I'm here to help you.'

There was no reply, but the man groaned once as she began to wash away the blood. She worked as swiftly as she could, glad now of all Jake had taught her. She had almost finished her task when the old sailor came in and stood watching her in silence.

'I thought I'd find you here,' he said. 'You've done well, Kit, but now you'd best go. Hades has been asking for you. I'll clear up in here.'

Katherine stared at him, mutiny flaring within her as

she considered disobeying Hades' command—but what was the use? She would have to give in in the end for there was nowhere on board she could hide which would not eventually yield to a thorough search. Shrugging, she nodded her assent, her mood bleak as she passed Jake on her way out.

He looked at her sympathetically. 'Try not to take it too hard, Kit.'

'He humiliated me in front of the crew. I hate him!' she retorted.

Jake looked grim but made no further attempt to persuade her, realising that she needed time to recover from her painful experience. Privately, he had been surprised at Hades' good humour, and wondered if she understood how foolish she had been to incite the crew to mutiny. Almost any other member of the ship's company would have been shackled with irons and thrown into the hold to cool their heels.

Katherine made her way quickly, now perfectly at home in any part of the ship, blissfully unaware of her friend's thoughts. Apart from the quarrels with Hades, she was enjoying her first sea voyage, and though the life was a little hard, it suited her. She was glowing with health, and her skin had ripened to the colour of pale honey. Entering the Captain's cabin, she had no idea of how lovely her young face and slim, lithe body looked to him, or what fierce emotion caused him to frown as he saw the sulky droop of her mouth.

'Your hair is growing,' he snarled. 'Get Jake to cut it for you, or you may find the crew becoming too curious for your liking.'

Katherine's hands clenched as she spat out, 'They cannot harm me more than you already have, sir.'

Hades' lips thinned to a forbidding line, sending a shiver of fear through her. 'You think not? You deserve that I should give you to the men as a plaything, and let you discover the worst for yourself. Have you ever seen a hare torn to pieces by a pack of dogs?' As Katherine's eyes widened, he nodded grimly. 'They would fight each other for the privilege of having you first, but eventually they would all get their turn.'

Having lived on board for some months, Katherine was no longer as innocent as she had been. The men did not watch their words when she was about, and thinking her a callow youth, had teased her often about finding a wench when they were next in port.

Hades' words sickened her, and she cried out for him to stop. 'Haven't you humiliated me enough for one day?' she asked bitterly. 'Must you insult me, too? As you think me a wanton, I'm surprised you don't carry out your threat—or are you still planning to sell me to the Don?'

An odd expression flickered across his face, and she saw a muscle tauten in his neck as if some strong emotion was working in him. 'I had to punish you, Kitty. You must see I could not favour you above the others.' He reached out to touch her hand, but she moved away sharply.

'Don't! Your attentions are as unwelcome to me as those of your crew would be. I see little difference between a pack of wild dogs and the wolf that leads them. I hate you!'

'Why, you little . . .' Hades began, his eyes going cold. 'I ought to . . .' He was interrupted by a shout from the deck above them. Walking to the window, he looked out, and his frown faded. 'We've reached the island, so we'll finish this discussion another day.' Suddenly he turned and grinned at her, his anger apparently evaporating as swiftly as it had come. 'Well, then, Kit, don't you want to get your first glimpse of our island?'

'Our island?' she asked, a queer little pain shooting through her as she looked at his smiling face. She wished he wouldn't smile at her like that—it was so much easier to hate him when he was being a tyrant.

'Yes.' Hades chuckled as he saw her reluctant curiosity. 'It is a base we all use to replenish our ships and spend time on shore. To many of the crew it is the only home they know.' His gaze was warm and friendly. 'Come on, young Kit, are you going to sulk for ever, or will you give me a smile and forget the past? There's no need for us to hate each other—you were not to know that Don Francisco is my sworn enemy.'

Katherine stared at him, feeling the power of his charm, and wondering what lay behind Hades' bitter hatred of the Spaniard. She had been tempted to ask many times, but now, for the first time, he seemed almost approachable. She looked at him uncertainly, remembering the way he had humiliated her earlier.

'Why do you hate Don Francisco so much?'

Hades' smile faded, and there was a strange bleakness in his eyes which puzzled her. He seemed to hesitate, and she thought he meant to tell her something very important, but then his face settled into granite lines.

'It is an old story and one which cannot concern you. Come, we'll go on deck together—if you've stopped sulking at last.'

Tossing her head with haughty pride, Katherine scowled at him. 'I'm not sulking, but I meant what I said. You're a tyrant, and I distrust you. Nothing you can say will change that.'

Hades inclined his head. 'So be it—I'll leave you to yourself. I've work to do on deck.'

He went out, and she sat down gingerly on the chair, stubbornly determined not to show any interest in the pirates' island. Why should she want to see it? She hadn't asked to come here. She was Hades' prisoner, and he had treated her shamefully. Ignoring the little voice in her head which told her she had brought most of her troubles on herself, she managed to control her curiosity for all of five minutes. Then she ran to the tiny window in the ship's side and looked out, straining to see the dark mass gradually growing larger on the horizon.

She watched from her vantage-point for some time, but as they sailed nearer the island, her impatience grew too much for her and she was soon scrambling up to the deck. Some of the crew called to her to join them. They were all grinning excitedly and eager to tell her about their island.

'There's all the booze you could want at Red Molly's,' one said, winking at her. 'Reckon you could do with some o' that, eh, Kit?'

Katherine smiled, her cheeks growing warm as their suggestions became more ribald, informing her explicitly what more delights and pastimes she might expect to find at Red Molly's place.

'Why, look at the lad—he's blushing!' one of them said with a guffaw.

'Leave him be; he's too young for your tricks,' Jake said, coming up to them. 'You tag along o' me, Kit, I've work for you to do.'

Grateful once again for his fatherly protection, Katherine went with him. She knew well enough that if it had not been for Jake she would have found life on board almost impossible. Without his watchful care of her, she was sure the crew would have discovered her true identity long since. And though she did not really believe that Hades would turn her over to his crew as a plaything, the threat had frightened her. There were one or two members of the crew who gave her odd looks sometimes, and she was careful to stay well away from them.

Helping Jake to bring up the scraps to throw overboard, she was able to catch glimpses of the island as it loomed even closer. At first it looked dark green, just a blur of shadow against the bright blue sky and sea. Then she saw the tree-covered hills beyond the fringe of golden sand, and white foaming water swirling around the barrier of rocks which appeared to surround the island completely.

'We'll smash against the rocks!' she cried, as they sailed closer, but Jake smiled and shook his head.

'Hades knows what he's doing—watch!'

Katherine did as she was bid, her heart pumping madly as they were carried dangerously near to the jutting rocks by the fierce waves. But she saw that most of the sails were being hauled down and that the sailors were taking soundings on either side of the ship by lowering ropes and waiting for the signal which told them the depth of the deep turquoise water. Hades was directing the helmsman as they crept through the narrow channel which was the only way into the island's lagoon.

Then a great cheer went up from the crew, and she saw they were through the reef. Here the sea was as calm and still as a pond, bright blue and very clear. She could see flashes of silver as jewel-coloured fish broke the surface of the water, and great white birds circled noisily overhead. Now the mass of green was pierced with bursts of brilliant colour, and the spicy scents of exotic blooms reached her as she heard the anchor splash its way to the bed of the lagoon.

Already the boats were being lowered over the side, but some of the men were diving into the lagoon, swimming strongly for the shore. And, as she looked towards the beach, Katherine saw men and women streaming from the woods on to the silver sands. They were waving and laughing, calling out to the crew of the *Golden Eagle*. The men waved back excitedly, pointing out faces they knew to each other and shouting greetings.

'You stick close to me, Kit,' Jake said, coming to stand next to her. 'I'll see as you're looked after, matey.'

'Thank you, Jake. I was wondering what I ought to do.'

He grinned at her. 'You can stay with a friend of mine. Her name's Lizzie, and she's got a tongue like broken glass, but her heart's as soft as butter. She'll take care of you while you're on the island.'

Katherine nodded, her attention straying. The Spanish ship they had taken as a prize was negotiating the narrow channel through the reef, and her arrival brought another burst of excited cheers from the watchers on shore. Because she was so engrossed in watching the other ship, she failed to notice Hades moving purposefully towards her, and the sound of his voice made her jump.

'And where do you think you're going?' he demanded, as she started to follow Jake.

Katherine swung round, her whole body sparkling defiance at him. 'With Jake. Didn't you say I'd be free to do as I please when we reached the island?'

'Kit can stay with Lizzie,' Jake said quickly, seeing the signs of a storm in Hades' face. ''Tis the safest place for . . . the lad.'

For a moment the golden eyes blazed, and Hades' lips compressed, then he nodded. 'Kit's your responsibility then, Jake. I'll hold you accountable if anything happens.'

'Fair warning, Cap'n,' he agreed. 'Come on then, matey, it's time we were gettin' into the longboat, or they'll go without us. You coming, Cap'n?'

Hades shook his head. 'Not yet. I've things to do on board, but I'll be there for the division tonight.'

'Ay,' Jake said easily, taking Katherine firmly by the wrist as she seemed to hesitate. 'Shake a leg, matey! It's many a month since I went on shore.'

She followed him, more reluctant to leave Hades than she would have believed possible only an hour or so ago. She turned back to stare at him standing alone on the poop, watching them depart. Suddenly she wished she could find the words to tell him how she felt, but even as she hesitated, he turned and walked away, disappearing down the hatch.

Katherine sighed, puzzled by the warring emotions inside her. She hated Hades, so why was she unwilling to leave the ship without him? Jake called to her impatiently, and recalling her wandering thoughts, she ran to the ship's side and scrambled down the rope-ladder to the waiting boat below.

Lizzie turned out to be a buxom blonde with a ravaged countenance, a harsh voice and kind, intelligent eyes. She roared a bullish greeting at Jake, hugged him to her ample bosom, and then turned her attention to Katherine.

'Who's this, then?' she asked. 'Another of your worthless mates, Jake? He's a mite young, ain't he?' Lizzie's gaze narrowed suspiciously. 'Well, bless me barnacles, it ain't a he at all!'

Jake looked startled, and then grinned at her. 'Never was able to put one over on you, Lizzie! This 'ere's Katherine—better known as Kit. No one knows she's a girl, 'ceptin you, me and Hades.'

Lizzie frowned. 'Hades' wench is she? What did you bring her here for, then?'

'I'm not Hades' woman; I'm his prisoner—or I was . . .' Katherine's protest ended lamely as she looked into the woman's bright eyes, eyes which saw more deeply into her heart than was comfortable. 'I went on board his ship by mistake, and he wouldn't let me go back to the shore.'

'You're a mite young to be going on board any ship alone, ain't yer?' Lizzie asked, somewhat mollified by the innocence she saw in the girl's face, but still wary.

'I wasn't meant to be alone. I was to have met a friend—only he didn't arrive . . .' Katherine felt the sudden tears sting her throat as she began to remember her mad plans to rescue her twin brother. Loneliness swept over her as thoughts of home entered her mind, and she wondered if she would ever see Lewis or Dunline Castle again. 'We were to have set sail in search of my brother . . .' She gulped as the tears spilled over. 'They said he was drowned at sea, but I know he's alive.'

Lizzie's expression softened as she saw the girl's tears. For a moment she stared at her, making vague clucking noises, then she drew her close to her, patting her back and glaring at Jake as if it was all his fault.

'Why, it's an innocent babe you've brought me, you ninny! Letting me think she was Hades' cast-off, indeed! There, don't fret, child; it's a terrible time you've had of it, I'm thinking. Come on into the house and tell Lizzie the whole story.'

Lizzie's house was a roughly-built wooden shack with palm thatching. Inside, it consisted of one large room, sparsely furnished with a table, stools, an old sea-chest bound with brass, and various utensils for cooking. At the back was a smaller room which contained a rather handsome bed covered by a crimson silk spread. Its presence in the tiny shack came as a surprise to Katherine, since it was the only sign of luxury.

Lizzie grinned at her. 'A present from a friend of mine many years ago. It was taken from a Spanish galleon, part of a high-born señorita's dowry, I'm told. It's my pride and joy, that bed. Ain't another like it on the island. Many's the offer I've had for it, but I'll not part with it while there's breath in me body.'

Katherine smiled, her tears drying swiftly. She felt she had found a friend in this extraordinary woman, and perhaps with her help, and Jake's, she might yet find a way of going on with her search for Lewis.

Soon she found herself telling the story of her twin's disappearance, and how she had planned to thwart her uncle's plans to marry her off to Don Domingues by escaping with Mathew. She explained how she had persuaded the gentle secretary to buy a ship and about the strange note she'd had from him, warning her to escape that night even if he did not meet her. Then she told how she had mistaken Hades' ship for the *Seabird*, omitting nothing but the time she had so nearly been seduced by the *Golden Eagle*'s captain. This, she found too painful to relate to anyone.

At first neither Lizzie nor Jake seemed to believe her when she spoke of her father as the Earl of Dunline, but as her story unfolded, Katherine saw acceptance in their faces.

'So, you see, somehow I have to find Lewis,' she finished. 'If I could search the smaller islands . . .'

Jake shook his head at her. 'It's an impossible dream, matey. Even if you could find a ship and crew willing to take you, there's so many islands that you'd never find him.'

'I must,' Katherine said, her mouth setting obstinately. 'I have to find him. I *know* he's still alive!'

'It would take a lot of money . . .' Lizzie said, staring at her pensively.

'I have money—or I had.' There was a flash of anger in Katherine's eyes. 'Hades took my jewels from me.'

'Then that's the last you'll see of them! Lizzie scowled. 'That Hades is a rare demon. He'll not give up lightly what he regards as his own.'

'They belong to me.' The girl's chin lifted stubbornly. 'Maybe I should just take them back?'

'Touch Hades' sea-chest, and he'll hang you from the yardarm,' Jake said. 'You wouldn't be the first to try it.' He shook his head sorrowfully. 'Forget the jewels, matey. With your share of the plunder this trip, you could pay an honest captain to take you back to England.'

'My share?' Katherine looked at him in surprise. 'What do you mean?'

'Every member of the crew gets his share. You worked your passage, matey, so you're entitled to your pay, same as the rest on us.'

Her face brightened. 'Would it be enough to hire a ship to look for Lewis?'

'I told you to forget it,' Jake growled, looking cross. 'It's a wild-goose chase.'

'You'd best listen to Jake,' Lizzie said. 'Now, come on, child, let me make you something to eat. And maybe I could find a dress to fit you.'

'A dress?' Katherine stared at her in dismay. 'Thank you, Lizzie, but I'll stick to my breeches, if you don't mind.'

Lizzie frowned, opening her mouth as if to protest, then changed her mind. 'Well, it may be for the best for the time being, but I'll give you something to wear while your clothes are in the tub. They look as if they could walk by themselves!'

Katherine looked down at her salt-stained clothes, realising just how filthy they really were. She had not dared to wash them on board ship in case someone came in while they were drying. Until now, she hadn't noticed their condition, as most of the sailors looked exactly the same. Smiling wryly, she met Lizzie's gaze. 'Do you think I could have a bath as well?'

Lizzie threw back her head and bellowed with laughter. 'Ay, that you can, child. I insist on it.' She glowered at Jake. 'Away with you, man! There's no more for you to do here.'

As Jake turned away, Katherine ran to him, kissing his weathered cheek. 'Thank you for everything,' she said. 'I shall see you again, shan't I?'

He looked pleased. 'I'll take you to the feast tonight, if you'd like. I'll see as you get your share, matey. Trust old Jake for that!'

Katherine smiled. 'I've always trusted you, Jake. I'll be waiting for you tonight.'

When he had gone away, Katherine spent a pleasant hour or so soaking in a tub of hot water and washing her hair with Lizzie's home-made soap. It smelt delicious, and she felt thoroughly clean for the first time in months, for though she had regularly doused herself in salt water, it could not compare with the luxury of a hot bath. She decided she was being spoilt when Lizzie produced a silk shirt and a pair of velvet trunk hose, with some fine red stockings besides.

The clothes fitted reasonably well, though she had to tie a sash tightly round her waist to stop the padded breeches from falling down. 'Where did you get these things?' Katherine asked. 'They are of good quality.'

Lizzie gave her a sidelong smile. 'They came out of my chest. A friend of mine gave them to me.'

'You seem to have some generous friends,' she commented innocently.

'And what if I have?' Lizzie's voice was suddenly

harsh. 'Them things is come by honest—which is more than most can say hereabouts.'

'Oh, I didn't mean to upset you!' Katherine looked at her in dismay.

'No more you have,' said Lizzie. 'I dare say as you'll hear soon enough. Everyone knows as Lizzie's the sharpest gambler on the island. Them things was not so much give as won, but it were done honest. Lizzie never cheats—and I'll kill the first one as says different!'

'I'm sure you don't.' Katherine looked at her in awe. 'Do you think you could teach me to gamble?'

'No, I don't! Eat them vittles, and don't plague me with foolish questions.'

Katherine did as she was told, realising she was hungry, and the food was very good. Clearing her platter and wiping up the last of the delicious gravy with her bread, she suddenly felt guilty as she remembered Fabius. Alone on his bunk with no one to help him, he must be hungry and in pain.

'Can I have this?' she asked, picking up a chunk of Lizzie's meat pie and some bread.

Lizzie nodded, looking surprised as Katherine jumped up from her seat and started towards the door. 'Where are you going, child? It will be dark in another hour or so.'

'Back to the ship. There's an injured man there, and I'm sure no one has thought to leave him food or water.'

'But how will you get there?'

'I'll ask someone to row me out.' And Katherine had slipped through the door before Lizzie could stop her.

She spent some minutes on the beach before spotting one of her former shipmates. He was not keen on the idea of rowing back to the ship, but gave in reluctantly when she told him her reasons.

'Come on then, Kit,' he said gruffly. 'But I'll not wait, so you'd best be quick.'

She scrambled into the boat, and smiled her thanks. He pulled strongly towards the *Golden Eagle*, resting his oars as they drew level.

'I'll wait here,' he called, as Katherine began to climb the rope-ladder that was still hanging over the side.

She lifted her hand in salute on reaching the deck. 'I shan't be long, Pete.'

Running swiftly towards the main hatch, she disappeared below with the agility of an old sea-dog. Fabius was lying exactly where she'd left him, his face buried in his arms. He stirred as she entered, smiling a welcome, his teeth white against the sweat-glistened ebony of his skin.

'I've brought you some food, Fabius,' she said. 'Shall I look at your back again?'

He shook his head, turning slowly on his side to take the food, and wincing. 'You're a good lad, Kit.' His voice was soft and deep. 'I shan't forget in a hurry.'

Katherine shook her head, smiling. 'I didn't want you to starve. Shall I fetch you some water now? Or perhaps I could find a little rum in the galley?'

'Bring both if you can.' Fabius sat up. 'How did you get back to the ship?'

'I persuaded Pete to bring me. Do you want to come to the island with us?'

'No, I'll bide here for a day or so. Fetch that rum then, Kit, there's a good lad.'

She hurried away, racing to the galley and then back to Fabius. 'I can't stop,' she panted. 'Pete won't wait long. I'll come again tomorrow.' With that she left him, scrambling up to the deck and then over the side to the waiting sailor below.

'Sorry, Pete, I was as quick as I could manage,' she

said as she noted his impatience.

She was completely unaware that her progress had been watched by Hades. She did not look back, so she failed to see him frown, hesitate and then disappear below deck once more.

Jake came to collect Katherine just as dusk was falling. She did not mention her return to the ship, thinking it unimportant. From his face, she could see he was excited as he led her through the trees into a large clearing.

At one side was a house much like Lizzie's, but larger and with an upper storey. Some of the sailors were lounging on the veranda, others were hanging from open windows; all of them seemed to be in high good humour, laughing and calling to each other. It was obvious from their behaviour that they had been drinking heavily, something Hades did not allow on board ship, and one or two scuffles broke out as Katherine watched.

In the centre of the clearing a bonfire was burning merrily, its red and gold flames licking into the darkening sky and sending up the occasional shower of sparks. A pig was being roasted on a slowly-turning spit, the tantalising smell of the meat making Katherine hungry again. At the edge of the circle were rough tables covered with palm leaves and laden with all kinds of foods; some of the fruits were completely unknown to her but were delicious, as she soon discovered, being tempted to try them all in turn by Jake.

Great casks of ale had been rolled out into the clearing, and several kegs of rum. The men helped themselves liberally, some of them already well on the way to becoming hopelessly drunk. Katherine began to understand why Hades was so strict about its rationing on board. Somewhere a fiddle was being played, and a woman dressed in a bright crimson dress with a low neckline began to dance, her body moving sinuously in a time to the haunting tune. One or two of the pirates made a grab at her, but she avoided them with a toss of her head, her face proud, eyes glistening as she weaved her spell of seduction, her ginger-red hair taking fire in the light of the flames.

'That's Red Molly,' Jake whispered, as they took their places in the circle of spectators sitting cross-legged on the ground. 'They say she ain't never been tamed by a man yet—not even Hades.'

Katherine stared at him, a sinking sensation in her stomach. 'Hades?' she asked in a small voice.

'She's his woman,' Jake replied, watching the climax of the dance. 'Some say she ain't faithful to him when he's away, but they don't say it loud enough for him to hear. He killed a man once in a fight over her.'

Katherine swallowed hard, wondering why it hurt so much to hear that. She really did not care what Hades chose to do. 'He—He must love her very much.'

Jake laughed harshly. 'Not him—he loves neither man nor woman! He ain't got no heart. I told you he was a demon, that one.'

'Yes, you did,' Katherine's voice was unsteady as she fought the stupid desire to weep. She concentrated her mind on Red Molly, thinking how beautiful and desirable she looked in the moonlight. So this was the woman who held Hades' heart! No wonder he hadn't been sufficiently interested in her herself to carry out his threats of seduction. Red Molly's eyes glowed like a cat's in the fire's glow, and her scarlet mouth was softly sensuous. She was a tall woman and well formed. Beside her, Katherine's slim body was childish and, to her own mind, uninteresting.

One of the pirates had risen unsteadily to his feet. He lurched after Red Molly, calling to her in a lewd tone.

She stopped dancing and turned to look at him, scorn in her eyes.

'What do you want?' she asked disdainfully.

'You, Molly. I've bin dreamin' of nothin' but you for months!'

A chorus of raucous laughter greeted the pirate's sally, and then it died away to a breathless hush as everyone's eyes turned to the same direction. Hades had entered the clearing and was standing watching the little scene, his face beaten copper in the glow.

The pirate froze, his face a comical mask of surprise mixed with fear. The silence deepened expectantly, and then Hades turned his back quite deliberately and went to fill himself a tankard from one of the casks of ale. His action was plainly intended to show that he was not interested in fighting over Molly. It brought a burst of coarse laughter from the sailors, and a spark of fury to Molly's bright eyes.

She tossed her long hair, giving such a venomous look that the laughter died in the men's throats. Then she strode from the circle of light into the large house at the edge of the clearing.

'There'll be trouble yet,' Jake said darkly. 'Molly's not the one to take an insult like that quietly.'

Katherine did not answer. It was spiteful of her, she knew, but Hades' public rejection of his rights over the ginger-haired beauty had made her heart sing. Perhaps he wasn't in love with Molly after all. He hadn't even bothered to go after her, but was chatting casually with some of his men. As she saw him turn and search the clearing with his eyes, and then begin to walk towards where she was sitting with Jake, her mouth started to curve in a gesture of welcome. Remembering just in time that she hated him, she did her best to turn the happy smile into a scowl.

Hades scowled at Jake. 'You shouldn't have brought Kit here tonight. You know what the men are like the first night on shore. There'll be fighting before long.'

Jake stood up, his mouth grim. 'I'm here to take care of Kit, Cap'n. Besides, it's time for the division, and Kit has a right to be here.'

Hades frowned. 'Kit has earned a share—that's true—but I intend to take charge of that myself. Kit has no need of money on the island.'

'That ain't fair, Cap'n,' Jake protested. 'She's entitled to her share.'

He was silenced by Hades' murderous look. 'Fool! Do you want everyone to know what we know? Kit is my property, and I'll take care of what belongs to me.'

'I'm not your property,' Katherine exclaimed indignantly. 'And I want what's mine!'

Hades took hold of her wrist, his eyes cold. 'Be silent,' he said, his voice dangerously quiet. 'I told you once that I would do as I pleased with you—and nothing has changed. You're coming with me now before you get into more mischief.' He glared at Jake, clearly angry. 'Since you obviously cannot control Kit, I shall have to see to it personally. I'll be back in time for the division of our spoils.'

With that, he strode out of the clearing into the darkness of the trees, forcing Katherine to run to keep up with him. Resenting the firm grip on her wrist, some instinctive caution yet held her silent until they had left the gathering well behind and there was no danger of being overheard; then, as he slowed his stride to a more normal pace, she looked up at him, her expression more curious than angry.

'Where are you taking me?'

'To my house.' Hades frowned. 'I'll lock you in, if I have to. Or will you promise to behave?'

'Why are you so angry with me?' Katherine gazed at him, watching the muscle pounding in his temple with fascination, and realising he was having difficulty in reining his temper.

'Why did you go back alone to the ship?' His eyes suddenly blazed at her. 'Have you made a fool of me, and does someone else know who you really are? Have you been lying to me, pretending to be innocent, while all the time you have a lover?'

His fingers had begun to bite deeply into her flesh, as if he did not realise his own strength. 'No one knows I'm a girl but you and Jake,' she said in a strangled voice, her face pale. 'You think I went to meet a lover . . . You think I have been . . . Oh, how dare you! How dare you say such a thing to me?'

She tried to wrench away from him, breathing hard as she fought to keep her emotions in check. Her eyes were stinging with tears she was too proud to let fall, and a terrible pain was twisting in her heart.

As Hades studied her face, his expression gradually lightened, chasing the shadows from his eyes. 'Why did you go back, then?' he asked in a softer tone. 'Not to see me?'

Katherine tossed her head as pride eased the aching pain inside her. 'No—I was glad to be free of you! I went to see that Fabius did not starve—or had you forgotten him?'

'No, I had not forgotten,' he said harshly, the muscles cording in his neck as he became angry again. 'Did you think I would leave him without seeing he had all he needed?'

'Yes.' She sparked defiance at him with every line of her body. 'You would.'

'So you believe me totally without feeling or sense of justice? Well, so be it.' His expression became distant, unreadable. 'It seems that I must still keep you a prisoner. I had hoped you might be sensible.'

Hades was striding towards a house similar to Lizzie's, but larger. He opened the door, thrusting Katherine inside before him. Letting go of her wrist at last to light a lanthorn, he faced her across the room.

'Will you go to bed and stay there until morning, or must I lock you in?' He sighed as he saw her sullen look. 'It's for your own good, Kit, I promise you.'

Katherine's mouth drooped, making her seem ridiculously childlike. 'Why must I stay here when all the others are enjoying themselves?'

The corners of his mouth twitched, and his tone had softened when he spoke. 'Don't hate me for it, Kitty. There will be other nights but tonight it's too dangerous. The men go wild after so many months at sea, and there's no telling what they might do. You will be safer here. I give you my word I am not doing this as a punishment.'

An odd tingling sensation swept over her as she heard the gentle note in his voice, making her limbs feel weak. 'I'll stay here,' she conceded. 'But I want my share of the prize we took. Jake says I've earned it.'

'And so you have: It will be safe enough with me.' Hades hesitated as if there was more he wanted to say, and Katherine's heart jerked as she saw the expression in his eyes. Then a shutter came down, closing off his thoughts. 'No one will disturb you here; we'll talk again in the morning. You'll find a bed in the other room. Good night, Kit.' He smiled at her, then turned and went out.

Left to herself, Katherine looked around the room she was in. Larger than the one at Lizzie's house, it was furnished simply with the same roughly-made tables and stools, but there was evidence that Hades had gathered some comforts about him in his island home, and it was stamped with his personality, just as his cabin had been. There was even the same smell of wood, spices and the masculine scent of him, which could have such a devastating effect on her senses. The bedroom floor had a carpet, and on the table were drinking vessels made of horn set with silver rims; several iron-bound chests and a small silver-framed mirror on the wall completed the furnishings.

As she looked in the mirror, Katherine studied her reflection eagerly, experiencing a shock as she saw her face for the first time in months. Her hair had grown since Jake cut it, but it was uneven, and straggling at her neck. Her skin no longer had the pale fairness of an English gentlewoman, and she stared at her complexion in dismay, hating what she saw. To her there was no merit in the healthy glow of her skin or the softness of her wide, generous mouth. She saw only the changes the months at sea had wrought, without noticing the brilliance of her eyes.

She turned away, angry with herself for caring how she looked—or what Hades must think of her. What did it matter?

Brushing away the tears of self-pity, she ignored the little voice inside her head that told her she was lying to herself. She went into the bedroom. The bed was not as grand as Lizzie's, but the covers were soft and it looked inviting. She crawled between the sheets without undressing, giving way to her tears as her face touched the pillow. For a while she sobbed as though her heart would break—then, gradually, the pain eased, and she slept.

It was there that Hades found her when he returned just before dawn, curled up like a child, one arm flung across the bed, the other tucked beneath her tear-stained face.

He lifted the covers carefully, easing in beside her and gathering her slim body close to him so that her head lay against his shoulder. Katherine sighed and stirred, but did not wake, nestling closer to the warmth of him like a sleepy kitten.

The sun was streaming in at the window as Katherine woke, wondering for a moment what was wrong. Then she realised she was missing the movement of the ship and the noise of the sea lapping against the timbers.

Turning with a sigh, she found herself pressed against the hard length of Hades' body. He was lying on his back with his eyes closed, breathing gently as if asleep. Since her side of the bed was set close to the wall, she would have to clamber over him to escape.

Katherine's heart began to hammer nervously at finding herself trapped so securely. The warmth of his body was sending heat waves coursing over her, making her blood pulse and her breath come out in little gasps. How long had he been lying next to her—and what had happened in the night?

Easing herself up on one elbow, she looked down into his face. In his sleep he looked younger and less frightening, and she felt a curious longing to touch his cheek. Her thoughts brought a sudden flush to her face. Surely nothing had happened while she slept, for she must have known if he had tried to make love to her. No, he would not take advantage of her as she was sleeping, but it would be a very different matter when he woke up! Alarmed at the prospect, she decided she must take the risk of climbing over him, unless she wanted to lie there until he began to pay her undesired attention. And that she most definitely did not want! The problem was how to avoid waking him.

She stood up on the bed, and hovered with one foot

over him, but he groaned and rolled towards the edge, leaving her no room to balance. Then she knelt down and prepared to slither across him, relying on speed to escape if he stirred. But as she arched herself over his body, a strong brown hand gripped her arm and she found herself pinioned to his chest. Looking into his tawny eyes, Katherine saw he was wide awake, and judging from his grin, had been so for some time.

'You wretch!' she cried. 'You were awake all the time!'

For answer, Hades' arms closed about her and he rolled over, trapping her beneath him as his lips came down to crush hers. The fierceness of the emotion let loose in her by his kiss surprised her, and she clung to him as sweet sensations spread through her body. Desire stirred in her, and a flame swept swiftly along her trembling limbs. Of their own volition, her arms went around him, caressing the smooth strong back, enjoying the feel of his flesh beneath her hand. His mouth moved down her throat, his hands straying to the firm curve of her breast, stroking and arousing.

Shaken by this unexpected surge of feeling within, Katherine made no protest as his mouth moved down to follow his gentle hands. He nudged teasingly at her nipples with his tongue, making a thrill of excitement shoot through her body, and a soft moan escaped her parted lips. She melted against him, her defences overcome by the aching longing inside her. She instinctively pressed herself against him, her lips soft and pliable beneath the demanding passion of his own. Suddenly she felt no fear of him, and the wanting grew in her as she strained against him, waiting for the inevitable. He had said that she belonged to him. Now, at this moment, she was ready to admit the truth of it in her heart.

'Am I still a loathsome vindictive beast?' he whispered

against her ear. 'Shall I give you a knife so that you can cut out my heart?'

Katherine tensed as she remembered when she had said those words. Stung by what she thought was mockery, she moved her face to one side, lying still and straight in his arms. For a moment longer Hades continued to stroke her, then he sensed the change in her and raised himself to look into her face.

'What's wrong? Have I hurt you?'

'Would you care?' she asked bitterly. 'You seek to use me only for your pleasure, or for revenge against the man you hate.'

His teeth clenched in a snarl of disbelief. 'It seemed to please you mightily a moment ago,' he said, watching her face intently. When she made no answer, he rolled away from her. 'Go, if you wish. I'll not force you.'

She made no reply. She could not, for fear of betraying herself. Her back turned to him, she slipped from the bed and fastened her shirt. She began to walk towards the door, halting as he commanded her.

'Where do you think you're going?'

'To Lizzie's.' She whirled round to face him, eyes suddenly blazing with anger. 'Unless you mean to keep me a prisoner. Or perhaps you will sell me to Don Domingues?'

She felt his fury stab her like a golden flame, piercing her breast. 'You deserve that I should,' he said coldly. 'But I would not condemn a dog to that fate.'

Katherine hesitated, aching for the word which would take her back to his arms. If only he would show some sign of softness, of needing her. She watched as he got up and walked into the middle of the room, her pulses racing, wondering if he would use force to prevent her going, half hoping he would beg her to stay, but he merely frowned and shrugged his shoulders indifferently.

'What are you waiting for?'

Gazing into his topaz eyes, tears caught in Katherine's throat as she forced them back. 'You think I'll come running back to you, don't you?' she choked. 'Well, I won't! I can manage well without your protection.' But not without your love, her heart whispered.

Then she ran to the door, wrenched it open and flew out before the tears could fall.

CHAPTER FIVE

THE SUNLIT days slid into each other and Katherine forgot how long she had been on the island, even though she could never quite forget the ache in her heart. Every morning she went fishing with Jake, cooking their catch for breakfast over an open fire. Fruit grew in abundance in their tiny paradise, and she soon learned to climb the trees, her lithe body agile as a little monkey's, throwing down her juicy prizes to Jake as he waited below. Sometimes she bathed in the clear springs while the old sailor stood guard to see she was not disturbed, their affection for each other growing in the warmth of the sun. And in the evenings, when dusk fell like a curtain over the magical isle, they sat together in Lizzie's house playing cards.

Lizzie had questioned Katherine fiercely when she returned after the night spent at Hades' house, but calmed down when the girl explained she had no choice but to go with him.

'He's cruel and I hate him,' she said, her eyes hard. Lizzie shook her head but said nothing, pretending to believe her.

Since Katherine's return, Hades had left them alone and the three formed a close companionship. Lizzie had taught the girl to play simple card games, though she would not gamble with her. Lizzie's cards were made of bone, delicately carved and painted. They were another of her most prized possessions.

'They belonged to a friend of mine,' she told Katherine with a twinkle in her eyes. 'Mad Jack they used to call him—bless his rotten soul, he's long gone now—and mad as fire he were when I won them from him. Lost everything else he had, so he wagered his cards. Some folk don't know when to stop!'

Katherine laughed delightedly. 'You tell such wonderful stories, Lizzie—how did you come to the island in the first place?'

Lizzie scowled at her. 'Ain't you no manners, child? There's some questions you don't ask, see, then you don't get told no lies!'

'Sorry, Lizzie,' Katherine apologised, knowing the other woman was not really angry with her. 'I didn't mean to pry.'

'All the same if you did. I ain't tellin' you.' Lizzie looked towards the door as it opened, and Jake came in. 'What do you want?' she barked.

Jake looked startled, then grinned at her good-naturedly. 'Got out of bed the wrong side, Lizzie? I come to tell Kit as they've started to provision Hades' ship, as he'll be leaving the island soon.'

'Leaving?' Katherine cried, alarmed by the news, though uncertain why. 'Is he going back to England?'

'Don't know.' Jake scratched his head. 'But are we sailing with him?'

'Do you want to?' Katherine asked, staring at him.

'Depends on you, matey. I go where you go.'

She smiled warmly. 'Bless you, Jake. What do you think we should do? Is there a chance of a passage back to England?'

'They ain't decided who's to be captain of that Spanish vessel we captured. There's a meeting in the clearing now. Shall we see what's happening, matey? Then we'll decide who to sign on with. Hades can be a demon, but he's honest, and that's more'n you can say for some.'

Katherine looked thoughtful. 'Couldn't you be the new captain, Jake? You know all there is know about sailing a ship, don't you?'

'Ay, matey. I reckon I could do the job, but I've no heart for it: there's more to bein' captain than knowing how to sail your ship. 'Sides, I doubt the men would sign on with me. I'm too old, now.'

'Oh . . . It was just an idea. And I don't think you're old, Jake.'

'You'd charm the birds out of the tree, Kit! Pity you ain't a man, for the crew would sail under you right enough.'

Katherine laughed and shook her head, saying nothing. They had been walking for a while, and as they reached the clearing, she could hear voices raised in anger. Taking their places among the others, they listened to the fierce arguments raging back and forth. It seemed as though the sailors could not agree about who should be the new captain, and as fast as one name was put forward so it was shouted down by a score of voices. Two evil-looking characters whom Katherine had never seen before were offering to fight each other for the captaincy. Before they could be stopped, one had drawn a dagger and stabbed the other in the chest. This foul act drew a howl of outrage from the men who wanted to see a fair fight, and both were pelted with fruit and cries of abuse.

Suddenly, without thinking what she was doing, Katherine found herself on her feet and in the centre of the clearing. She heard her name called by several of the men she knew, and waved to them, chuckling as the daring idea came to her.

'What's up, Kit? Settin' yourself up for captain, then?'

cried one, his words bringing forth a burst of genial laughter all round.

She grinned at him. 'Why not? I'd make a better one than you.'

Her saucy reply made him shake with laughter. 'That you would, matey,' he replied. 'And than a good many more here, I reckon.'

'I've learned to read the charts,' Katherine said, 'and I can navigate by the stars. Why shouldn't I be captain, since none of you can agree?'

More laughter and jeering greeted her words, but she stood her ground, giving back as good as she got. Some of the sailors called out encouragement, others shouted abuse, telling her to sit down, but she refused to be intimidated.

'Give me a sword, and I'll fight any man here,' Katherine said, her chin going up proudly.

This made the pirates roar with laughter; then a curious hush fell over them as they realised that she was serious.

'No, Kit! Come here, lad,' Jake said, rising to his feet in alarm.

'I'll fight the young cockerel! He wants teaching a lesson.' The man who had spoken was the one who had stabbed his first opponent in the chest. At his words, an uneasy rumble went through the assembly.

'Kit won't stand a chance,' Jake protested.

'He asked for it. Let them fight.'

'No. The lad's game enough, but it wouldn't be fair. Black Rod'll have an easy win.'

'Give me a sword,' Katherine said, her eyes alight with excitement as she was seized by a mood of recklessness. 'I'll show you I can fight as well as any man here.'

The men looked at each other uneasily; those that had sailed with Katherine had a warm affection for the young lad they thought they knew. They thought of Kit as a spirited youth, and did not doubt his courage, but Black Rod was a powerful man and a skilled swordsman. It was obvious that there could be only one outcome, and most of them wanted no part in the death of a comrade they liked. Finally, it was a stranger to Katherine who threw a sword to her: it was a wicked-looking cutlass and she rejected it, taking instead a light rapier from one of the men she knew, who parted with it reluctantly.

'Kit, give it up, lad,' Jake called despairingly. 'He's too strong for you.'

'No. The challenge has been given, and Kit must fight.'

A hush fell over the clearing as Hades stepped into the circle. 'I claim my right, as captain of the ship which took the *Santa Maria*, to fight all challengers.' He turned the menace of his golden eyes on Black Rod. 'You'll fight me first, the winner to take on the boy.'

Black Rod glared at him furiously. 'He challenged me. It weren't my doing. It ain't fair I fight you first.'

He was shouted down by a score of voices.

'Hades is right. He has the first pick of any challengers.'

'Ay, Hades is abiding by the rules. What's wrong, Black Rod? Lost your guts all of a sudden?' A burst of coarse laughter followed this taunt.

Black Rod scowled at the speaker. 'You fight him, then. I ain't a fool. I ain't mad enough to challenge Hades.' He slunk off into the trees with a ferocious scowl at those who dared to laugh, and there was a sigh of relief all round that a massacre had been avoided.

Hades joined in the general laughter. 'Reckon we could all do with a drop of Molly's rum—ay, mates?'

A buzz of approval met his suggestion, and everyone began to talk. Katherine's words fell into the ripple of relief like a stone into water, shocking them to sudden silence.

'You can drink after you've fought me, Captain Hades. This affair isn't settled yet.'

His grin froze on his lips as he looked at her. 'Do you mean that?' The golden flame leapt in his eyes as he saw the stubborn set of her chin. 'By heaven, it's time I taught you some manners, Kit! I've had enough of your games. I'll fight you, if that's what you want, and with one hand tied behind my back to even the score.'

'I want no favours from you,' Katherine snapped, her face proud.

'Then you'll get none.' Hades' mouth was hard as he drew his sword. 'You've asked for this, my lady!'

A gasp of surprise went through those close enough to hear his words, but in his fury he did not realise what he had said. His gaze was fixed on Katherine's face as he waited for her to move, hoping she would come to her senses and apologise, but he had not reckoned with her stubbornness.

Tossing her head with haughty pride, she took up the stance her father had taught her was correct for duelling, one hand on slender hip, her sword-point to the ground. 'I await you, sir,' she said coolly.

Surprise registered on Hades' face as he saw the grace and confidence of her movements, realising for the first time that she was not quite the novice he had thought her. His curiosity was aroused, and a tiny smile played across his mouth; this little exercise might prove interesting after all. He brought his sword up to touch Katherine's in courtly fashion, making her an elegant bow.

'At your pleasure, Kit,' he murmured.

They drew apart, circling each other warily, eyes locked in bloodless but intense combat, as both knew that there was much more to this struggle than the captaincy of a pirate ship. The sailors called out encouragement to Katherine, excited now by what they sensed was a private battle between the two. Seized by a mood of recklessness, and wanting to hurt Hades for some reason she herself did not fully understand, she suddenly rushed at him with a flurry of blows. A little surprised by the fierceness of her attack, he managed to parry her thrusts with consummate ease, yet making no attempt to attack.

A loud cheer broke from the excited spectators, as much for Katherine's courage as for her undoubted skill at fencing. She had been taught well and made a pretty sight as she parried and feinted, whirling swiftly aside as Hades tried to flick the rapier from her grasp. She was light and fast on her feet, and he found himself hard pressed to parry her thrusts without actually attacking her, something he had no intention of doing as he waited his chance to disarm her. A flicker of admiration gleamed in his eyes; she was a delightful opponent in the art of fencing, though he could at any time have pressed home his advantage of strength and superior experience; but it pleased him to play with her, to let her come at him with all her might and turn the blows aside.

After a while, Katherine realised that he was playing with her, indulging her, as if he enjoyed watching the flames of anger spark from her eyes. In her father or Lewis the indulgence would have been acceptable, but somehow in Hades it was not. She wanted him to take her seriously, to respect her for what she was and stop treating her like a foolish child. Anger made her thrusts grow wilder, and by some chance her blade slipped against his, flying off at an angle and cutting a jagged slash across his forearm. As she saw the blood spurt crimson, she gasped, and her guard lapsed as she felt instant remorse. In that moment he brought his own sword up sharply, and with a deft twist of his wrist sent Katherine's blade swirling through the air to land harmlessly in the sand.

Hades watched as she stood there panting, all anger gone from her face, and he sensed the anguish in her. He brought his arm up so that the point of his blade touched a spot just above her heart, seeing the look of bewilderment and pain in her lovely eyes; then he sheathed his sword and made her a graceful bow.

He was smiling as he came to her and offered his hand. 'It was a fair fight, Kit,' he said, in a voice loud enough for all to hear. 'You are a brave heart, and you have won your right to be the *Santa Maria*'s captain.'

Katherine stared at him, suspicion and disbelief in her face. 'You won,' she said breathlessly.

'But you drew first blood.' Hades looked ruefully at the scratch on his arm. 'I shall not underestimate you again.' Turning from her, he faced the silent spectators. 'By our laws, anyone may challenge the winner. Does any man here wish to fight me?'

There was silence, and the Captain smiled, hands on his hips as he surveyed them.

'Then, as the victor, I claim my right to the *Santa Maria*, and I nominate Kit as her captain. We shall sail together, my friends, and between us we shall sweep the seas free of the accursed Spaniards!'

There was loud, excited cheering at this point. With Hades in charge, there was no one who would dare to deny Katherine's rights. All at once she found herself surrounded by her shipmates, who were laughing and slapping her on the back.

'Damn it if you ain't the only one among us with enough spunk to stand up to Hades,' one of them said.

'I'll sail with you, Kit.' Fabius walked into the

clearing, his ebony skin glistening with sweat in the heat of the midday sun. His dark eyes travelled slowly round the men. 'I'll take Kit as my captain. Who will join us?'

'I'm with you, matey.' Jake came to stand beside them. 'You all know the lad has courage—you've seen it often enough. Are there any of you brave enough to sail with us?'

There was an immediate buzz of argument, as the sailors tried to decide whether to sail in the *Santa Maria* or in the *Golden Eagle*, but silence fell as Katherine held up her hand.

'If you sail with me, any prizes we take will be equally split among you. I want nothing for myself but a safe passage back to England when I'm ready, and your obedience to my commands until we part company.' She lifted her head, looking at Hades proudly, but with a new warmth in her eyes. 'I'll wager you we take more prizes than the *Golden Eagle*!'

His eyes sparked at the challenge of her words, but then he saw the warmth in her face and he began to grin, throwing back his head to roar with laughter.

He slapped his thigh. 'By thunder! I'm not the man to refuse a challenge, Kit, and I'll not do so this time, even though you've stolen my best gunner'—he nodded at Fabius—'and the only decent cook we've ever had. Here's my hand on it.'

Katherine gave him her hand, a faint flush stealing into her cheeks at his touch. 'Then we'll sail together,' she said, though the look in his eyes told her what he was asking.

Hades inclined his head, a gleam of mischief in his eyes. 'I leave you to instruct your crew, Kit. Since we sail tomorrow, may I invite you to dine on board the *Golden Eagle* tonight?' As she hesitated, his lips twitched. 'A meeting of captains to discuss strategy?'

Suddenly, Katherine was no longer afraid of him, and her eyes began to twinkle. 'Only if you allow my cook to prepare the meal, sir.'

He bowed his head, unable to hide the look of satisfaction on his face. 'Until tonight, Captain Kit.'

Katherine watched as he turned and strode from the clearing, her heart suddenly free from the ache she had carried for so long. Now that she was no longer Hades' prisoner, they could meet on equal terms.

Her eyes followed Jake and Fabius as they moved among the sailors, persuading those they trusted most to join the *Santa Maria*. Now, at last, she was free to search for Lewis at any island they chanced to pass, but first she must win the confidence of her crew. The men wanted plunder, and she must prove her worth as their captain. Her mind shied away from what it might mean in terms of lost life, but she stifled any guilt she might have felt. She must let nothing stand in the way of her determination to find Lewis—not even this feeling in her heart for her fellow-captain.

Katherine sat in the rowing-boat as her two most trusted friends pulled strongly towards the dark shape of the *Golden Eagle*. The moonlight played temptingly on the calm waters of the lagoon; it was a clear, warm night and there was something magical about the sound of the gentle waves lapping against the shore.

Lizzie had wanted her to wear a dress, offering a tempting one of black lace in the Spanish style, but Katherine refused it. Although she had stopped hating Hades, she needed the protection of her manly garb; to dress as a woman would once more give him the advantage, and he already had too much. Her heart was thudding with such excitement that she found it difficult to hide her feelings from Jake and Fabius. They had become so close to her that she felt they could almost read her thoughts.

Fabius had been told of her real identity. He showed little surprise, confessing he had suspected as much for some time.

'Does anyone else know?' Katherine had asked apprehensively. 'Would they still sail with me, if they knew the truth?'

'They respect you for standing up to Hades. Besides, he had the right to choose, and he nominated you. But the men will be satisfied only when we've taken our first prize.'

'So, until then, I'm on trial? If I fail, they'll demand a new captain.'

Fabius grinned. 'You won't fail—not with me and Jake to help you. There ain't much Jake don't know about ships, and I'm the best gunner you'll find hereabouts. Between us, we'll make the Spaniards give up their gold before we send them to the bottom of the ocean.'

Katherine nodded. She knew Fabius's story: he had told her how he had been a galley-slave for the Moors for years, then captured by the Spanish and tortured at the hands of the Inquisition. He had escaped by killing the prison guard, joining the pirates as a free man.

'I'm free now,' Fabius told her. 'I sail with whom I choose; and I chose you.'

'And I'm grateful. Without your help, I'd have found it harder to enlist a crew, no matter what Hades said. The chance to find my brother means a great deal to me.'

'He might have given you that chance, had you asked. He can be reasonable when he wishes. I don't blame him for having me flogged; I broke the the rules and got drunk on duty, so I earned my punishment. But you cared enough to help me. No one ever did as much for me.'

Katherine merely smiled and shook her head. He had repaid her small act of kindness by standing by her in the clearing, and she knew she would need to rely heavily on his advice in the coming weeks . . .

Her thoughts were brought to an abrupt end as the rowing-boat touched against the *Golden Eagle*'s side. Hades was waiting to welcome them on board, and the girl's eyes widened as she saw him. His trunk hose and doublet were of black velvet slashed with gold, and his silk shirt had ruffles of fine lace at throat and wrists. It was the first time she had seen him dressed in the garb of a gentleman, and she almost regretted the gown Lizzie had offered her.

'Welcome aboard the *Golden Eagle*,' he said, his manner respectful, despite the gleam in his eyes.

'Good evening, sir.' Katherine took the lead from him, averting her gaze as her heart began to pound. 'Have my crew permission to go below?'

'I never go back on a bargain, Kit.'

She heard the hint of laughter in the softness of his voice, and raised her head. 'Shall we go to your cabin and discuss your plans, Captain Hades?'

He bowed. 'As you wish, Captain Kit.'

As he stood aside to let her go first, she straightened her back, her head high. Why was it that they must always clash, even now that they were on equal terms? she wondered. The answer came swiftly to her mind: Hades was a man who needed to be in command. He demanded complete surrender, and she was too proud to give it.

Entering his cabin, she drew a sharp breath as she saw that the table had been set with a silken cloth and silver.

She turned and looked at him in surprise. 'I had not expected this.'

Hades' brows went up. 'You thought me a total savage, didn't you, Katherine?'

She flushed. 'You gave me little cause to believe otherwise.'

'Touché.' He grinned at her, sending tiny shivers down her spine. 'Who taught you to fence, Kitty? I enjoyed our sport today.'

Katherine raised her head with a touch of defiance. 'I took lessons with my brother.' She scowled at him. 'Don't laugh at me! I know you could have disarmed me sooner, had you wished.'

'Not so,' he lied, his soft voice making her tingle with pleasure. 'It's true that I'm stronger than you, but you fought well.'

'I'm sorry I hurt you,' she said. 'I was angry, but I shouldn't have done it. I've behaved like a fool, haven't I?'

Hades chuckled. 'A handsome apology—though I'm not sure I deserve it. I've given you cause enough to hate me.'

But I don't hate you! her heart cried. Katherine sensed the intensity in his burning look and turned away, needing to catch her breath. 'Shall we look at the charts?' she asked, seeing them spread on top of his sea-chests. 'Have you plotted our direction?'

'I see you mean to take your duties seriously.'

'Did you think I would not?' she replied, a touch of belligerence in her tone.

He smiled, shaking his head. 'If I did, then I was wrong. Come, we'll discuss this after dinner. First, you must have some wine.' He took a jug and poured red wine into the silver cups. 'We'll drink a toast to our new alliance.'

Katherine took a cup from him, her hand trembling as their fingers touched. He noticed the tinge of colour in her cheeks, but made no mention of it.

'To us,' he said, lifting his cup to toast her. 'To our partnership and the future—whatever it may bring.'

She sipped her wine, feeling unable to echo his words because of the tumultuous beating of her heart. Then he put down his goblet and moved towards her, his eyes promising so much that she could scarcely breathe. Very slowly he reached out and took her in his arms, drawing her against him. She felt the throbbing of his heart as his lips came down to brush lightly over hers, teasing and arousing the flickering desire within her.

As his kiss deepened, his tongue invading the sweet freshness of her mouth, inflaming her to careless passion, she pressed herself against him, melting into the iron hardness of his body. Her lips parted in breathless awareness of the fierce wanting inside her, the longing to be his—his woman. She was surprised when he let her go.

'That kiss will seal our bargain, Kitty,' he murmured. 'It is a promise for the future. Remember it, and when we return to the island, come to me if you will.'

Katherine stared at him, puzzled. She had been so certain that he meant to seduce her tonight, and in her heart she had been ready to accept the inevitable as the price of his protection.

Hades smiled wryly as he read the thoughts reflected in her eyes. 'Think well, Kitty. For once I have you, you belong to me.'

'I—I shall give you my answer when we return to the island next,' she breathed, her heart thumping.

'So be it.' He walked to his sea-chest and opened it, taking something out, then came back to her. 'These are yours. Take them if you wish, or let me guard them for you. I hope you will be satisfied with what I chose as your share of the prize on our last voyage.'

As he held up the necklace of huge black pearls, Katherine gasped. 'Are—Are they for me?'

'You earned them, as you have told me several times.' He grinned at her. 'Well, do you want your property, or shall I keep it safe you you?'

Katherine looked at him then, her eyes bright. 'Keep them for me until—until the day I come to give you my answer . . .'

To Katherine's surprise, the Spanish vessel they had closed with surrendered the moment a shot was fired across her bows. The white flag went up and her captain made a great show of laying down his sword.

She looked at Fabius. 'What do you think this means?' she asked anxiously. 'I expected they would put up a fight.'

'It may be a trap. I think we should put a hole in her and wait until Hades comes up with us.'

'No, I'm going on board, Fabius, and I want twenty of our best men in case they try to deceive us. But if they do intend to surrender, we'll not harm them—make sure the crew understand that.'

'Ay, ay, Cap'n.'

Fabius did not argue. Katherine had already proved herself a worthy leader in the past weeks, and he knew she preferred to deal with the capture herself because Hades would have given no quarter to the Spaniards. He was but an hour's sailing behind them, having stopped to take on water at an island they had passed earlier in the day. Only three days previously her ship had taken a merchantman laden with precious silks and spices, and once the cargo was transferred to the *Santa Maria*, she had allowed the crew to sail on, against Hades' advice. If he were here now, there was no doubt he would order the sinking of this galleon.

Katherine led the way across the rigging, too impatient to wait for the gangplank to be laid in place. Sword in hand, with feet apart and one hand on a slim hip, she looked haughtily into the Spanish captain's face.

'Well, sir, do you surrender?'

'I want to speak with your captain,' the Spaniard replied coldly in perfect English. 'This is an outrage—we are not at war with England. Your Queen has promised that this piracy will stop.'

Katherine smiled mockingly. 'Ay, she'll hang us if we're taken, I'll grant you that, sir, but we're a long way from home. I am the captain of the *Santa Maria*.' She raised her brows as she saw disbelief in his eyes. 'These are my men. If you doubt me, I shall have one of them cut off your left ear to prove it.'

Fabius took a step towards him, knife in hand. 'Let me do it, Cap'n.'

The Spaniard paled. 'No, no, that will not be necessary, Captain, I shall take your word. Please, sir, will you be good enough to speak with me in private?'

Katherine looked at him. He was slight of stature with a little beard and pale eyes. She could see beads of sweat on his brow.

'Certainly, sir.' Katherine turned to look at Fabius. 'If I'm not back by the time you count to one hundred, you know what to do.'

Fabius nodded grimly, turning his eyes on a Spanish seaman who was fidgeting with his sword-hilt. 'I'll know what to do.'

The Spanish captain saw his look and frowned at the sailor. 'Remember my orders—no resistance.' He turned to Fabius. 'I mean your captain no harm, I give you my word.'

'The word of a Spaniard—pah!' Fabius spat on the ground. 'I've started to count.'

'Please come with me, sir.' The fussy little Spaniard beckoned anxiously to Katherine. 'I must talk with you.'

She nodded, her hand resting lightly on her sword-hilt as she followed him along the deck and down the hatchway, doing her best to scowl ferociously. As they reached what was obviously his cabin, he turned to plead with her.

'As you will appreciate, Captain, our surrender has made the capture of this vessel easier for you, with no loss of life to your crew. My reason for so doing is inside. I am begging you as a gentleman—please, sir, do not rob me of my dearest treasure.'

'You will deliver your gold and jewels to me, sir, or I shall not be responsible for the actions of my men.'

The Spaniard threw open the cabin door. 'Take everything of value—but please do not harm my Isabella. She is my only child, and I would die to save her.'

Inside the room, Katherine saw a pretty girl of little more than ten years. She was weeping and clinging to her duenna, a woman of perhaps thirty, well fleshed and handsome.

The child looked at Katherine fearfully. 'Are you going to kill us all?' she asked.

Katherine almost smiled at her, then remembered her role just in time. 'I hope it will not be necessary to harm anyone, Señorita. You must tell your father to surrender his treasure, and then we shall let you go on your way in safety.'

The young girl released herself from her duenna and ran to Katherine, seizing her hand to kiss it. She looked at the child's pale skin against the tan of her own, experiencing a strange emotion. She was about to rob Isabella's father of his possessions, and yet it was not so long ago that she had been as innocent as this child. How had it come to this? She steeled her heart, remembering that it was because of a Spanish Don that she had run away from her home. Yet she was not proof against the child's sweet smile.

'No, you may keep that,' she said, as Isabella began to unfasten a heavy gold cross and chain set with tiny pearls that was round her throat. 'But everything else must be delivered to my men—and I want your duenna's prettiest dress.'

'Thank you, sir, I knew you were a man of honour,' Isabella said, her eyes shining. 'Father, you must do as the Captain asks.'

'Yes, yes, I will give him everything, my love, do not fear.' The Spaniard looked at Katherine. 'We should go back. Your men will be growing impatient.'

Katherine agreed, feeling reluctant. She would have liked to stay and talk to the child, but she knew Fabius would be anxious and likely to tear the ship apart if she did not return as promised. Besides, she doubted if he could count to one hundred.

Returning to the deck, she found her friend about to come in search of her. He looked relieved when she came towards him, sheathing the sword he had already drawn.

'Is everything safe?'

Katherine nodded. 'They will give up their gold in return for a safe passage. We shall take what we came for, and let them go on. And Fabius . . .' He paused to look back at her. 'Tell our crew there are a woman and child on board. If any man lays a hand on them, he forfeits his share of the prize. The child is allowed to keep her trinket, by my orders. I'll have no flogging on my ship, but I'll be obeyed!'

Fabius did not smile. Over the past weeks his liking for

Katherine had grown to a deep respect, shared, he knew, by the rest of the crew. Her orders would be obeyed equally out of that respect and the knowledge that she was under Hades' protection.

The Spaniard's treasure was brought up on deck: three chests of rich materials, one of silver, one of gold and a small casket containing the finest emeralds and rubies Katherine had ever seen. There was also a dress of black velvet trimmed with lace with a low neckline and wide, panniered skirts. Katherine had it taken to her cabin with the rest.

'This is everything?' she asked, her eyes steady on the Spanish captain's face.

'All I have, Captain,' he replied. 'You will leave us now, as you promised?'

Katherine nodded. 'Yes, you may go on, sir, we shall not hinder you further.'

The pirates left, and the *Santa Maria* began to draw away from the other vessel; but as they did so, Jake shouted a sudden warning. Looking towards the galleon, Katherine saw a puff of smoke and flame as a cannon fired at them, the ball falling harmlessly into the water some feet from their stern.

Fabius was instantly at her side, waiting for her signal. 'Shall we sink them?'

Katherine looked at him thoughtfully. 'Can you bring down their mainmast?'

Fabius grinned. 'Ay, ay, Captain.'

He barked his orders at the crew, waiting until the helmsman had brought the *Santa Maria* on to the right tack. 'Now!' he yelled at the eager torch-man.

The *Santa Maria*'s cannon roared, belching smoke as the iron ball sped on its way, finding its mark with a deadly accuracy which gave proof of Fabius's boast. He truly was the best gunner on the Spanish Main.

A cheer went up from the pirates as the Spaniards mast went crashing down, causing confusion and fear amongst the crew. Screams and shouts rent the air, and figures could be seen beneath the wreckage. Katherine's face was grim as she gave the order to close in once more when a white flag was shown.

'Shall we put a hole in them?' Fabius asked.

'No. We are boarding again. Make ready with the grappling-hooks.'

'But why?'

'I've an idea our friend has been less than honest with us. This time we'll search the ship ourselves.'

Fabius stared at her. 'You think there is more treasure on board?'

Katherine nodded grimly. 'I would have let them keep it, but for that shot.'

A very frightened captain greeted them as they re-boarded the galleon. He dragged forward one of his men, forcing him to his knees on the deck in front of Katherine.

'This is the culprit—against my orders. I shall see he hangs for it.'

'That is your affair,' Katherine replied. 'We shall now search your ship ourselves. I advise you to keep better order among your men, sir, for if my crew becomes nervous, I cannot answer for them. We have no love for Spaniards.'

A thorough search of the ship unearthed three more chests packed with silver, and another of gold was discovered beneath Isabella's bed. The little Spaniard wrung his hands in anguish as the pirates brought them up, shouting and laughing triumphantly.

'We ought to kill the dogs!' Fabius growled, and the others chorused their agreement.

'No!' Katherine cried. 'They broke their word, but

we'll keep ours—like the English gentlemen we are, lads.' The crew laughed at her jest, their tempers cooling as they gloated over the rich prize they had taken. 'But this time we'll spike their guns before we leave—they'll not fire on us again.'

As they climbed back on board the *Santa Maria*, Fabius looked at Katherine curiously. 'How did you know there was more?'

'Our little friend was too nice, too pleased to hand over his treasure—and much too happy to see us leave.'

Fabius threw back his head, laughing long and loud. 'By heaven, but you're a wily one, Kit. Not even Hades himself could have done better. He'd have sent the galleon to the bottom with half her treasure still on board, given the chance. After this, the men will follow you to hell and back if you command it.'

Katherine smiled. 'Perhaps I shall ask something of them one day—for now we shall wait for Hades to come up with us. Our holds are full, and it is time we returned to the island.'

The *Golden Eagle* was already anchored in the lagoon as Katherine took her ship slowly through the white water. Once, the bottom scraped against some rocks and she held her breath, afraid that the *Santa Maria* might come to grief on this last stage of her triumphant voyage. But Jake's presence steadied her, and Katherine kept her fears well hidden, only her closest friends guessing her relief as they passed into the calm lagoon.

She smiled as a cheer went up from her crew, watching the shore anxiously as men and women began waving and calling greetings. This time it was almost like coming home, and like her crew, Katherine was eager to feel the earth beneath her feet once more. She searched the now crowded beach hopefully with her eyes, looking for

Hades' commanding figure, but he was not among those who had poured out on to the shore to greet them.

He had been a day's sailing ahead of them, as Katherine had stopped to visit two islands they passed on their way home. The *Golden Eagle* was riding quietly at anchor, her masts empty of sail, the decks bare as if she were deserted. Katherine bit her lip: Hades had obviously gone on shore, and would be waiting to see what she intended to do. He would make her come to him, just as she had promised.

Boats were being lowered over the side, and the men were eager to depart. Katherine had the treasure brought up and placed in one of them under the guard of her most trusted men. The keys were in her possession, and should the locks be tampered with before the division, those responsible would be torn to pieces by their companions. Therefore she had little doubt that the chests would remain intact until she opened them herself.

She had her own sea-chest, containing the black dress, taken to Lizzie's house. The woman came out to greet her, clasping her so tightly that she could hardly breathe. 'You've changed,' she said, her eyes going over Katherine's face shrewdly. 'I think you've left childhood behind you now.'

'Perhaps. I've brought you a present, Lizzie. Look.' Opening her sea-chest, she took out the black velvet gown which had belonged to Isabella's duenna. 'If you let out the seams a little, I think it will fit you.'

Lizzie's eyes gleamed with pleasure. She pounced on the dress, holding it against herself. 'Why, bless you, Katherine, it's fit for a princess! You should keep it for yourself.'

Katherine shook her head. 'I've no use for a dress, Lizzie. It's for you.'

She stroked the dress lovingly, folding it carefully before putting it away with her other treasures. She was thoughtful as she looked at Katherine. 'You can bathe while I get you something to eat—and I'll trim your hair for you, if you like.'

'I would be glad if you could make it look a little tidier, Lizzie.'

After the girl had bathed and eaten, Lizzie took out a tiny pair of silver scissors, snipping at the ragged edges of her hair. When she had finished, she gave Katherine a shiny pewter plate so that she could see her image in its surface. The reflection was blurred, and Katherine merely glanced at herself.

'I'm sure it's better than Jake's handiwork. Thank you, Lizzie.'

She had a nervous fluttering in her stomach, but she didn't want Lizzie to guess that she cared what she looked like.

'I wish I had a mirror, so that you could see yourself,' Lizzie sighed. 'There's a difference in you since you were last here.'

Katherine shrugged. 'I've grown a little. I'll buy some new clothes.'

Lizzie pulled a face. To her, the changes were obvious: Katherine's figure was beginning to fill out a little and it was becoming harder to disguise the fact that she was a beautiful woman. The men who sailed with her were not blind; most of them must have guessed her secret, and in Lizzie's opinion it could only be a matter of time before there was trouble.

Jake confessed to some anxiety when he came to fetch Katherine that evening, though he maintained that the trouble would not come from her crew. 'I doubt there's a man who doesn't know the truth by now,' he agreed, 'but they'll not harm her—Fabius has seen to that.

Besides, Hades has his mark on her, and none of them dares risk his displeasure.'

'And what of him?' Lizzie asked with a frown. 'He's a man without a heart, Jake, and he'll break hers if she lets him.'

Jake pulled his lip. 'Kit has more sense than that.'

'I'm not sure,' Lizzie replied doubtfully. 'She's a woman, and Hades has a certain attraction . . .' She broke off as Katherine came out of the bedroom, dressed in the clean breeches and silk shirt that she had borrowed before.

'I'm ready,' she said, looking at them. 'Tell Fabius to have the chests fetched to the clearing. I'll join you there in a little while.'

Jake stared at her. 'Aren't you coming with me?'

Katherine shook her head. 'I've something I must do first—but I'll be there in time for the division.'

She smiled at him to hide her nervousness, and went out.

CHAPTER SIX

KATHERINE'S HEART was thumping as she reached Hades' house. It had taken her a long time to make up her mind—but she had a promise to keep. Besides, she longed to be with him again, and her pride had given way to the stronger emotion. During the weeks of their voyage they had met only briefly to discuss tactics, and she had been surprised at how much she missed the sight of his tall figure striding about the deck.

If she accepted his invitation to be his mistress, it would mean that she must give up her position as captain of the *Santa Maria*, but in her heart she knew she could not carry on with the masquerade for much longer. Perhaps he would take her back to England with him . . . At this point Katherine's thoughts became confused. She dare not think far ahead; the future was too uncertain.

Reaching Hades' house, she knocked and waited; then, receiving no answer, she opened the door and went in. It was empty, and she felt a sharp disappointment as she turned to leave. She had been so sure he would be here, waiting for her.

Darkness was falling as she began to make her way towards the clearing. Knowing her crew would be impatient for the division of their spoils, she quickened her step; then she halted, drawing a sharp breath as a shadow fell across her path.

'Hades?' she said, her voice eager. Then the shadow moved into the moonlight and she saw it was one of her former shipmates who had chosen to sail on the *Golden Eagle*. 'Oh, it's you, Ram. Have you seen Captain Hades?'

The pirate's small eyes narrowed. 'He's away over the other side of the island on a hunting trip. We needed fresh meat for tonight.'

'I see,' Katherine said, feeling uneasy. She had never liked Ram, and had been secretly glad he was not one of those who had chosen to sail with her. 'Well, I must go. My crew will be waiting for me.'

'Captain Kit . . .' Ram leered at her, leaning towards her so that she could smell the strong odour of rum on his breath. 'Or is it Captain Kitty?'

Katherine stared at him haughtily. 'I think my name can have nothing to do with you. Please stand aside. I'm already late.'

'Why the hurry?' Ram asked, his lips curving in a sneer. 'Allus did think yourself too good for the likes o' me, didn't you?'

Katherine's eyes flashed darts at him. 'You're drunk,' she said scornfully. 'Or you wouldn't dare to speak to me like this.'

Ram sniggered. 'If you're expecting Hades to protect you, you're out of luck. He spent the night at Red Molly's.'

'I can protect myself,' Katherine snapped. 'And you're lying . . .'

She went to push past him, but he grabbed her arm, twisting it behind her so that she almost cried out with the pain, but would not give him the satisfaction of knowing he had hurt her. She tried to wrench away from him, kicking at his shins and struggling to free herself. His fingers tightened on her arm, digging into the fleshy softness. As a small gasp escaped her, Ram laughed, his other arm going round her throat from behind, pressing hard and choking her.

'I've got you now, Kit,' he muttered. 'I've bin' waiting for this a long time, my pretty, and now I'm going to have you. You've been giving it to old Jake and that tame Moor o' yourn—and a few more besides, I shouldn't wonder.'

'How dare you say such filthy things!' Katherine cried, anger making her redouble her struggle. She managed to free herself sufficently to sink her teeth into his hand, wriggling out of his grasp as he howled with pain. The next moment her sword flashed in the moonlight. Ram blinked at her in bewilderment, surprised by the sudden reversal. Her eyes were glacial as she faced him. 'Well, I'm waiting. Or shall I just slit your throat?'

Ram was not wearing a sword. His eyes rolled uneasily as he saw the purposeful way she was holding her weapon. 'Now you don't want to take it like that, Kit,' he said. 'I were only teasing . . .'

Katherine's scornful look seared him. 'You miserable coward! You thought to take advantage of a defenceless woman, but you're not so brave now that you've discovered I'm not so weak as you thought. I ought to run you through . . .'

'Bravo, Kit! I've a mind to do it myself, but I'll not spoil your triumph . . .'

Hades' voice startled them both. Katherine glanced quickly at his face as he walked out of the shadows, a grim smile flickering about his lips.

'How long have you been there?' she asked, her heart missing a beat as their eyes met.

Hades' smile deepened. 'Long enough to see you were in control of the situation, but not in time to prevent this creature from attacking you.' He turned his gaze on

Ram, and the pirate's mouth went slack with fear as he read his fate in the hard eyes. 'Shall we kill him now, or later—after he's suffered a little?'

He sounded as if he were asking her if the weather was fine, and Katherine shivered as she looked at the thin line of his mouth. Even now there was a side of him that terrified her. 'He's not worth the trouble,' she said. 'I'm not hurt, and I don't think he'll accost me again in a hurry.'

Hades' nostrils flared as he looked at Ram, who had started to sweat profusely. 'It seems you've a short time left to you,' he said in a deceptively mild voice. 'If I were you, I should make the most of it . . .'

The man's eyes bulged and he made a sound that was half a moan, half a protest, and then he turned and went crashing through the trees in a blind panic.

Katherine drew a deep breath to steady her fluttering pulses, then she raised her eyes to Hades', almost frightened by the anger she saw there, even though it was not for her. 'There's no need to kill him.'

'No?' His brows rose. 'That's my affair, I think, but surely we have other, more important, business to discuss?'

She bit her lip, suddenly feeling unsure. It was impossible to read his thoughts, and the memory of that kiss was all she had to help her.

'The wager. I came to find you so that you could be present at the division, to see for yourself . . .' Her words ran into a breathless whisper as the golden flame in his eyes reached out to sear her.

'Ah yes, the wager. I had forgotten that.' His voice was soft, caressing her like a velvet glove. 'I had something else in mind—a promise that you made me. But we shall settle the wager first. How many ships did you take in all?'

Katherine's heart raced madly, her eyes suddenly alight with mischief as she gazed up at him. 'Two—a galleon and a merchantman. How many did you capture?'

Hades laughed, matching his longer strides to hers as they walked through the woods together. 'You know the answer well enough, Kit. The *Golden Eagle* took two ships, both galleons on their way home from the New World. Oh, and there was another, but it was of no account, since the holds were empty.'

'Then you have won,' Katherine said. 'For a merchantman does not match a galleon, even though we captured gold, silver and some fine emeralds as well as silks and spices.'

'I think we'll agree to a draw,' he said, his eyes a deep gold in the moonlight. 'You've changed, Kit, and I like it.' His gaze roved over her appreciatively.

She flushed and turned her head aside, not wanting him to see how easy his victory over her really was. 'Lizzie says I've grown up. Perhaps I've learned that it is not always easy to take the decisions which must be made . . .'

It was an admittance of something felt between them, a bridge over which they both could pass. Hades was silent for a while, his face thoughtful; but when he spoke at last, Katherine heard a new tenderness in his voice which made her tremble.

'Then I have won that prize I most desire,' he said, a faint smile dawning in his eyes. 'I shall have to decide what forfeit you must pay . . .'

Katherine smiled but made no reply. At that moment she had no words to convey her feelings, and could only hope that she was not deceiving herself when she believed there was a new tenderness in him. Perhaps it was possible that he loved her as she loved him—

as she had loved him for so long.

They had reached the clearing. The pirates were gathered round the huge bonfire, waiting eagerly for their share of the spoils. A huge cheer went up as Katherine and Hades entered the circle of light together, standing side by side.

Katherine knew that her happiness must show on her face, for she could not stop smiling; and she realised that the men were instantly aware of the change. She heard laughter and a few sly jests, whispered just loud enough for her to hear. They left her in no doubt that her secret was a secret no longer: they were calling her Hades' woman. He stood beside her, tall and strong, the firelight falling on the carved features, his hand resting lightly on her waist with an air of possession that was plain for all to see. And she no longer cared that it was so.

Taking the keys to her sea-chest from the fine chain around her neck, she handed them to Fabius. He opened the sturdy trunks, and the task of sharing out the captured treasure began. There was some dispute as to the emeralds' value, and to settle this, they were put up for sale to the highest bidder. Red Molly bid for them, but Hades seemed determined to have them, and in the end Molly tossed her mane of ginger hair and walked off in disgust. Hades sent a member of his own crew to fetch a small chest of silver, which was then divided among the *Santa Maria*'s crew.

Katherine looked at him curiously. 'Why did you want the emeralds so badly? You paid a high price for them.'

'I have my reasons. They're some of the finest stones I've ever seen.'

She nodded, remembering for a moment the face of the child whose father had surrendered his emeralds to preserve her life. Her conscience was disturbed vaguely by the child's delicate looks, and she wondered what would become of Isabella now that her father had lost so much. Then, as she felt the pressure of Hades' arm about her waist, she forgot Isabella and her father. She forgot everything but the look in his eyes as she glanced up at him.

'Your work is done here,' he murmured close to her ear. 'Are you ready to leave?'

Katherine drew in her breath sharply, her heart racing wildly as she saw the golden promise in his eyes. Her head was whirling as the word seemed to move away, leaving just the two of them in all eternity. She felt a quickening in her limbs, and knew that it was desire.

'Yes, my love,' she whispered. 'I'm quite ready.'

They left the clearing with a wave of the hand to their friends, most of whom had begun to celebrate with a vengeance, walking through the welcoming darkness of the trees, their minds and bodies in perfect communion with the night and the peace of knowing that the struggle between them was at an end. Somewhere a night bird's jarring broke the velvet softness of the evening, startling Katherine. Hades' arm tightened protectively round her waist and she leant against him, smiling. As they neared his house, she thought he would take her there, but instead he drew her past it, towards the beach.

A crescent moon had turned the sands to silver. The waters of the lagoon whispered gently against the shore, and a faint breeze rippled through the trees, cooling the scented air. It seemed that they were alone in some magical place of their own. Hades stopped walking, gathering her into his arms as though he could wait no longer to taste the nectar of her lips, his body shuddering with desire as he gazed hungrily down at her lovely face.

'Katherine, my proud warrior queen,' he whispered huskily against the freshly-washed silkiness of her hair.

'Have I truly won at last?'

Her lips curved in a teasing smile. 'Our wager—have I not conceded defeat, sir?'

The fire leapt up in Hades' eyes, enfolding her in its white heat, scorching her and turning her blood to molten honey. 'Still she defies me,' he murmured, smiling oddly. 'Then shall I play the victor's part and take my prize, or will you give it willingly, Katherine? Sweet, lovely Kitty . . .'

Katherine trembled, her limbs aching to be pressed against him, her hands reaching out as she remembered the smooth feel of his flesh beneath hers. Desire churned in her, melting her very bones. For a moment longer she held back, hoping for those special words she longed to hear, but they did not come and she could restrain herself no longer. With a cry that was half pain, half passion, she arched her slim body against the lean, hard length of him, feeling the throb of his maleness and his need of her, the heat of him burning her up so that she was one living, breathing, flame of desire. In an instant his arms closed around her, and in his face she saw a fierce triumph that sent fiery thrills coursing through her body like a river in full flood. Then his mouth came down to take possession of hers, and she surrendered to his mastery.

All else was forgotten as the hot desire churned in her. She clung to him, crying his name wildly as he rained passionate, hungry kisses on her lips and throat, and the sweet silken valley between her breasts. Her body was consumed with a fierce wanting; she moaned, her lips parting for the invasion of his tongue, her thighs moving against his in aching suspension, instinctively knowing that only the meeting of their flesh could bring relief from the madness pulsing in her blood.

Hades' hands were unfastening her shirt, slipping it

back from her shoulders so that it fell to the sand. His mouth moved down her throat, his tongue licking, teasing her nipples to twin points of arousal as he caught them gently between his lips. Then his big hands were tearing at the velvet breeches in sudden urgency as he pushed them down over her narrow hips. The moonlight washed her skin in a silver glow, making him groan as he witnessed her beauty. His clothes joined hers on the sand, the muscles rippling in his shoulders as he swept her up and laid her gently down.

As flesh touched flesh, Katherine gasped her pleasure aloud, her hands stroking the steely firmness of his back, her nails digging in to him as his caresses drove her wild. Flesh burned flesh as they came together in delicious urgency; burned, cooled and burned again as they slaked their mutual thirst like two travellers in the desert.

Her first cry of pain as he entered her was forgotten in the pleasure which followed, sweeping them on to planes of unknown sensation. Katherine moved wildly beneath him, crying out as she dissolved in ecstasy.

'Kitty, my wonderful Kitty,' he murmured. 'I have never known a woman like you! You're like a fever in my blood, a sweet madness that won't be stilled. You belong to me,' he muttered hoarsely, as they lay entwined in each other's arms, reluctant to be parted even now that their first urgency was quenched. He buried his face in the softness of her breasts. 'Tell me, Katherine—say it now.'

She trembled as his hands began their seductive stroking again. 'I belong to you,' she whispered.

Her cheeks were wet with tears. He demanded total surrender, yet he did not say the words which she so desperately needed to hear. His lips moved against her throat, arousing that wild throbbing in her limbs once more, and she knew she could not fight it. No matter what he was or what he did, she belonged to him: she was his woman.

He raised his head to look into her eyes, which were just now the colour of the ocean, green and mysterious but full of moonlight. 'You will never leave me—say it, Katherine. Say it now!'

'I shall never . . .'

The words was lost as he gave a cry of savage triumph, his mouth devouring hers as he trapped her beneath him in the sand. Once more Katherine was swept away on a tide of passion, her cries of pleasure mingling with the beating of the waves against the reef.

Her surrender was total as she gasped out his name. 'Hades, I love you . . . love you . . .'

And still he did not say, 'I love you, Katherine.'

Katherine woke, stretching her hand across the bed in search of Hades' body. The sheets were cold to the touch, and she sighed, her lips curving in a smile of satisfaction as she remembered her lover carrying her to the bed last night. They had quarrelled earlier, as they still did quite frequently, but the argument had been forgotten as she discovered anew the delights of love in his arms. A month had passed since her return to the island: a month of love-filled nights and lazy days.

She sat up in bed, hugging her knees to her breast. Hades was nowhere to be seen, and she wondered if he had gone fishing, as he often did while she still slept. He would return with his catch, clean it, and bring it to her when it was cooked.

Katherine had offered to cook the fish one morning, but he made her sit and wait until it was ready, watching her with that half-mocking smile on his lips that she found so tantalising. He was, she thought, a curious mixture that defied her understanding. One moment he could be gentle and tender, the next cruelly possessive, demanding total obedience to his commands. It was as though he had a demon hidden in his heart, as though some secret from his past haunted him, never letting him be at peace; when that bleak look came into his eyes, she knew that it would not be long before they quarrelled. Yet even their fiercest rows ended when he took her in his arms, for Katherine was not proof against the sweeping desire he aroused in her so easily, and she melted before the heat of his passion.

Sometimes her mind struggled against his dominance, still fearing to trust him, despite her burning love. She felt herself his possession, something valued. But for how long? Without his love, she felt his desire for her must burn itself out eventually . . .

Thrusting such unwelcome thoughts from her mind, Katherine rose, splashed herself all over with the cold water Hades had fetched from the spring, and dressed in the velvet breeches which had been her brother's, now almost worn out. She looked at herself, wondering how it would feel to wear a dress again, remembering for a moment the life at Dunline Castle before her father and Lewis had quarrelled. Suddenly a clear picture of her brother came into her mind. She could see his face, thinner and paler than she remembered it, but still the same dear face. He was calling to her, begging her not to forget him.

'Lewis,' she whispered, guilt striking at her heart like a blade. 'Lewis, where are you?'

'Breakfast . . .' Hades came in, his arms full of fruit and a string of fish he had caught. He looked solemn as he saw the look of pain in her eyes. 'What is it, Kitty—are you ill?'

Katherine's face was stricken as she turned to him. 'It

was Lewis—my twin—he called to me. He needs me, Hades. He needs me!'

He frowned, laying down his burdens. 'Your brother, who was lost at sea . . .'

She sobbed, 'He is in trouble! I know it. I must find him. I must!'

Hades' eyes took on a distant expression. 'You could search these islands for years and never find him, always supposing he is still alive.'

'How do you know I wouldn't find him?' Katherine demanded, her guilt making her angry. 'You don't want me to try. You want to keep me here as your—your plaything.' She stopped in horror as his mouth tightened and his eyes narrowed to tawny slits. 'No, I didn't mean that . . .'

He made no reply, moving outside to clean the fish and cook it over an open fire. Katherine watched from the doorway, torn between resentment and regret for what she had said. It was not fair, and she knew it: she was as eager for their loving as he, and he treated her more as a prized possession than a plaything. Her anxiety for Lewis had made her speak without thinking.

She went and knelt by his side, touching his hand. 'I'm sorry, Hades,' she whispered. 'I spoke in haste.'

He looked at her, and she gasped as she saw the agony in his eyes. 'You're right, Kitty, I'm selfish to keep you here. You were not meant for this life.'

'What do you mean?' she asked fearfully.

'You were gently born. I kidnapped you and took you from your home—and for what? To bring you to a pirates' nest . . .' Hades stood up and walked in to the house, and Katherine followed him.

'What are you doing?' she asked, as he went to his sea-chest and unlocked it.

Hades turned to her, and his eyes had a curious blind

look as though he was hardly aware of her. 'I am returning your property, Katherine. Take it and go home. Go back to England, where you belong.'

'No!' Katherine refused to take the pouch he held out to her. 'No, I won't leave you. You can't send me away.'

He hesitated, and she saw he was torn by indecision. 'I want you to go.' He held the pouch out to her.

Katherine struck it from his hand, her eyes blazing with anger as it fell to the floor and the contents scattered. 'I'll not be sent away like a common whore!'

'It's for your own good,' he said. 'Find your brother and go back to the life you were intended to live. Don't waste your time with a man who has nothing to offer you.'

Hades bent to gather up the fallen jewels, and Katherine saw a heavy gold cross and chain set with pearls in his hand as he stood up and once more offered them to her. A cold chill ran down her spine as she recognised it.

'That chain is not mine! Where did you get it?'

'I bought it for you from a sailor,' he said. 'I wanted you to have something, even though you refused your share of . . .'

'Liar!' A tide of sickness rose up in her as she looked at the chain she had last seen hanging about the child Isabella's neck. Her eyes widened with horror as she recalled him speaking of a galleon they had taken with empty holds and realised it must have been the one that had surrendered to her. 'What did you do with the child? May you burn in Hell if you killed her, you demon!'

Anger registered in Hades' eyes, replacing the look of sadness. 'What are you talking about?'

'That ship—the one with empty holds you spoke of. What did you do with her?' Katherine laughed bitterly. 'Need I ask? She was a Spaniard, so you sent her to the bottom of the sea with all her crew to satisfy your hatred of Don Francisco, didn't you?' She stared at him hard. 'Why will you not tell me the reason for your hatred? Perhaps then, I might understand why you act as you do.'

The muscles corded in Hades' neck, and his mouth became a hard line. 'You call me a murderer,' he muttered. 'Then you ask me to explain—why? So that you can heap more insults on my head? Perhaps one day I will tell you my story—but it will be when I decide. It is enough for you to know that I have sworn to sweep the Spanish from the seas, and not even you will sway me from my purpose.'

His stubborn refusal to trust her enough to confide in her made Katherine lose all control. 'Murderer!' she screamed. 'There was a ten-year-old child on board. I let her keep that chain—and you took it from her before she died!'

Hades' face was dark with anger. For a moment Katherine thought he meant to strike her, then an icy coldness settled over him. He tossed the jewels on the table and strode past her, out of the house.

She gasped, clutching at herself as the pain struck her. She sank to her knees, weeping wildly, her mind tortured and confused. She was not sure whether she was weeping for herself, the child or Hades. After a while the storm of weeping passed and she began to feel the ache in her breast. What had she done? She had said unforgivable things to him, accusing him of murder when in her heart she knew instinctively that he would not have deliberately killed an innocent. She looked at the chain again, wondering now if he had told her the truth. Was it possible that one of her own men had taken it as revenge when they went back on board for the second time? She decided that she would apologise to Hades when he returned, and listen to his story; then they would make up their quarrel and he would take her in his arms. There would be no more talk of her leaving.

Katherine sat down to wait, deliberately numbing her mind to keep at bay the terrible thoughts which tormented her. The hours passed, hours that seemed a lifetime in their loneliness and the despair which held her chained to the house. She was afraid to leave the shack lest Hades return and find her gone.

When the door opened, she jumped to her feet with a glad cry. 'Hades . . .' Her words trailed away as she saw it was Fabius. 'Fabius . . .' she faltered. 'I'm glad to see you.'

'I should not have come here,' he said, 'but the men are talking about choosing a new captain for the *Santa Maria*, unless you tell us your plans.'

Katherine stared at him. 'We did well last voyage, didn't we?'

His face was grim. 'They think you'll sail with Hades next time.'

'I'm not sure . . .'

'I've persuaded them to wait thus far, but they're growing restless. They want to know what your thoughts are, Kit.'

She turned away, hiding her tears. 'Another day or two . . . Give me two days, Fabius.'

He nodded. 'I can hold them together as long as that, but no more.'

'You'll have my decision by then, I promise you.'

'Why don't you go with him?' Fabius asked, frowning. 'It's what you want, isn't it?'

Katherine closed her eyes for a moment, her throat aching with the pain of her despair. She knew that what Fabius said was true, but was it wise to sail with a man who could tear her apart so easily? Might it not be better to go back to England as he had suggested?

She turned to look at Fabius, her eyes very bright. 'I'll give you my answer in two days,' she whispered.

When morning came, Hades had not returned to the house. Katherine woke feeling stiff and sore from crouching tensely as she lay waiting for the sound of his footsteps; she had succumbed to her weariness at last, sleeping only fitfully. Now, a glance around the house showed her that he had not been near since their quarrel.

Jumping up, she did not stay to tidy her hair. She was fully clothed, not having undressed the night before, and she ran straight out of the house, panic flaring in her. Where was Hades? Why hadn't he come home? Was he hurt . . .

The questions pounded in her head as she raced through the trees to Lizzie's house, banging on the door like a madwoman and yelling for her friend at the top of her voice.

Lizzie came to answer the door, yawning and scowling as she saw who it was. 'In heaven's name, what's the matter, Kit? You made enough noise to waken the dead!'

Katherine grabbed at her arm. 'It's Hades—he didn't come home last night. Oh, Lizzie, I'm afraid something has happened to him.'

The woman sniffed, annoyed at being woken at what she considered an unearthly hour. 'Him! Sleeping it off, I expect. He was drinking himself silly at Red Molly's last night.'

Katherine stared at her, eyes dark turquoise as the pain moved in her. 'Drinking at Molly's . . . He was with her?'

Lizzie saw the hurt in her eyes and cursed herself for being a clumsy fool. 'No, Kit, it weren't that way. He were just drinking in a corner by himself. Molly were with some other man.'

'But he didn't come home . . .' Katherine whispered. 'He stayed there all night . . . with her.'

'You can't be certain. He might have curled up under a tree somewhere and fallen sleep. He was probably too ashamed of himself to come back in that state.'

'No.' Katherine felt oddly calm. 'I know he was with her, and I'm going to prove it. I'll ask her.'

'Let it be, child. Like as not, he'll slink back with his tail between his legs and say he's sorry.'

But Katherine wasn't listening. She had turned away and was already walking towards the clearing and Molly's house. Her face was tight and cold as she marched through the trees. Already she knew she would find Hades there, at his old love's house. She felt numb, too shocked to feel pain. How could he do it? How could he betray their love in this way? But he had never said he loved her . . . He had told her to go back to England . . .

There were a few pirates standing around in the clearing. Katherine saw them, but their faces were only blurs of shadow. Nothing seemed quite real to her; she was moving through a nightmare. As she reached the veranda of Molly's house, its owner came to the door. Her yellow eyes glittered with dislike as she looked at the girl.

'What do you want?' Molly asked, hostility in every line of her face.

'I've come to see Hades.'

'Why? He don't want to see you. He's finished with you for good—told me so last night.'

'I don't believe you,' Katherine said, though the other woman's words were like a knife thrust in her heart. 'I want to see him for myself.'

Molly jerked her head towards the back. 'He's in

there. See for yourself if you don't believe me, but don't say I didn't warn you. He spent the night with me, in my bed.'

Katherine passed through a long room scattered with small tables and benches, the tables still strewn with dirty pots from the night before. She halted in front of a door which she guessed led through to a bedroom. The door was closed, and Katherine hesitated, almost ready to turn back as doubts assailed her. Perhaps Lizzie was right . . .

'Well, what are you waiting for? Scared you'll find something you don't like?'

Molly's goading made Katherine open the door. Hades was lying on his back, naked beneath the sheets and fast asleep. Hearing the mocking sound of Molly's laughter, Katherine was suddenly furiously angry. Without thinking what she was doing, she picked up a half-full tankard of stale ale from the table beside the bed and emptied the contents straight into his face.

He jerked awake, spluttering and coughing. Then he noticed Katherine, still holding the empty tankard, and his eyes filled with fury as he threw back the bedcovers and got up. She saw then that he was still wearing his breeches, but before she could think what that might mean, he had reached her and seized her wrist.

'You little wretch!' he snarled. 'What the hell did you do that for?'

'You slept with Molly last night,' she accused, too upset to think clearly. 'You walked out on me, and went to her. You're a demon, Hades; a cheating, lying . . .'

'Murderer.' He finished for her. 'Isn't that what you called me, Katherine? Am I not the kind of man who would murder an innocent babe for the sake of a gold chain?'

Katherine went pale. 'I would have asked your pardon

had you come back, but you stayed with Molly instead. You left me for her.'

'Katherine, I . . .' he faltered, seeming uncertain. 'I didn't mean to do that . . . I thought you hated me. I'm sorry, Kitty.'

He was admitting that he'd slept with Molly. Katherine backed away from him, tears rising in her throat to choke her. She turned and ran blindly from the room, hardly seeing the look of satisfaction on Molly's face as she passed her.

'Kitty, come back . . . Listen to me!'

Katherine heard his cry, but did not stop. If she let him near her, he would force her to listen, and bend her to his will. Once he held her in his arms, she would be his willing slave, his property. Her only chance was to put as much distance between them as possible.

Katherine stood alone on the deck of the *Santa Maria.* They were through the white water; the sails were being unfurled and soon the island would be left far behind, a tiny dot on the horizon, to be seen no more for many months.

Until the very last moment, she had believed that Hades would come for her. Watching the loading of stores, she had been in a fever of impatience to be off. If he came, she was lost. One kiss, and she would melt into his arms, a victim of that desire which raged in her even now, making her sick with longing. But he was a cold-hearted womaniser who had used her for his pleasure. He did not love her. He did not love her . . .

Fabius came to stand beside her, glancing at her strained face. 'It has been arranged. We'll search every island we come to, but not at the expense of losing a prize.'

Katherine nodded and smiled. 'Thank you, Fabius.

I'm sure we'll find my brother if he's in the islands. Hades said it wasn't possible . . .'

'Forget him. He's not worth your tears.' He spat on the deck. 'I should've killed him.'

'No.' She sighed and turned to look out to the open sea. 'I always knew he did not love me . . . It was my own fault. I do not blame him.' She raised her head proudly. 'Are the water-casks secure?'

Fabius saw the subject was closed. 'Ay, ay, Cap'n. All secure below.'

'Good!' She smiled a little too brightly. 'I'm going to my cabin to check the charts, and I don't want to be disturbed.'

The storm had raged all night. The wind so fierce that the mizen-mast had come crashing down with all its canvas still unfurled, resulting in one man dead and two injured. Katherine made a tour of the deck, her face grim as she looked at the damage.

'Can we make the repairs?' she asked Fabius.

'Not at sea. We'll have to return to the island, and it may take some time.'

'Since we have no choice . . .' Katherine broke off, as a cry came from aloft.

'Sail on the starboard!'

She went to the side, straining to see the ship approaching swiftly to their right. They were in a vulnerable state after the ravages of the storm and would be hard put to it to defend themselves. Even before she saw the black flag with the golden eagle flying proudly in the wind, she knew that it must be Hades. Panic swept through her. With her mizen-mast down, she had no chance of escaping.

'Shall I fire a warning shot?' Fabius asked, but Katherine shook her head.

'No, we could not win a fight against Hades in this condition. Heave to, and let him come up with us. I shall wait in my cabin.'

Katherine was aware of the crew watching her as she went below. She knew that many of them had not wanted to sail without Hades; they were afraid of his displeasure, and would blame her if he took his revenge on them.

Yet somehow she had no fear for herself as she sat calmly, waiting for the inevitable. Hearing the shouts on deck as the *Golden Eagle* came alongside, she tensed, her nails digging into the palms of her hands. She looked up as the door opened and Hades stood on the threshold, her heart jerking as she saw the coldness in his eyes.

'You will come with me, Katherine,' he said. 'I am relieving you of your command of this ship. Fabius will take over—at least until we return to the island. Once my ship is properly provisioned, I intend to sail for England.'

'And what of me?'

'I shall take you home. It may be that your brother has been found in your absence.'

'And if he is still missing? Will you send me back to my uncle?'

'You will be safer there than roving the seas on a pirate ship.' He held out his hand imperiously. 'Stop sulking, Katherine, and do as you're told for once.'

Her eyes snapped with anger as she brushed by him, ignoring his frown. 'Very well. I'll come with you, since I have no choice, but don't touch me. I don't want you near me, do you understand? I hate you now, and I always shall.'

'You've made that very plain.' Hades looked through her, his eyes icy. 'So the sooner we stop wasting time and get back to the island, the sooner we can leave for England—and then you'll never have to see me again.'

The *Santa Maria* was limping slowly behind them as they neared the island. Hades had stayed with the crippled ship throughout the five days it took to complete the return journey, knowing that she would be helpless without his protection, and he had no intention of loosing the vessel; it was important to his future plans.

Katherine was standing on deck as they approached the reef. She did not turn her head to look at Hades as he came to stand beside her.

'I did not sink the galleon, Katherine,' he said, watching her stony face for any sign of a change. 'We must have passed her in the night. I bought the chain from one of your own men—He has since confessed that he disobeyed your orders.'

'Then I acquit you of the charge,' Katherine replied coldly, moving away from him.

'And will you not also forgive me?'

She stood with her back to him, her shoulders stiff and straight. 'I cannot,' she choked.

'Very well. I shall not ask again.'

Hades walked away, and she heard him giving orders as they entered the narrow channel between the sharp rocks. Then they were through the foaming water into the blue calm of the lagoon. A ragged cheer went up from the crew as they dropped anchor, and everyone watched as the *Santa Maria* negotiated the treacherous passage. The ship had begun to list as she took on water, and Katherine caught her breath as the hull scraped against the reef, but at last she was safe in the lagoon. Instead of the expected cheer, there was a hushed silence, and on the island, the beaches were strangely empty. No one had come out to greet them. She frowned as she noticed a pall of smoke in the sky; there was too much for it simply to be a bonfire.

Hades had also noticed it. Their quarrel was forgotten, as they looked at each other.

'Something's wrong,' Katherine said.

'Yes.' He did not try to hide his fears. 'It must have been a raid.'

'A raid! Has it happened before?'

'Not here—but at other islands, yes.'

'Spaniards?'

'Who else?' Hades' eyes glittered with anger. 'Now you may begin to understand why I show no mercy, Katherine.'

'What do you mean?'

'You have friends on the island?' His face was grim, as she nodded. 'Then pray you find them alive.'

Katherine gasped, her face turning pale. 'I'm going ashore.'

'You will wait here until I know it's safe,' he said, scowling as he saw the protest in her face. 'I shall send a boat for you when I've made a thorough search of the island.'

She turned away, tossing her head angrily. It was always the same: *his* law must be obeyed! In her heart she knew that he merely sought to protect her, but she could not forgive him for betraying her, and nothing else would bring understanding between them.

She watched resentfully as Hades and the small party of men with him in the longboat pulled towards the shore. Part of her had wanted to go to him and beg him to take care, but pride held her back. He had chosen to revert to their old relationship, so he could expect nothing from her. Once more, she was his prisoner.

Even when the boat came to fetch her the next morning, she sat in silence as she was rowed ashore, asking no questions, although it was plain from the men's faces that something was seriously wrong.

She was angry because Hades had left her on board for so long. Waiting was far worse than being involved, even if there had been danger, and she was sure the Spaniards had long gone. They would not have remained to be caught by pirate ships returning to the island: he must have known that, and it was just another case of his arrogance.

Once the boat beached on the shore, Katherine made her way to his house, determined to vent her anger on him; but when she got there, she saw that only blackened timbers were left of the house she had shared with him. She stared at it, her eyes wide with shock. If he had not come after her, he might have been sleeping inside when it was set on fire . . .

Katherine shuddered at the thought; sickness churned inside her and she wondered at the strangeness of fate. Remembering Lizzie, she turned and ran through the trees, her heart pounding as she feared for her friend. With a sigh of relief she saw that her house was still standing, and whispered a prayer of thanks. It seemed to be untouched, but when the door was opened to her knock, Katherine saw it was not so. The furniture had been smashed to pieces, and even Lizzie's precious bed was broken and ruined. Nothing was left but a few pewter plates and the iron-bound chest which had proved too strong for the destroyers.

'Lizzie, do you know where I can find Hades?' Katherine asked, gasping as she saw the look on the other woman's face.

Lizzie ignored her question, staring at her with hard eyes. 'So you've come back, now that it's too late.'

'Too late? What do you mean?' Katherine asked. 'We'll help you start again, Lizzie . . .'

'You can't give me back the memories.' The woman's eyes were cold with dislike. 'You brought this on us. They came for you, and when they found you had gone, they took their revenge on us all.'

'Looking for me?' A trickle of fear ran down Katherine's spine. 'Who were they? It wasn't—It wasn't Don Francisco Domingues?'

'Ay, that's the bastard,' Lizzie said bitterly. 'He ordered his men to smash everything I had because he believed I knew where you were. He only let me live so that I could pass on his message if you came back.'

'But how could he know I was here?' Katherine asked, bewildered.

'Ram told him. He led them here because of what Hades threatened to do to him—because of you. I knew you'd mean trouble for us the first time I saw you . . .'

Katherine saw the bruises on Lizzie's face and heard the bitterness in her voice. 'I should have let Hades kill Ram that night,' she said ruefully. 'I'm sorry you were made to suffer because of me, Lizzie. I have money. I shall pay for anything you need.'

'You can't give me back my bed, or the lives of those who were murdered.' Her friend's eyes were cold. 'Hades should never have brought you here, knowing who you are.'

'Who I am?'

'You were promised to Don Francisco's son in marriage. Isn't that why he came for you?'

'Yes, but I never agreed to the marriage. I was running away from him. I hate him as much as you do. You must believe me, Lizzie!'

Katherine gazed into the other woman's hard eyes and knew that their friendship was at an end. Lizzie blamed her for what had happened on the island, as others would. She had brought death and destruction to her shipmates, and they would not forget it.

'Did—Did many die?'

'Those that were fool enough to stay and fight. They burned Molly's place to the ground, though she escaped. And they killed Ram when he was of no more use to them. There's a feeling against you, Kit. You'll not be welcome here in future.'

She nodded. 'I understand how you feel, Lizzie. I can only say how sorry I am.' She turned to leave, pausing to glance back over her shoulder. 'You said the Don gave you a message for me. What was it?'

For a moment Lizzie's eyes softened, and there was a hint of pity in them. 'The Don told me he has your twin brother in custody. Unless you are delivered to him safely, Lewis will die, as will the hostages they took from the island.'

'Delivered to him safely . . .' Katherine frowned. 'Then the Don believes I am a prisoner?'

'Yes. I did not tell them otherwise, though others may have.'

How can I send the Don word that his terms will be met?'

'The Don himself has returned to Spain with his prisoners, but one of his ships waits at Eagle Island for word from you.'

'I see,' Katherine said quietly, keeping her raging emotions in check. 'I shall have the money I promised you delivered later to day. Goodbye, Lizzie.

She went out, closing the door behind her.

'Kit.' Lizzie cried, but Katherine did not hear her.

She could think only of her beloved brother, and how he must be suffering as the Don's prisoner . . .

CHAPTER SEVEN

'HOW SOON can the *Santa Maria* be ready to sail?' Katherine asked Fabius as they walked along the shore together. 'I have sent word to Don Francisco's men that his terms will be met.'

'I won't take you to him,' Fabius said. 'You'd rather die than agree to the marriage with his son. You told me so.'

Katherine's eyes were sad as she looked at him. 'I cannot leave my brother in his hands, Fabius. You must see that?'

Fabius shook his head stubbornly. 'I cannot obey you, even if I would. Hades has given orders that the *Santa Maria* must not sail until he gives the word. The men dare not disobey him again; he would sink us if we did.'

'Would you sail with me if Hades were no longer in command, Fabius?'

'You know I would, but . . .'

'Then I shall buy the ship from him.' Katherine's face was pale but determined. 'When I tell him that Lewis is a prisoner, I believe he will allow me to go my own way.'

'If he agrees, I will guarantee you a crew, Kit.'

She smiled at him. 'You're a good friend, Fabius. I shall let you know his decision tomorrow. I must go now to meet him. He sent Jake to tell me he would be waiting for me on the *Golden Eagle*. He is staying on board since his house was burned.'

Turning she walked towards the boat waiting to row her out to the *Golden Eagle*. Her face was pensive as she looked back at the island, remembering the happy times she had known there before the Spaniards' raid. Soon she would be leaving it behind her for ever.

Dusk was falling as she climbed on board. There was no sign of Hades, so she went below to his cabin, but that was strangely empty. She began to wander about the room, touching familiar things; she picked up a doublet he had discarded, holding it to her nose to inhale the remembered scent of him, dropping it quickly again as she heard a sound behind her. Whirling round, she saw Hades watching her, an odd expression in his eyes.

'I was checking the stores,' he said. 'We shall be ready to sail in the morning, Katherine.'

She looked at him in alarm. 'I can't come with you to England,' she said quickly. 'I must go to Lewis.'

He frowned. 'England must wait. I have a long overdue score to settle with Don Francisco, and now payment becomes urgent.'

'So you intend to seek revenge for what was done here?'

'Did you think I would not?' Hades' eyes were hard as he looked at her. 'These people were my friends; because of me they have suffered death and destruction. Do you not think some payment should be made for the harm done to them?'

'Yes . . .' Katherine looked at him uncertainly. 'I—I feel guilty, too, of course I do!' She raised her eyes to his defensively. 'I wish I could undo what harm has been done here, but you must see that my brother comes first. I must keep my bargain with the Don. You will let me take the *Santa Maria*, and go? Please?'

Fire glowed briefly in his eyes, and then the shutters came down. 'I have been told of the message Lizzie gave you, but it makes no difference. You will do as I tell you. I warned you, Katherine, when I have something I do not let it go easily.'

'But you meant to take me back to England,' she said in dismay.

'That was before Don Francisco raided the island.'

Katherine stared at him, a tiny shiver running down her spine. 'You—You mean to use me in some way to gain revenge on the Don?'

'Do I, Katherine?' Hades' face was grim. 'There are many on board this ship who would think it only just if I did.'

'No!' Katherine cried. 'You must let me keep my bargain with the Don, or Lewis will die.'

'Do you think he will spare your brother, once he learns you have been my mistress?' He stared at her, his expression unreadable. 'If your brother is not already dead, he will be once Don Francisco has you. Our only hope now is to take our revenge.'

'No. You must let me go! You must!'

'You will remain in this cabin until we sail,' Hades said. 'I shall bring food myself, and perhaps we shall dine together.'

'You can't do this!' Katherine said angrily. 'I told Fabius what I intended, and when he learns you have kidnapped me, he will come after us.'

Hades smiled. 'I have already sent word to Fabius to follow as soon as he is ready. We shall need all our guns against the Don.'

'But he will kill my brother!' Katherine said in desperation. 'Don't you understand that Lewis is in danger?'

The smile faded from his face and his eyes became bleak. 'We may all die, Katherine, but at least we shall take Don Francisco with us to Hell . . .'

* * *

Katherine stood watching the swell of the waves. It looked as if a storm was on the way, and she almost welcomed it. A prey to frustration and the thoughts which tormented her day and night, she was finding the voyage unbearable. Not least because of the way Hades had decided it was time she became a woman once more. He had brought a dress to her the day after they sailed, tossing it on the bed in front of her.

'Put that on,' he commanded. 'It's time you gave up this masquerade, Katherine. Don Francisco will expect to see you wearing a gown, and I think you've forgotten how.'

'I'll wear what I please,' she yelled with anger. 'Neither you nor Don Francisco shall tell me how to behave.'

Hades did not move, but his mouth hardened. 'Put it on, Katherine, unless you want me to do it for you.'

Meeting his gaze defiantly, she was shocked by the sudden gleam of excitement in his eyes and she backed away from him in a panic, knowing that he meant what he said.

'Go away and leave me to change alone, then.' The wild beating of her heart brought a flush to her cheeks.

'Are you sure that's what you want, Kitty?' His voice dropped to a caressing whisper. 'This may be our last voyage together. Why don't you stop this foolishness and admit you want me as much as I want you?'

'As much as you wanted Red Molly?' Katherine asked, her face hard. 'Go away, Hades, unless you mean to rape me!'

A pulse flicked in his cheek and she saw him clench his fists. 'I might kill you, Katherine, but I'll not force you to my bed. It wouldn't be worth the effort.'

'Oh, you—you arrogant man!' she screamed, seizing the dress and throwing it at him. 'Leave me!'

He grinned. 'Just be wearing that gown when I come back, or . . .' He went out, with the threat lingering in the air between them.

Katherine screamed her frustration, throwing a pewter tankard at the door as it closed behind him. For at least half an hour she stamped about the cabin, complaining aloud about the man's arrogance and planning all kinds of revenge, but in the end she calmed down and stripped off her clothes. It felt strange to be wearing a gown after so many months, and her temper was not improved by the look of approval on Hades' face when she went up on deck, neither did she enjoy the stares of the crew.

'The skirt is too long,' she complained bitterly when Hades was foolish enough to come near her.

'I'm sure you can manage to turn it up,' he replied calmly. 'You'll find a needle and thread in my chest.'

'It's black, and it makes me look like an old hag,' she muttered resentfully.

'Do you want me to tell you that you look pretty?'

She ground her teeth. 'No! And you needn't grin like that. I don't care what you think of me. I hate you.'

'Do you, Kitty?' His voice was soft and husky. 'Then why are you making so much fuss?'

'Because you are a brute, and—and . . .' She stared at him suspiciously as she saw the gleam in his eyes. 'Oh, damn you, Hades!' She turned and flounced off, nearly tripping over her skirt.

'There you are,' he called. 'I told you that you've forgotten how to be a woman.'

Katherine clenched her fists, but would not grant him the satisfaction of an answer. The truth was that she was finding it increasingly difficult to keep her distance from him. It still hurt her that he had gone to Molly's house, but somehow, when he looked at her in that special way, it no longer seemed to matter.

Now that they were nearing the end of their journey, she had begun to fear for the future. She was torn between her longing to be in Hades' arms and the need to keep her distance from him. She was still uncertain of his plans, and did not know whether he meant to attack the Don with his flag flying or to sell her to him for a king's ransom, knowing what it would mean when Don Francisco learned that she had been the mistress of his most hated enemy.

The wind was rising now, casting spray high into the air. Katherine shivered as she saw the dark clouds gathering and felt the cold settle about her. The storm was coming on them fast, and there was little they could do but ride it out.

'Come below, Katherine, I want to talk to you.'

She felt the touch of Hades' hands on her shoulders, and her heart jerked with pain as she looked up into his face. Perhaps it was the charged atmosphere or the pounding of the waves against the ship's timbers that made her blood begin to pulse in her veins, she could not be certain; she knew only that suddenly her aching need of him meant more than all the rest.

He read her expression truly. Without a word, he drew her into his arms, his lips moving over hers with infinite tenderness.

'Come with me now, Kitty,' he whispered. 'For this night, let us forget all the world. Tomorrow will be time enough for talking . . .'

Dressed in a wide-skirted gown of black lace and wearing a string of creamy pearls around her throat, Katherine waited on board the *Golden Eagle*'s deck as the *Hispaniola*, Don Francisco's flagship, sailed closer.

After the night of the storm, Hades had agreed to meet his enemy for Katherine's sake, and she knew it was a great concession. His own inclination was to run up the skull and crossbones and go in with all cannon firing.

The rendezvous had been arranged in open waters so that there was no danger of a trap, for neither party trusted the other. As the *Hispaniola* anchored alongside, Katherine felt her stomach twisting with nerves: it was a dangerous plan they had made, and she was suddenly afraid of the consequences if it should go wrong, but she hid her fears as Hades came to her.

'Are you sure you want to go through with this, Katherine?'

'I have no choice,' she replied, her nails digging into the palms of her hands. 'I cannot leave Lewis to die.'

'Then you must trust me,' he said softly. 'Come, it is time to go on board the *Hispaniola*.'

'I shall never forget this, no matter what happens,' Katherine replied with a misty smile. 'I know how much you hate Don Francisco.'

'I do not want your gratitude, Katherine.'

'Then—what?'

Hades shook his head. 'Do you not know me even yet, Kitty?'

How could she know him, when he kept his past a secret from her? And yet there was something in his smile which made her long to understand this thing inside him that had caused him so much pain. Perhaps one day soon he would tell her what lay behind his hatred of Don Francisco.

As she hesitated, Hades took her hand and held it lightly, a teasing light in his eyes. 'Surely you don't need me to say it, Kitty?'

Her heart stopped beating for one moment. Was he saying that he loved her? He had never said as much even when they lay together in his bed, their bodies entwined as one. She wished suddenly that she had not persuaded him to this madness, that they were free to sail away together this very moment . . . But it was already too late. The boat was waiting to take her on board the *Hispaniola*.

With Hades at her side, she was helped into the longboat and rowed the short distance to the Spaniard's ship. Don Francisco was waiting to greet the small party as they went on board. Glancing nervously about the deck as she saw several armed men, Katherine felt her sense of foreboding increase. Had she been a fool to agree to this? Could the Don be trusted to honour the pledge of a safe passage he had made for the crew and captain of the *Golden Eagle*?

'Don Francisco—we had come, as you see.' Katherine held out her hand.

The Don raised it to his lips. 'Lady Katherine, I am delighted to see you looking so well. These dogs have not harmed you, I trust?' His cold eyes swept over the three pirates who had accompanied her, dwelling for a moment on the Captain's face. 'I believe you are the one they call Hades?'

He inclined his head mockingly. 'I have that honour, sir. Your countrymen know me well enough.'

'You have cost me five ships to my certain knowledge, Captain Hades. We have never met before, and yet there is something familiar about you . . .'

'We have never met.' His eyes were dancing, and his hand moved involuntarily towards his sword-hilt. 'However, you knew my father well.'

'Indeed?' Don Francisco's brows rose. 'And what was your father's name, sir?'

Hades shrugged his powerful shoulders. 'What does a name signify? I doubt that you knew it.'

'Then your father was not my friend, but an enemy.' The Don frowned as if trying to recall something. 'No matter. There are other more important details to discuss.'

Hades smiled unpleasantly. 'You agreed to pay a ransom for the safe delivery of Lady Katherine Winters. As you see, she is here.'

Katherine gasped. This was not what they had planned! She was to have offered the Don a ransom for her twin's life. Why had Hades suddenly changed his mind? Or had he always planned to sell her to the Don?

Don Francisco's lips curved in a sneer. He pointed to an iron-bound chest near by. 'Would you care to examine the contents?'

'Yes.' Hades threw open the lid and glanced at the silver coins inside, then he nodded to his two companions. 'Take this back to the *Golden Eagle*, and then return for me.'

Katherine stared at him, bewildered. The heavy chest was lowered over the side and the longboat began to pull towards the *Golden Eagle*. What was Hades doing? Surely he was not planning to secure the Spaniard's silver and then turn the *Golden Eagle*'s guns on the galleon?

The longboat had reached the pirate ship, but even as they were hauling the chest on board, a shout went up from the look-out. 'Sail on the horizon!'

Two ships had appeared on the horizon, and they were clearly Spanish galleons, part of Don Francisco's fleet. It was obviously a trap: the Don had planned to sink the pirate vessel once he had Katherine safely on board his flagship!

Hades drew his sword, his face cold with anger. 'So I was right,' he snarled. 'I knew you could not be trusted to keep your word, Domingues.' He waved his sword over his head as a signal to the *Golden Eagle*'s crew, shouting at the same time, 'It's a trap! Get away now, and save yourselves!'

In the confusion that followed, Katherine had time only to see that the pirates reacted swiftly to their captain's warning. Even as she struggled to understand what was happening, she found herself seized from behind. Kicking and screaming, she was dragged away as Hades was surrounded by armed Spaniards.

'Hades!' she cried. 'Behind you!'

Her warning came too late. He was defending himself against five Spanish swordsmen and fighting valiantly, but he had no defence against the cowardly blow which struck him down from the rear. Katherine saw him slump to the floor, seconds before she was carried forcefully below deck.

Don Francisco's fortress home was built into the rocks overlooking a wide bay. The road to the forbidding *palacio* was steep, and the horses found it hard going to pull the unwieldy carriage up the last few yards. It was accomplished with much shouting and urging by the driver, and some pushing by the Don's servants; but at last they drew to a halt in the courtyard and Don Francisco dismounted from his horse, coming to help Katherine down.

She shook out the stiff folds of her silken gown, one of the many unwanted gifts he had pressed on her, and looked at him without interest. Seeing the gleam of satisfaction in his eyes, she turned aside, letting her gaze wander to the grey stone arches guarding the entrance to the *palacio*. The building itself was of the same stone with narrow windows, brightly-coloured domes, turrets and crenellated battlements. Ugly gargoyles protruded from the roof-gutter, and there were strange carvings above the many arches built into the walls.

The courtyard was pleasant enough, with enclosed walks, flowering shrubs and a cool fountain cascading into a tiny pool. But Katherine was not allowed to linger in the warmth of the sunshine. Don Francisco hurried her inside to the coolness of rooms shaded and shuttered from the heat of the day.

Katherine shivered, oppressed by the echoing emptiness of these dark chambers. Outside, at least there had been sunshine and the sound of bird-song to lift the ache in her heart: here there was only silence and an air of unhappiness.

The silence was broken by the tapping of a woman's heels on the tiled floor. Tall and pale, with large, sad eyes, and dressed all in black, she came into the salon to meet them, greeting the Don in her native tongue.

He frowned at her, replying in English. 'It is no matter, Margarita, Catalina is here now, and the boy will be happy.' His words had the ring of a command about them, Katherine thought as he turned to her. 'This is my sister, Doña Margarita. She will show you to your rooms. If there is anything you need, Margarita will be happy to arrange it for you. Now, if you will excuse me, it seems there is business I must attend to.'

Margarita smiled as the Don departed. 'Doña Catalina, I am pleased to welcome you to our home. I hope you will be happy here.'

Some of Katherine's depression left her as she saw the genuine warmth in the older woman's eyes. At least here there was someone she could talk to without feeling threatened. Don Francisco had been attentive to her after she had been released from her cabin, and when the sound of guns firing had been left far behind, but he would not answer her questions about the fate of the pirate ship, neither would he tell her whether Hades was alive or dead, merely turning aside her demands for the truth with a shrug of his shoulders.

Beneath the smiles was a ruthlessness she feared, and she had not dared to protest too much, sensing that he would crush any sign of disobedience with alacrity. She could only wait until he chose to tell her his plans.

'Your rooms are all prepared,' Margarita was saying, as she led the way through endless chambers, all with the same atmosphere of oppression and all dark. 'I do hope you will like them.'

Katherine forced herself to smile. She wished she could throw open all the shutters—better still that she could be back on board the *Golden Eagle* with Hades by her side. The thought of him brought a sharp pain to her breast as she recalled their last moments together. Why had he changed his plans so suddenly? She could not believe that he had really meant to sell her to the Don, but the doubt added to her burden of misery.

Where was he now? Was he still alive, or had he died when that cowardly blow struck him down from behind? The uncertainty was tearing her apart.

Her rooms were similar to those through which they passed; the walls half covered with patterned tiles of blue and white, the floors of large stone flags and cold beneath her thin shoes. The meagre furniture was dark and heavily carved, as sombre as the chambers themselves, though the bed-hangings were of the finest silk and a small vase of flowers stood on the windowsill.

Katherine walked to them and bent her head to inhale their exotic scent, feeling cheered. 'You picked these? You are thoughtful, Margarita.'

Margarita frowned, seeming uneasy. 'No, they are a gift from Esteban. He picked them himself not an hour ago, to—to make you happy.'

'It was a kind thought." Katherine was puzzled. Don

Esteban had picked the flowers, but had not come himself to greet her. 'Where is Don Esteban? When shall I meet him?'

A look of fear passed across Margarita's face. 'When my brother decides that it is time. Please, you will not let him know that Esteban has been to your room? He would be so angry with me.'

'No, I shall not tell him.' Katherine was surprised. 'But why should he be angry with you?'

Margarita faltered. 'It—It is improper for your—your betrothed to visit your apartments. Francisco is very strict in these matters. Please let us say no more of this. Are you hungry? Shall I tell a maid to bring food or wine, or would you rather rest?'

'I am a little tired. Will you come back and talk to me later?'

Margarita smiled. 'Yes, I should like that very much. I shall send a maid to you in one hour. Then, when you have changed your gown and refreshed yourself, I shall show you where we dine.'

'Thank you.'

Margarita smiled again, her eyes darting nervously about the room before she left. Listening to the sound of her departing footsteps, Katherine shivered, feeling the claustrophobic atmosphere close in around her. Dunline Castle was full of bright colours, the walls covered with rich tapestries and pictures, and there were servants everywhere, going about their business with a cheerful smile. Here there was nothing but silence. It frightened her, and all her instincts told her to run as far and as fast as she could, but it was too late for escape. She was the Don's prisoner as surely as her twin. Besides, there was no one she could run to now.

Where was Hades? Her heart cried out to him, and tears rose in her throat to choke her. Was he hurt and in pain, or was he already dead? Even if he lived, she knew the Don would show no mercy to his enemy; he would hang Hades just as soon as it pleased him, and there was nothing she could do to prevent it. If only there was some way she could send word to the *Santa Maria*, perhaps Fabius could help. But it was useless to dream, Katherine knew. The *Santa Maria* had not joined them as Hades had ordered, and there was no means of knowing where their companion ship was: she might still be at the island or scouring the seas in search of treasure ships.

Walking to the window, Katherine opened the shutters and looked out over the bay. The blue waters of the sea called to her, and she knew a desperate longing for the freedom of her former life. She had called herself Hades' prisoner, but how much she longed for the sweet captivity of his strong arms at this very moment, to feel his lips on hers and surrender her very being to his demand.

'Hades, my love . . . my love . . .' she whispered, as the tears coursed down her cheeks. 'How can I bear it if you are dead?'

'Why are you crying? You're a pretty lady. I don't like to see you cry.'

Katherine was startled by the high, childish voice. She searched the seemingly empty room with her eyes, feeling she was watched, though she could see no one.

'Who are you? Where are you?'

The laughter was high pitched, echoing around the large chamber with an eerie strangeness that chilled her. She felt prickles on the back of her neck. Was the room haunted?

'Who are you?' she cried again. 'Come out and let me see you! You're frightening me.'

The laughter rose to a shrill pitch, then there was a movement behind the bed-hangings and a figure came towards her. At first glance it seemed to be that of a young man in his twenties, but when she lifted her eyes to his face, she was shocked. His face was that of innocent childhood, smooth and soft with the paleness of ill health. As he came closer, she saw that his lips were red and pouting like a girl's, his hair long and curling on his shoulders; but his blue eyes were curiously vacant, yet full of secret thoughts.

'You are Don Esteban,' Katherine said, his likeness to the miniature close enough for her to be certain. 'You startled me! What are you doing here?'

The young man put a finger to his lips. 'Mustn't say, mustn't tell . . .' He giggled foolishly, a trickle of saliva running down his chin. 'I know a secret, pretty lady.'

'A secret? What secret?'

He cocked his head to one side, his eyes suddenly very bright and knowing. 'Mustn't say, mustn't tell. He would be angry!' His face creased and tears welled up in his eyes. 'He would lock me away again, but you won't let him beat me, will you? When you marry me, he won't hate me any more. Margarita says so.'

Katherine looked at him with pity in her eyes. The childish voice coming from a man of her own age was pitiful. It was clear that though his body had developed normally, his mind had not. She was reminded of a simple-minded lad who worked in the kitchens of Dunline Castle. The other servants called him names and said he was crazy, but he was quite harmless and seemed happy to laugh at their cruel jests, not understanding that they were mocking him. But they had never really harmed him, and he had never been beaten. Esteban was very much like that boy, Katherine thought, except that he was obviously desperately afraid of being beaten.

She felt sorry for him, and smiled encouragingly. 'Do you want to marry me, Esteban?'

He nodded, his pale cheeks flushing. 'Yes, I like you, you're gentle. Margarita says he will let us go away when he has you. I shan't be locked up any more. Margarita says so.'

There was pitiful eagerness in his voice, and Katherine shivered. She was beginning to understand why the Don had been so anxious to arrange a marriage for a woman who could not know that his son was not a normal man, but she did not yet see what he had to gain from the marriage, or why he was so determined that she should be Esteban's wife. Such a marriage could never be more than a mockery . . .

'Esteban! What are you doing here?'

Don Francisco's voice cut through her thoughts, making her shudder. Her eyes flew to the doorway, even as she heard the terrified gasp from the young man beside her. She glanced at him, noting his bulging eyes and his mouth slack with fear. He was shaking from head to foot. Instinctively she moved towards Esteban as if to protect him from his father's anger. Sensing this, the young man darted behind her, taking hold of her hand like a frightened child, and whimpering.

'He came to greet me and bring me some flowers,' Katherine said, facing the Don proudly across the room. 'He is doing no harm.'

There was a look of surprise in the Don's eyes. 'So, you would protect him. What an unusual woman you are! I expected you to be disgusted by this charming son of mine and weep all over me. Well, perhaps no harm has been done, though I had not intended you to learn the truth so soon.'

Katherine said calmly, with a look of pride, 'You plan to marry me to this child? What can you hope to gain from it?'

'Esteban, leave us!' Don Francisco turned his glittering gaze on the frightened boy, who ran from behind Katherine, darting past his father and disappearing through the open door. 'Since there is no way you can escape me now,' the Spaniard went on, ignoring his son's departure, 'I may as well tell you the truth. Please come with me, Katherine. I have something to show you.'

'Where are we going?' Katherine asked, following him from the room. 'When am I to be allowed to see my brother? You said he was your prisoner . . .'

The Don inclined his head. 'Very well, since you are impatient to be reunited with your brother, we shall visit him in his apartments first, Catalina.'

'My name is Katherine.'

'Your pardon, my dear. She was called Catalina, and you are so much like her that I sometimes forget you are not she.'

'Who is this woman you speak of?'

'Catalina was the woman I loved—the woman whose portrait I was about to show you. It is all I have left of her, since she herself was stolen from me by your father.'

They had reached the lofty entrance hall, and Katherine stopped to stare at him in astonishment. 'My mother's name was Katherine . . .'

'I called her Catalina. We were betrothed to one another as children. I loved her as I have never loved anyone else. Then one day an Englishman came to her father's house. He spoke of friendship, but he stole my Catalina.' Don Francisco's eyes glared. He took out a key and opened an iron-bound door at the side of the porch, which swung back to reveal a flight of steep stone steps. 'Be careful of the steps, Catalina. They are dangerous, and it would be a pity if you fell.'

He held her arm, guiding her down a winding flight of stairs which seemed to lead deep into the bowels of the *palacio*. The walls were cold to the touch, and damp. After a while they entered a long, dark passage, and the Don took a torch from a sconce in the wall, lighting it and beckoning to Katherine to follow, since they could walk only in single file in the narrow opening.

Conversation was at an end for the moment, and she tried to gather her thoughts. Her mother had been a Spanish woman and betrothed to Don Francisco! She tried to recall something from childhood which should have given her the clue, but there was nothing—except her father's hatred of Spaniards. She could never know the whole truth. Memories of her lovely mother were vague and shadowy. Katherine was very young when she had died, and she had only a faint picture in her mind of a beautiful face and a soft, sweet voice.

At the end of the passage were more steep stairs, twisting futher down into a murky blackness. Katherine had guessed at the start that she was being taken to the dungeons, and her heart was beating wildly as she prayed that both Lewis and Hades were alive. Would the Don allow her to see Hades? she wondered. Please God, let him not be dead!

The last flight led down into a huge cellar. In the middle was a circular fireplace similar to that used by the blacksmith at Dunline, but with a more sinister purpose here. Iron bars were laid across it, and instruments which were obviously used for torture. She averted her eyes as she saw brown stains which could only be dried blood, and shivered.

The Don had paused to speak to two burly men, using his native tongue so that she could make out only an odd word here and there. Then he took her arm, and they passed into a smaller chamber, which had several cells built into the thick walls. Here the air was foul with the stench of human sweat, excrement and fear. Katherine trembled as she heard moans coming from inside the cells. It was a terrible place—and somewhere here was her brother! Perhaps Hades as well . . .

Don Francisco unlocked one of the doors with a key he took from a bunch on the wall, an unpleasant smile on his lips as he looked at Katherine. 'Please go in, Catalina. Do not fear that I shall lock you in this wretched place. My plans for you are quite different.'

She hesitated for a moment, then went inside the cell, choking as the fetid air caught in her throat. Blinking in the darkness, she was unable to see anything until the Don entered behind her, and the light from his torch fell on the figure of a man lying on a pile of filthy straw.

Katherine stared at the man's pale face, half hidden by a ragged beard. His hair was straggling on his shoulders and matted with dirt. He looked thin and gaunt, his eyes bewildered in the unaccustomed light, but Katherine recognised him at once.

'Lewis . . .' she whispered, tears starting to her eyes. 'My dearest brother, what has he done to you?' She knelt at his side and put her arms around his thin body. 'Oh, Lewis . . .'

'Katherine?' Lewis blinked his eyes warily. 'You've come to me . . . I've called to you so often . . .'

'I know, my beloved . . . I know. I've heard you calling,' she said, her cheeks wet against his. 'Oh, my poor darling!' She looked up at the Spaniard as he stood over them. 'How could you do this? Why?'

Don Francisco's face was cold. 'Long ago I vowed I would be revenged on your father. I planned to tell him of his son's imprisonment, but he denied me that pleasure by dying too soon.'

'My father is dead, sir. What can you hope to gain from this now?'

'Revenge, Catalina. You I shall take to my bed once you are wed to Esteban. Your brother shall continue to partake of my hospitality until he dies.'

Katherine stood up, shaking with anger. 'You are ruthless and cruel. I would rather die than bed with you!'

He laughed harshly. 'How lovely you are when you are angry, Catalina! I thought you might answer me thus, but perhaps you would rather see your brother hang?'

'Lewis would rather die than live on in this misery!'

'Then perhaps I shall improve his lot—if you please me.'

She stared at him, a cold chill running down her spine. 'You are a monster . . .'

The Don took her arm, forcing her out of the cell as she hung back and tried to cling to her twin. Lewis called her name despairingly, struggling to his feet in an effort to follow, before he fell to his knees.

'Katherine, don't leave me . . .'

'Lewis! Lewis . . .' she screamed his name, fighting the Don with all her strength. 'Lewis . . .'

He dragged her away from the door, locking it behind him while she stood panting and staring at him with hate-filled eyes. She flung herself against it, sobbing and beating at it with her fists, repeating her brother's name over and over.

'His fate is in your hands.' The Don's voice broke through her grief. 'It's your choice, Catalina.'

Katherine stared at him, feeling sick. 'No! No . . .'

'Do not disappoint me. I believed you had more spirit. But perhaps this will restore your humour.'

He dragged her after him, back to the torture chamber, his fingers biting into the flesh of her arm.

Her eyes widened in horror as she saw that the men Don Francisco had spoken to earlier were chaining a third man to the wall. He was struggling violently, and cursing them.

'Hades!' she cried, breaking free of the Don's grasp and running towards him.

His face was contorted with pain. 'Katherine!' he roared. 'My God! What have I done? May his rotten soul burn in hell . . .'

His cry pierced her to the heart. 'Oh, Hades my love, it doesn't matter about me, as long as you're still alive!' She tried to touch him, but the Spaniard seized her arm, dragging her back.

'What a touching scene—and so revealing.' He smiled cruelly. 'Now, Catalina, how shall I entertain you? A little sport with the handsome captain, perhaps?' He heard her gasp of horror as she saw the red-hot irons, and laughed. 'No? Well, perhaps not—I have a score to settle with Captain Hades and it would be a pity to end the fun too soon. We must give him the pleasure of witnessing your marriage to Esteban before he dies. I want him to realise fully that you are my idiot son's wife, and that I shall use you for my own pleasure whenever I wish.'

'No!' Hades cried, straining at the chains which bound him. 'I'll see you dead first.'

'Unfortunately, sir, you are in no position to do anything. Perhaps we should use the hot irons on you. What do you say, Catalina?'

'No,' she whispered, her face ashen. 'I will do anything you ask of me, but I beg you not to torture him!'

'Ah, so you begin to understand me.' The Don took her hand and stroked it softly, making her shiver. 'Very well, I shall spare him for today. But the first time you refuse me anything, he will suffer for it.'

'I—I shall not refuse you,' Katherine said, closing her eyes as she heard Hades' groan of agony. 'Please, I beg you, sir, give him an honourable death.'

'Perhaps, if you please me well enough, I may even give you his life.' He stroked her cheek, making her tremble and causing Hades to swear and tug at his bonds like a madman. 'There, forgive me, Catalina. I do not want to hurt you. I find you beautiful and exciting. There is no reason why we should not deal well together.'

'What do you want of me?'

Katherine let the Don take her arm, going with him without resistance. She heard Hades call her name, but she dared not look back, knowing that to do so would be fatal for him. If she did not do exactly as Don Francisco wanted, both her brother and Hades would suffer cruelly for her defiance. She blinked, holding back the tears.

They had reached the entrance hall again. The Don relocked the door to the cellars, placing the key inside his doublet. He frowned as he saw the sparkle of tears on her lashes.

'Weep no more for him,' he commanded. 'If you smile for me, I will see he is not tortured. If you weep, he will feel each tear.'

Katherine brushed her eyes with the back of her hand, lifting her head in a brave smile. The Don was a monster, but she would do anything to save her loved ones from further suffering. If that meant that she must become this man's whore, then she would do it, and laugh as if it pleased her—her tears would come when he left her alone. Once he was sure of her, he would hang Hades and probably Lewis as well. It was better that they should die swiftly than be left to endure the misery of those horrible cells. And when they were dead, she could die, too.

'I shall do whatever you ask of me if you will give Hades an honourable death.'

The Don reached out to draw her close to him, his mouth covering hers greedily. Katherine suppressed the shudder that ran through her, letting him have his way.

When he let her go at last, she looked at him. 'And my brother? What of him?'

His hand traced the proud line of her white throat. 'You are so cold to me, Catalina; yet I will swear there is fire in you. When you beg for my kisses, I shall set your brother free . . .' The hand moved beneath the silken gown to caress her breast.

Katherine could not quite suppress the shiver of revulsion she felt at his touch, and he saw the rejection in her eyes.

'So you are not yet ready to obey me in all things,' he hissed. 'Take care, Catalina! If you break your word, I shall make you watch Hades die slowly, painfully, little by little, until he screams for mercy.'

Swallowing hard, she forced herself not to flinch beneath the searching of his hands. 'Do with me as you will,' she whispered. 'I shall not deny you.'

'Catalina . . .' Fire burned in the Don's eyes as he reached out for her once more, but even as he did so, there came the sound of hurried feet, and a startled oath broke from him. 'Margarita! What is it?'

Doña Margarita stared at him with wild eyes, her chest heaving. 'It's Esteban—he has gone.'

'Gone! What do you mean—gone?' Don Francisco barked. 'He cannot be far.'

'But he is . . .' Margarita wrung her hands in anguish. 'He was so frightened, Francisco. I'm sure he has run away.'

The Don's face darkened with fury. 'The servants have orders never to let him leave the *palacio*. If he has escaped, someone will pay for this! It's your fault, Margarita! You should not have begged me to give him his freedom within the *palacio*. I'll speak with you later!'

He strode out, shouting orders loudly in Spanish, leaving Katherine and Margarita together. Doña Margarita was shaking, her face deathly pale. Katherine went to her and took her hands, holding them tightly.

'What is it? Why are you so frightened, and why is your brother so angry?'

Margarita glanced over her shoulder. 'Come! We cannot talk here. Follow me quickly!'

Katherine allowed herself to be hurried away into a part of the *palacio* that she had not yet seen. Margarita opened a door and pushed her inside, locking it behind them. She drew a deep, shuddering breath, hiding her face in her hands until the shivering subsided; then she raised her head to look at Katherine.

'If anything happens to Esteban, all Francisco's plans will be ruined and he will go wild—we'll none of us be safe from him!'

'But why? I know he wants me to marry his son, but that is only a part of his plan to humiliate me. Why is it so important to him?'

Margarita pressed her ear against the door, listening for a moment, then she came back to Katherine, lowering her voice. 'How much do you know?'

'Only that he plans to marry me to Esteban, and then—then force me to bed with him. He wants revenge for something that happened years ago . . .'

Doña Margarita nodded, her face grim. 'This much is true—but revenge is only to pleasure himself. Esteban's mother was the daughter of a very wealthy noble. She had royal blood, did you know that?'

'No—I had no idea.'

'She was the bastard of a member of the Spanish royal family. It is a secret long kept, that only we and a few others know. Esteban is the heir to a great fortune, and my brother is deeply in debt. But if it were known in certain circles that the boy is insane, then the money would pass to the King.'

'So he planned to marry me to his son, and get me with child himself, pretending it was Esteban's, then . . .' Her voice faded to a horrified whisper.

'Yes, your marriage would be quite legal. Your child would inherit Esteban's fortune if he should die.'

'Then the Don meant to kill him once I had borne a child—to kill his own son? He couldn't!'

'He hates him because of what he is,' Margarita said, her eyes sad. 'He has always hated him since we knew he would never really grow up. If Francisco could only get the money without him—but Esteban cannot inherit until he marries. If he should die unmarried and without an heir . . .'

'Don Francisco would lose everything.'

Margarita nodded. 'Esteban was safe until you came. Francisco would not dare to bring a Spanish girl of good family here. I begged him to let me take the boy away when the wedding was over. He promised to allow us to leave, once you were with child, but I do not think he will let him go . . . ever.'

Katherine stared at her. 'You love Esteban, don't you?'

'Yes.' Doña Margarita smiled for the first time. 'I have never married. Esteban has been my life.'

'Then if I were not here to marry Esteban, he would be safe?'

'Perhaps—at least until Francisco could find someone else to take your place.'

'Could you not find a way to take the boy away from here?'

'Do you think I have not tried? The servants are all terrified of Francisco; they watch us all the time. Why—Why do you ask?'

'If I were to leave here before the marriage could take place, it would give you time. Perhaps you could find a way of escaping before it is too late.'

'I might . . . I have thought recently there could be a chance . . .' Doña Margarita stared at her, fear in her eyes. 'You are asking me to help you to escape. No! Francisco would kill me and punish Esteban if he discovered what I'd done. No! It's impossible.'

'Perhaps you could escape with me,' Katherine said, eagerness in her voice as the idea came to her. 'Yes, I would take you and Esteban with me. You could go where you liked.'

'I have friends who would protect us if we could once escape Francisco's power,' Margarita said, her eyes narrowing in thought. 'Once it were known that Esteban is what he is, my brother would have no further use for us . . .' She turned to pace about the room in agitation, then came back to stand in front of Katherine. 'If Esteban is still alive when they find him, I shall help you, on condition that you take us with you. Now tell me your plan. What is it you want me to do?'

Katherine took a step forward and embraced her. 'It is a faint chance. But, I think, our only one. Listen carefully, this is what you must do . . .'

CHAPTER EIGHT

KATHERINE STOOD stiff and straight as the maids came to dress her in her wedding gown, made of ivory silk heavily embroidered with silver threads and seed pearls. It had wide, panniered skirts which fitted over a slim silk petticoat and tied at the waist with a silver girdle. The neckline was cut very low to enhance her lovely shoulders, the bodice dipping to a V shape at the front and thickly encrusted with pearls. Her hair had been brushed until it shone, and arranged in the Spanish style.

When they showed her her image in a little mirror, she scowled, wishing she could tear off this unwanted finery and don the salt-stained breeches she had become accustomed to. Yet it was a small sacrifice when the lives of her brother and Hades were at risk.

'Hades . . .' Katherine closed her eyes as a picture of her lover chained to the wall flashed into her mind. 'My dearest love,' she whispered, tears catching at her throat. 'Pray God that Fabius has kept faith . . .'

It was three days since the *palacio* had been turned upside down in the hunt for Esteban. The young man had eventually been found hiding in a gloomy passageway he foolishly imagined was a secret place. He was chilled to the bone and shaking with fear when they dragged him out, still babbling of his secret hideaway.

That evening he had been taken with a fever which lasted for two days and nights, thus preventing the marriage being celebrated sooner, despite his father's impatience. Don Francisco had been in a terrible temper all the time, fearing his plans might yet come to naught if the boy died. The physicians had been threatened with death themselves if their patient did not recover, and Esteban's body-servant had been whipped for allowing the boy to go missing.

Katherine expected hourly that the Don would burst into her rooms and force her to accede to his demands. Although she would have wished to die before he laid his hands on her, she knew she would do anything rather than watch Hades being slowly tortured to death. So far, however, Don Francisco had left her in peace, perhaps because he was too busy terrorising the servants and physicians. She was sure it could not be long before he turned his attention to her once more, but she would not let herself give way to despair.

All was not yet lost. There was a chance that Fabius had followed them and had learned what had happened to the *Golden Eagle*. It was possible that he might have brought the ship secretly to one of the sheltered bays further along the coast; she did not doubt his loyalty to her, and she believed he would at least try to find out what had happened to her. If Margarita's friend had done as she asked . . .

During all the confusion when Esteban was missing, Margarita had slipped away to the village at the foot of the hill. Among the folk who lived there was a young fisherman she sometimes spoke to after visiting the church on Sundays, the one day of the week her brother allowed her to leave the *palacio*. Of course he knew nothing of her secret friendship, and would have forbidden her to visit the village had he guessed what was happening.

When Katherine asked if she knew someone who

could search for the *Santa Maria*, Margarita had suggested the fisherman. He was braver than many of the village folk, who lived in fear of Don Francisco, and he had agreed to the plan. But even though he had taken his fishing boat out immediately, Katherine knew his task was not an easy one. There were many small coves where a ship might hide—and Fabius would not want to be found.

Katherine turned as the door opened and Margarita entered. She handed the bride a lace kerchief and kissed her cheek. 'I made this myself,' she said. 'I wanted you to have it.'

Katherine smiled. 'Thank you, Doña Margarita.'

'The villagers have gathered in the courtyard to serenade the bride,' Margarita said, her hand pressing urgently on Katherine's. 'Come to the window and listen.'

In the courtyard below, a group of men and women dressed in bright colours had begun to sing an old Spanish love-song.

'Have you news?' Katherine whispered. 'Tell me quickly!'

Margarita glanced back at the servants. 'José's sister is with the villagers. She told me he went out last night after hearing rumours of a ship sheltering in a cove he had not searched. He has not yet returned.'

Katherine bit her lip. 'He knows they must come today? If he fails to find Fabius it will be too late: Don Francisco will hang Hades once I am Esteban's wife.'

'We have done all we can.' Margarita's tone was harsh.

'Yes, I know. I am grateful, believe me.'

'We must pray that José returns in time and brings your friends with him.'

'Is everything else as planned?'

'Yes, but if Francisco ever discovers what I've done . . .' She broke off, her face turning pale as her brother entered, carrying a silver casket.

He came towards them, his eyes narrowing as he saw them standing close together. 'Have you come to wish Catalina luck, Margarita?'

'Doña Margarita brought me a present,' Katherine said, holding out the kerchief for him to see.

'A pretty trifle,' Don Francisco commented. 'But I have a gift more fitting for such a beautiful bride. 'Come, my dear, let me see you smile.' He opened the small casket and took out a magnificent collar of diamonds, dangling it in front of her so that she could appreciate its magnificence. 'Worthy of a queen, I think? Allow me to fasten them for you, Catalina.'

Katherine forced herself to smile, managing to suppress the shiver which ran through her as Don Francisco touched her neck. He bent to kiss her naked shoulder, making her draw a sharp breath.

'How lovely you are, Catalina,' he murmured close to her ear. 'And how I long to make you my own, to hear your cries of passion. It will not be long now, my dear.'

Don Francisco's voice was soft and persuasive, but his eyes were hard and greedy as they fastened on Katherine's pale face. She felt terror rise in her as his fingers closed round her wrist—supposing Fabius did not come? How could she bear to let this man make her his slave? Yet there were Hades and her brother to consider. She was caught fast in the Don's trap, and there was no escape for her, unless the fisherman had found the *Santa Maria* . . .

'Come, Catalina, your bridegroom awaits you.' Don Francisco took her arm, to lead her from the room.

Katherine felt as if she were living a nightmare as they walked through the echoing passages. Was it fate that

Hades should die and she should be forced to a life of shame? As they reached the great hall, she saw a blur of faces: servants and guards assembled to witness the wedding at the Don's command. He was making certain it could not be questioned in the future.

At the far end of the hall a dais had been set up with an altar and a silken canopy. A solemn-faced priest waited, cross in hand, as he chanted a prayer. Esteban stood before the dais dressed in black and silver, his elegant clothes giving him the appearance of a bridegroom until one looked at his face.

Moving forward to take her place at his side, Katherine heard a shuffling sound somewhere to the side of the hall, and then a cry of protest. Turning her head, she saw that three of the Don's guards had entered from the door leading down to the dungeons, thrusting their prisoners before them. Hades and Lewis had been brought up from their cells to witness the wedding!

Lewis was swaying on his feet, blinking in the unaccustomed light of day, a guard at each side of him to hold him steady. Hades had a bruise on his face, and his golden hair was matted with dried blood, but he stood proudly with his head high, despite the chains binding his wrists.

This last cruelty of the Don's was almost more than Katherine could bear. For a moment the world went black and everything swam before her vision. Then she heard Hades cry out in anger, and opened her eyes in time to see one of the guards hit him so hard that he sank on his knees.

She blinked back her tears, looking at Don Francisco. 'I'm ready,' she choked. 'Please don't hurt him again.'

He made a sign to the guard, and Hades was jerked to his feet. Katherine looked at him and smiled, praying he would understand why she had agreed to the marriage. Then she knelt beside Esteban on the silken cushions at the foot of the altar.

Listening to the priest intoning the marriage service, Katherine made her responses as instructed by the Don, hardly knowing what she did. Every nerve in her body was on fire, straining towards the man who stood in chains just a short distance away. Her eyes moved to his face, drinking in every feature as if she would hold them in her memory for ever.

Hades seemed not to see her. His eyes were remote, as if he was refusing to watch what was happening. Don Francisco might force him to be present, but nothing could break his pride. Looking at Hades now, Katherine knew just how much she loved him, and was fiercely glad to have been his woman if only for a short time.

'Come, Catalina . . .' Katherine became aware that the priest had finished his blessing. Don Francisco was beckoning to her. 'Esteban! Give your hand to your wife.'

Katherine threw a despairing glance at Hades. This time their eyes met, and she saw a golden flame blaze out from him, and suddenly he seemed to come to life. Moving swiftly towards the guard who had felled him to his knees, he lifted his arms and brought them down on the man's head, jerking the chain hard against his throat. The guard choked, his face going purple and his eyes bulging as he slumped forward and slithered to the ground.

One of the guards supporting Lewis ran towards Hades, and was brought down by a tremendous two-fisted blow on his head. Becoming aware of what was happening, Don Francisco shouted for more guards. Half a dozen men started towards the golden-haired giant, their swords drawn. Katherine screamed, and tried to go to him, but the Don seized her arm, holding her back.

'I'll make him beg for death after this,' Don Francisco hissed. 'And you shall watch every moment of his agony.'

Katherine tossed her head, pride and anger making her speak out. 'If Hades dies, I'll die too,' she said, and before anyone realised what she meant to do, she broke free of the Don's grasp. Running to the guard Hades had killed, she drew his sword from its scabbard, taking her place at her lover's side to face the circle of guards advancing on him warily. 'Kill us both if you can!'

Don Francisco swore furiously. 'She is not to be harmed,' he said. 'I want them both alive!'

The guards hesitated, unsure of how to capture their quarry without disobeying the Don.

With one deft movement of her wrist, Katherine untied the girdle at her waist, kicking aside her heavy overskirts. Dressed only in her bodice and slim silk petticoat, she attacked the nearest guard, surprising him with her skilled swordplay. He fought back, forgetting his master's orders until one of his companions shouted a warning. He faltered, looking nervously over his shoulder at the Don, and received Katherine's blade in his upper arm. Dropping his sword, he clasped his wound and retreated.

Everyone was so busy watching Katherine and Hades that no one noticed Lewis crawling towards the dead Spanish guard. He ran his hands over the man's body, finding the key he was looking for on a ring at his belt. Then he pulled himself painfully across the floor to where Hades was standing, and pushed the key into his hands. Even as the Don shouted a warning to his men, Hades was free.

Moving with great speed, he picked up the sword

dropped by the guard Katherine had pricked. At once the situation was altered. There were six armed Spaniards in the hall besides Don Francisco, but Hades was an awesome sight as he stood facing them, eyes glittering, lips curved back in a savage snarl. Katherine moved closer to his side, both of them prepared to sell themselves dearly before they died.

'Kill him!' Don Francisco screamed. 'Take her alive—but kill him!'

The guards rushed at Hades, deciding that there was safety in numbers. His sword flashed out at them, and one fell, mortally wounded in the throat. They came at him again, and found there were two blades as Katherine joined the attack, pressing hard with no care for her own safety.

Another guard fell to Hades' blade, and the Don went wild. Rushing to the main door of the hall, he wrenched it open to call for more guards, but the words froze on his lips as he found himself looking into a pair of cold eyes in an ebony face. A sword-point was delicately poised at the base of his throat. His eyes widened in disbelief as he backed away, shouting for help.

The guards heard their master's cry, and three of them rushed to his aid, leaving their companion to face Hades alone. The Spaniard fought on desperately, but without help he was no match for the golden-haired avenger and he fell dying at Hades' feet. Now a score of pirates had streamed into the hall, and women's screams could be heard as the servants fled.

The guards were still fighting bravely, but one was wounded and the end was in sight. Don Francisco had retreated to the far end of the hall. Hades saw him, and realising he meant to escape, started after him. Suddenly a knife flashed in the Spaniard's hand. He drew back his arm to throw, and Katherine screamed. At that moment, Esteban sprang at his father. It was not clear what the boy meant to do: no one could guess the thoughts that went through his tortured mind in those seconds before he died. Perhaps the sight of so much bloodshed had touched some darkness in his mind, so that the fear he had always felt for his father became so strong that he reacted like a wild beast driven into a corner. Certainly, the scream which issued from his lips as the Don's knife entered his throat was barely human.

Margarita's cry was agonised as she ran to catch the dying youth in her arms. Her action hampered Hades, preventing him from reaching the Don before he escaped through a small door behind him.

When Hades tried to open the door, he found it had been locked from the other side, and though he charged at it with all his strength, it would not give. Frustrated and angry, he yelled for Fabius to bring him a pistol, and fired at the lock. Still the door held, and he knew it was useless.

'Damn his soul to hell!' Hades roared. 'I'll see him dead before we leave.'

'He's not worth the trouble,' Fabius said. 'We were lucky. Most of the Don's men had been locked in the guardroom, but they may have managed to get free by now and we'll have a fight on our hands. Besides, three of his ships are anchored in the bay. We left the *Golden Eagle* and the *Santa Maria* further up the coast and came in a fishing-boat. We should leave before Don Francisco's crews realise that something is wrong up here.'

Hades stared at him, rage making him want to break down the stubborn door and seek out his enemy, but commonsense told him Fabius was right. He called to his men to follow as he started towards the main door.

Katherine had gone first to her brother when the

pirates came swarming into the hall, but having seen him cared for by one of the pirates, she had done her best to comfort Margarita, and she was still kneeling by the Spanish woman's side.

Margarita was weeping over her nephew's body. 'Francisco killed him. It was my fault for helping you . . .'

'No, Margarita, he always meant to kill Esteban. You cannot blame yourself for this. Come with us now. Let us take you to safety,' Katherine begged.

Doña Margarita shook her head. 'No, I shall go to my friends: my life is finished here. Francisco will not care what becomes of me. Escape yourselves while there is time. My brother will have raised the alarm by now.'

'Come, Katherine.' Hades bent to take her arm. 'She is right; we must go.'

Katherine nodded, pausing only to kiss Margarita's cheek. 'Thank you! You were a good friend to me. I am sorry . . .'

Margarita nodded, but said nothing. Lewis was being carried from the hall by two of the strongest pirates as Katherine joined Hades. No one tried to stop them leaving, but in the courtyard they met several guards who had heard the noise and had come from their posts on the battlements to investigate. As yet they had not discovered those who had been locked in the guardroom by Margarita, but there were enough of them to delay the pirates' escape, and some fierce fighting ensued before they reached the horses stolen from the Don's stables by José. Several Spaniards and two of Hades' men were killed. Even as Hades mounted, sweeping Katherine up with him, they heard the sound of running feet.

'Don Francisco has released the guards!' The warning cry went up.

'Come on,' Hades cried, kicking his heels against the horse's flanks. 'We must go now!'

One of the others had taken Lewis up before him. Now they were all mounted and following their leader as he galloped through the courtyard and down the steep hill. Several shots were fired after them, but the remaining guards were too late to stop their escape. As they rode furiously through the hilly countryside, the peasant folk watched in wonder but made no attempt to hinder them.

Katherine glanced fearfully over her shoulder for some sign of the pursuit which surely must come, but Hades' arms tightened protectively round her. 'Let them come,' he said. 'We'll fight if we have to.' His voice was sharp with hate, and Katherine sensed the bitterness in him.

Fabius drew his mount level with them. 'They cannot follow us by road,' he shouted, grinning. 'The fisherman drove off the rest of the horses. It seems that he too had a score to settle with the Don. He promised to do what he could to delay them.'

Hades scowled. 'I pray that Domingues does come after us with his ships. What condition is the *Golden Eagle* in, Fabius? I've some unfinished business with our friend, and next time we meet I mean to kill him!'

Fabius laughed. 'The *Golden Eagle* is undamaged. We arrived in time to join the attack, and between us we sank one of the Don's ships and sent the other running for home.'

'Then this time we'll finish the task you began!' Hades cried triumphantly.

Fabius laughed again. 'Leave a few Spanish dogs for me,' he retorted. 'Now, swing to your right when we reach the fork in the road just ahead—it's not much further now . . .'

* * *

Half an hour's fast riding brought them to the bay where the two pirate ships were anchored. High cliffs rose on either side, sheltering the ships from view until they came quite suddenly upon the cove. Abandoning the horses at the top of the cliffs, they paused to look at the treacherous path leading to the beach.

Lewis was unable to climb down, as what little strength he had had been exhausted by the hard ride. Hades ordered a rough stretcher to be made from two of the horses' saddles and bridles; then, with one of the other pirates to help steady the load, he carried the almost unconscious man down the steep path.

In her petticoats and bodice, Katherine was able to negotiate the rocky path with a little help from Fabius. As they neared the bottom and the going became less difficult, she paused for breath, smiling at him.

'Thank God you came after us and stayed to discover what had happened,' she said.

Fabius grinned. 'It was always Hades' plan that I should arrive in time to surprise the Don. Unfortunately, we suffered slight damage in the storm and did not catch up with you until it was too late to save you from being taken by him.'

Katherine stared at him. 'You mean that Hades intended to trap Don Francisco? Is that why he was playing for time by sending his crew back to the ship with the silver?'

'Of course!' Fabius looked at her in surprise. 'He didn't tell you he intended to take the Don and his flagship? You cannot have thought the Captain would be stupid enough to walk into a trap as easily as that?'

'But he said we would try to ransom Lewis . . .' Katherine frowned.

'The Don would never have agreed to that. Hades knew that his only chance was to take the Don himself and use him to win your brother's freedom.'

'So that was why he suddenly pretended to agree to sell me!' Katherine said. 'He must have realised you were not coming to the rendezvous in time . . .'

'He obviously sensed a trap when he sent his own men back to the *Golden Eagle*. He was willing to risk his own neck, but not his ship or his men.'

Katherine nodded, but had no time to reply. They had reached the beach now and she could see the boats waiting for them in the shallow waters.

Hades turned to look for her, beckoning to her to hurry; then he bent and picked Lewis up in his arms, carrying him to the nearest boat. Katherine followed with Fabius, scrambling into the second boat to be greeted with grins and jests from the sailors. Immediately they began to pull towards the ships with long, sure strokes. A feeling of urgency was in all their minds: Don Francisco's ships would show no mercy if they were trapped in the bay.

Jake was waiting for Katherine as she climbed on board the *Golden Eagle*, tears of joy pouring unashamedly down his weathered cheek.

'Thank God Fabius was in time,' he said gruffly, hugging her to him. Katherine hugged him back and kissed his cheek. 'Beggin' your pardon, Cap'n,' he said. 'I got carried away!'

Katherine smiled and shook her head. 'Hades is the only captain aboard this ship.'

The sound of Hades' laughter behind her made Katherine turn. His eyes were glittering with a fierce triumph as he looked at her.

'Do my ears deceive me?' he asked, a note of mockery in his voice. 'Can this really be our Kit?'

Katherine's eyes caught fire and her mouth curved in a wicked smile. 'Fie on you, sir! You waste time in idle chatter when there's work to be done—or must I do it for you?'

He threw back his head and roared with laughter. 'By heaven! For a moment I thought you finally tamed! Peace, wench, I'll attend to you later.' With that, he strode away, barking orders at the eager sailors.

The anchor was hurriedly hauled up and the sails unfurled. As they headed for the open sea, a cry came from aloft and in the distance three ships could be seen rounding the coast. Now the men worked with feverish haste. In deep water the *Golden Eagle* was more than a match for the Spanish vessels, but trapped in the narrow cove with little room to manoeuvre, his chances would be halved.

It was a race against time as the Don's ships sailed closer and closer—could they manage to slip through before the gap was closed? The tension grew as every sail was unfurled in an effort to speed the *Golden Eagle* through the water. Hades knew that he must be free to attack the Spanish ships first, before they could trap the slower *Santa Maria* in the cove.

A puff of smoke issued from the first of the Don's ships, but the ball fell short. The *Golden Eagle* slipped out of the bay with only minutes to spare; the *Santa Maria* was not so lucky, and some damage was done to her bowsprit.

Hades' face was an unreadable mask as he gave rapid instructions which brought the *Golden Eagle* round on a new tack. Fabius was watching his moves closely, and he, too, brought his ship round to the attack. The two pirate ships fired together, catching the Spaniard in a deadly crossfire. The Spaniard's mast came down, and the ship shuddered from bow to stern as the other guns pounded against her sides. The Spanish captain gave the order to fire, but his ship was slow and clumsy and could not turn fast enough to catch the *Golden Eagle* broadside; his shot did some small damage to the foremast.

Meanwhile the gunners on both pirate ships were reloading with feverish haste, while Hades ordered his helmsman to bring the *Golden Eagle* round to the attack once more. The Spanish galleons were being out-sailed, out-gunned and out-thought. Topheavy in the water, they simply could not turn quickly enough, and Hades' manoeuvring was brilliant. All twelve cannon belched smoke at the same moment, bombarding the Spaniard with instant death.

Screams could be heard across the water as the mainmast of the flagship came crashing down. The *Hispaniola* was now floundering helplessly with two of her masts gone. Fire and smoke could be seen pouring from the forecastle, and some of the crew were diving overboard in an effort to reach the shore. Fabius had attacked the second ship and was engaged in a deadly battle; they were of similar design and the *Santa Maria* had not the same manoeuvrability as the *Golden Eagle*, but Fabius was proving his worth as a master gunner and the outcome was in little doubt.

But now a new danger was imminent. While the *Golden Eagle* was engaged with the flagship, the third vessel had sailed in closer. A shudder ran through the *Golden Eagle* as a broadside hit her, damaging both the mizen-mast and the gun-room. A fire started, and Jake assembled a team of men to put it out with sea-water.

Hades brought his ship round once more. Before the Spanish gunners had time to reload, his cannon fired within seconds of each other, finding their mark. But then, instead of ordering the helmsman to bring her round again, he deliberately sailed in closer.

'Prepare to board!' he cried.

'To board?' Katherine heard the order, and looked at him in surprise.

He neither saw nor heard her; his eyes were blazing with hatred and he was staring straight at the Spanish vessel. Following his gaze, Katherine saw Don Francisco on the deck of the ship. For some reason, he had not sailed on board the *Hispaniola* this time.

Suddenly, she felt terribly afraid. Hades had let his hatred of the Don cloud his judgment. He was going in for the kill too soon! As they closed on the Spaniard, Don Francisco gave the order to fire. Only two of his cannon were still able to operate after the damage sustained by Hades' first attack, but it was enough. The first ball ploughed into the forecastle, starting a fire; the second struck the already weakened mizen-mast, bringing it crashing down.

Katherine screamed as she saw that Hades would be trapped beneath it, but it was no use; he could never have avoided it in time. She ran towards him, neither knowing nor caring that Jake had taken command of the ship and was bringing the *Golden Eagle* sharply about. She heard their cannon fire again, but the ragged cheer from the crew meant nothing to her.

Kneeling by the wreckage of the mizen-mast, she could see that Hades' eyes were closed, and a terrible fear grew in her heart. 'Please, God, don't let him be dead,' she prayed, taking his head on her lap as the pirates began to clear away the splintered mast and torn canvas.

As luck would have it, the mast had been deflected by the wheel-house, so that only a part of it had fallen across his body. As they pulled him free, Katherine bent her head to his chest, straining to hear the faint beating of his heart. Tears streamed down her cheeks. 'He's alive!' she whispered. 'Oh God, he's alive . . .'

CHAPTER NINE

HADES WAS carried below to his cabin. Katherine could still hear the boom of the cannon, but she knew the order had been given to retreat, leaving the *Santa Maria* to finish the battle.

Glancing at Jake's grim face as he bent over the still figure of the *Golden Eagle*'s captain, she felt her heart contract with pain. 'Is he going to die?' she asked fearfully.

'Well, he don't look too good, matey.' Jake sounded doubtful. 'We'll just have to patch him up as best we can. There's a broken rib, and his leg's badly cut.'

'What can I do?' Katherine asked, blinking away her tears.

'You can help me clean up his leg, if you've the stomach for it?'

Katherine nerved herself as she saw the bloody mess where Hades' leg was badly gashed. 'Just tell me what to do.'

Jake smiled at her. 'That's it, matey. Now first we've got to see if there's any bones broken in that leg, then we'll patch up his thigh. Don't worry! I've seen men with wounds as bad as this pull through. Hades is strong, and he ain't dead yet.' Jake didn't tell her that it was the head wound which was worrying him most. Torn muscles and cracked ribs were something he could deal with, but his experience had taught him that head wounds could prove fatal.

She smothered her fears as she helped to wash away the blood. 'No,' she said. 'He's not dead yet!'

Hades did not recover consciousness as they bound his wounds, nor did he stir as Katherine sat by his side long after Jake had left her to attend to his other duties. Later that night, when the guns had been silent for some time, she heard a commotion on deck and guessed that the *Santa Maria* had come alongside. Soon afterwards, she heard heavy footsteps outside, and Fabius entered the cabin.

'How is he?' he asked, glancing at Hades' white face, and then at her.

'He has not opened his eyes yet, and his breathing is uneven, but Jake says his leg has not been broken.' She sighed. 'So you managed to follow us. What happened after we broke off the engagement?'

'The Don's ship was on fire, the *Hispaniola* was sinking fast, and we crippled the third vessel. Even if Domingues manages to escape alive, he cannot come after us.'

'Then we are safe for the moment.' Katherine smiled wearily. 'And what will you do now?'

'I shall sail with you to England. The *Golden Eagle* needs repairs, as she is taking in water, but we can control it until we can put into port and carry out the necessary work.'

'But what of the *Santa Maria*?'

'Her crew have decided to return to the island. Besides, with Hades ill, you need me. Did you imagine I would desert you, Kit?'

Katherine smiled mistily, realising something she should have guessed long ago. Fabius loved her. She knew he would never speak to her of his feelings, but it was there in all he did for her sake.

'Thank you,' she whispered. 'Now I must come with you. My brother is asking for me, and there are other wounded to attend to.'

Katherine heard the faint moan, and her eyes flew open. She had closed them from sheer weariness, having slept little in the two days and nights which had passed since Hades was injured. Bending over the bed, she saw his eyelids fluttering, and then he was looking at her.

'Hades,' she said, smiling down at him.

'Kitty . . .' His lips moved in a painful whisper. 'Water . . .'

She lifted a cup to his lips, slipping her arm beneath his head to support him while he drank. He swallowed with difficulty, falling back against the pillows as if exhausted by the effort.

'How long have I lain here?'

'Two days. Fabius is in charge of the ship. The *Santa Maria* has left us to return to the island and the Spanish Main.'

'And the Don?'

'His ship was on fire, the *Hispaniola* sunk and the third vessel badly damaged.'

'May the Devil take his soul!' Hades muttered, trying to sit up, but falling back as he felt the pain of his wounds. 'Curse it!'

'Lie still,' Katherine said. 'You need to rest, and there is nothing to concern you. We shall put in for repairs soon. Then I am taking you home to Dunline Castle. Lewis has said that you will be welcome to stay there as long as you wish.'

'Dunline Castle? I am honoured, my lady.' His lips twisted wryly.

Katherine was hurt by the bitter note in his tone. 'Where else should I take you but my home?'

Hades' eyelids fluttered as the weariness swept over him. 'I'm tired,' he said. 'We'll talk of this another day . . .'

For much of the homeward journey, Hades was forced to keep to his cabin, though it was only a matter of days before he had Jake shave him and insisted on getting out of bed.

The carpenter was sent for, and a crutch solid enough to bear Hades' weight was made. Despite the pain it caused him, he spent hours learning to hobble about the cabin until he could do so without help. His temper was volatile, flaring at any minor disobedience; there was no doubt that he had resumed command of his ship, even though he could not yet climb up to the deck.

'I've seen him in a few rages,' Jake said to Katherine one day when they had been at sea for some weeks. 'But I've never seen him quite as bad as this. I think that blow on the head must have addled his brain.'

'No, he's sane enough, Jake, but he's frustrated because he's tied to his cabin. And there's something more . . .' She frowned. 'I think he's angry with me for some reason.'

'Ay, the ungrateful fool! If it wasn't for you, he'd be dead or rotting in a Spanish dungeon.'

'It was because of me that he was there in the first place,' Katherine reminded him. 'Perhaps that's why he's so angry with me.'

'Mebbe.' Jake scowled. At least his leg is healing; he'll walk on it by the time we reach England.'

She gave a sigh of relief. 'Where is my brother? Have you seen him?'

Jake's face softened. 'He's on deck, getting some air

into his lungs. This voyage is building up his strength, and he'll soon be fit and well again.'

'Yes, he is better. And you've been so good to him.'

'I like the lad. He's had a hard time of it. All those months in Domingues' cells, when you thought he was marooned on an island!'

'I could have searched for years and not found him.' Katherine's face was serious. 'I think I'll go up and join him.' Leaving Jake, she scrambled up the wooden ladder to the deck.

Since the gown she had worn for her short-lived marriage to Don Esteban was torn and bloodstained, Katherine had discarded it in favour of breeches and a shirt borrowed from the smallest member of the crew. She sometimes wondered if she would ever feel comfortable in female clothing again, though she knew she would have no choice once the voyage was ended.

Going to her brother's side, she watched the blue-grey water parting as the ship ploughed her way through the waves. Salt spray touched her face, and she laughed, loving the sense of freedom she felt at being on deck.

'In a few days we shall be home,' she said. 'Uncle William will be surprised to see us.'

Lewis frowned. 'I mean to call him to account for what he tried to do to you.'

She sighed. 'Could we not just forget the past?'

'No.' Lewis looked at her, his face grim. 'I shall never forget the hell of being Don Francisco's prisoner! I need to know whether our uncle knew where I was.'

Katherine's eyes were anxious as she looked at him. Lewis was recovering his health, but the inner scars would take much longer to heal.

'Oh, Lewis . . .' Sometimes he seemed almost a stranger to her now. 'How I wish I could have prevented your suffering!'

His face softened. 'It was none of your doing, Katherine. I have much to thank you for, and your friends, too.'

She saw the darkness of his expression and tried to change the subject. 'Why did you quarrel with our father? I know he regretted it so much after you went away.'

'As I have regretted it so many times. It haunted me—especially when the Don told me he was dead . . .' He looked out towards the sea, his face working with emotion. 'Father wanted me to go to Court. I refused. I am a Protestant, Katherine, and my faith means a great deal to me—more than ever now. I could not bend the knee to a Catholic queen who was stained with the blood of Englishmen.'

Katherine's hand closed over his. 'But Father was of the same faith, Lewis. He only pretended to adopt the Catholic faith, as so many others were forced to do.'

'That is why we quarrelled. I would not accept that doctrine simply to keep my place at Court. Not while others of my faith were dying because they refused to renounce it.'

'Father said that Mary was a sick woman, and that one day Elizabeth would be queen.'

'That day cannot come soon enough!' Lewis said strongly.

'Amen to that! A man after my own heart, I see.'

Brother and sister turned at the sound of Hades' voice.

'How did you get here?' Katherine upbraided him. 'You might have fallen!'

'By heaven! Will the woman give me no peace?' He glared at her. 'Would you have me lie abed so that you can weep over me?'

Katherine's eyes flared. 'Weep for you? I'd sooner cry over a snake!'

He grinned. 'Go away, Kitty, and find something ladylike to do—if you can remember how . . .'

'Oh, you—you arrogant man!' she shrieked. 'I hope you fall down the hatch and break your neck!'

'Now that's the Kit we all love so well,' Hades said, his eyes gleaming. 'Leave us, child. This is men's business.'

'You—you . . .' Katherine exploded as she saw the mockery in his face. 'I hate you—do you hear me? I hate you . . .'

'Then nothing's changed, Kitty.'

She gasped. His black mood had passed. She stared at him, wondering what had worked the miracle. 'Hades?'

'Go below, Kitty. I have something to discuss with your brother.'

Katherine swallowed hard. Could he—did he—mean . . .? A little bubble of happiness began to rise inside her. If he had something to discuss with Lewis, it must concern her. He must be going to ask her twin for her hand in marriage!

Hades frowned as she still hesitated. 'I punished you once for disobedience, Kit, and I can do it again, even if I've got only one good knee to put you over.'

She giggled. 'You'd have to catch me first, and I don't think you could!' Then, as he glared at her, 'I'm going . . . I'm going . . .'

She gave him a wicked smile, then ran across the deck and disappeared below.

If Hades had spoken to her brother of a marriage between them, neither man mentioned it to Katherine. She waited in vain for a sign that something had been arranged, but none was forthcoming. That the two men had reached an understanding was obvious, however, for they had become firm friends and spent most of their time together during the remainder of the voyage. But whenever Katherine approached, she felt they changed the subject and began to speak of something quite different.

She struggled to hide her annoyance, knowing that it amused Hades to see her temper flare. The hatred and pain she had seen in him in the early days of his illness seemed to have drained out of him. He had thrown away his crutch, and though he still walked with a limp, his strength was growing every day.

Sometimes she remembered their love-filled nights when she had been just Kit and not the sister of an earl. It no longer mattered to her whether he had bedded with Molly or not. Now she wished only for a sign that Hades still wanted her, but though he always had a smile for her, he never tried to take her in his arms.

She began to dread their arrival in England, fearing that he would not consent to accompany them to the castle, but her fears were groundless. He and Lewis went together to meet her uncle, and she was told to stay on board ship until they sent for her. Her protests met with a frown from Lewis.

'Come with us in those clothes?' He shook his head. 'If Lady Margaret sees you like that, she will assume the worst. I must have a care for your reputation, if you have none. I shall have your clothes brought to you.'

Katherine flushed, shamed by her brother's criticism. She made no further protest, and so was never really sure what took place at that first meeting. However, one glance at Sir William's face when Lewis brought her home, suitably attired in a gown of blue silk, told her all she needed to know.

Lady Margaret looked older, and there were streaks of grey in her hair. She embraced Katherine with more warmth than she had been used to show. 'Dear child, we thought you dead!' she cried. 'Forgive me. I should not have stood by when your uncle pressed you to an unwanted marriage.'

Katherine kissed her cheek. 'It was not your fault.'

She allowed her aunt to lead her to her uncle. She curtsied to him with a natural grace which had not been lost during her months at sea. 'I am glad to see you, sir.'

Lewis had told her he was satisfied that their uncle had known nothing of his imprisonment. Now she looked into Sir William's eyes and saw acceptance there.

'So you offer me forgiveness,' he said, not quite able to meet her eyes. 'I thank you, Lady Katherine, but I shall not try your goodness too far. I shall leave here as soon as my baggage can be packed, and shall trouble you no more.'

Katherine nodded. She looked towards her aunt. 'Do you go with him, aunt?'

'Lewis has said I may stay. If you want me, Katherine?'

'I should be happy if you wish to make your home with us.'

This gentleness was too much for Lady Margaret. She nodded, kissed her niece and then excused herself before the tears could flow. Her husband followed with a curt nod of his head.

'I believe your uncle is still reeling from the shock of finding you alive and well, Lewis.' Hades chuckled.

'He will trouble us no more, thanks mainly to you, my friend.'

'I think you could have handled him yourself, Lewis! Your scowl makes me shake in my shoes. It is so like Katherine's.'

Her eyes took fire; then she saw that Hades' words

had been meant to cheer her brother. Lewis was laughing, and the shadows had gone from his face.

He laid his hand on Hades' shoulder with the ease of friendship. 'How good you are for me. I shall miss you when you go. I wish I could persuade you to make your home with us.'

Hades' smile faded. 'You know why I must go, Lewis, but I hope we shall meet again one day.'

Katherine watched in silence. Somewhere inside she was hurting, but she fought the pain. 'You are leaving us?' she asked, unaware that her pain showed in her eyes. 'When must you go?'

'In a few days.' Hades spoke softly, his face gentle as he looked at her. 'I shall stay until you are settled here, then I must go.'

'But your leg . . .' she protested, knowing it was a vain hope. His leg was almost healed; it would not serve to hold him if he wished to go. 'You will leave me . . . Shall I see you again?'

'You have things to say to each other,' Lewis said. 'Excuse me.' He walked swiftly from the room.

Katherine stared at Hades. 'You were going—without telling me?'

'No. I meant to tell you myself.' Hades reached out to her, but she moved away from him, and he frowned.

She turned away, pride banishing her tears. 'Yet still you will go, and all that was between us is as nothing?'

'You would have left me once, Katherine,' he said softly. 'You hate me—how often you have said as much?'

Katherine kept her face averted as the pain twisted inside her. 'And if I loved you, would you stay?'

'I cannot.'

She turned to face him then, near to tears. 'Then go,' she whispered. 'Go now . . .'

A golden flame flared in his eyes. He stared at her like a man possessed, and then he drew her into his arms, crushing her against him so hard that she could scarcely breathe. His mouth came down to cover hers, bruising her with the hunger of his kiss. She clung to him, tears coursing down her cheeks as he held her.

Then she looked up at him, all pride gone. 'Don't leave me,' she begged. 'I love you so much . . .'

'Kitty,' he choked, and she saw agony in his eyes. 'I cannot stay—don't ask it of me.'

Then he stepped back, staring at her wildly for a moment before he turned and strode away. Katherine watched him go, her heart torn and bleeding as she longed to call him back, to plead with him again. The words stuck in her throat. What was the use? Now, or in a few days' time, he meant to leave her . . .

Katherine's fingers were clumsy as she drew the silken thread through her tapestry. She threw the needlework to the floor impatiently. Such pastimes were tedious to her now, and the walls of her solar seemed to close in around her. Her heart yearned for the motion of a ship beneath her feet and the salty tang of the wind in her face, but most of all for the man she loved.

She walked to the window, gazing out at the grey sky. 'How dull England is in winter. Will the sun never shine?'

Lady Margaret watched her anxiously. 'You are restless, Katherine—but it will pass, as everything does in time.'

'I think I shall go for a walk. It is oppressive in here.'

She left the room, intending to walk in the courtyard, but as she reached the great hall a man came towards her.

'Lady Katherine, may I speak with you, please?'

Katherine frowned. 'Mathew! It is Mathew Sommers, isn't it?'

He looked hurt that she should need to ask. 'I believe I need not tell you how delighted I am at your safe return. I have been away on business for Sir William, and when I arrived at Dunline this morning his lordship told me Sir William has gone.'

'Yes, some three weeks since. I believe my brother can furnish you with his address.'

The colour rose in his cheeks. 'I shall of course acquaint Sir William with my intentions, but his lordship has offered me a position at Dunline. He was good enough to say I would be a great help with the estate, having been Sir William's . . .' He broke off as he saw the impatient look in her eyes. 'But I have not asked if you are well, though I can see for myself how lovely . . .'

Katherine smiled, feeling herself ungracious. 'Yes, I am quite well, Mathew. I was about to walk in the gardens—if you would care to accompany me?'

He fell into step beside her. 'I have never ceased to blame myself since the night we were to have met in the cove. If I had been with you . . .'

'You could have done little to change what happened. I persuaded you to a course of action you felt unwise. The blame is my own.' Katherine glanced at him. 'Yet I have often wondered why you did not meet me that night.'

'But did you not send me a note to say you had changed your mind?'

'No! I went to the secret room, and found a letter from you urging me to escape that very night because I was in danger.'

'I left no such note.' Mathew seemed bewildered. 'I did not know you had gone until Sir William told me the next day. Naturally, I contacted the *Seabird*'s captain, but discovered he had never left port . . .'

Katherine frowned. 'Someone left the note for me. Obviously our secret was discovered, probably by Don Francisco himself. He knew I would never agree to the marriage, and so he found a way to trick me. It was no accident that his ships were in the bay that night. The Don meant to kidnap me himself! How angry he must have been when he discovered that Hades had taken his prize.'

'You mean the pirate captain who brought you home?'

'Yes.' Katherine looked thoughtful. 'The *Seabird*—where is she now?'

'Somewhere between here and France. Sir William has been using her as a trading-vessel. It was to arrange the sale of her last cargo that I left Dunline.'

'You will deliver to me the bill of sale for the *Seabird*, and any profits from the disposal of her cargo. Since she is my ship, they rightfully belong to me.'

'Yes, Lady Katherine, though perhaps his lordship . . .'

'My brother will agree with me. I have a use for the *Seabird*: I owe a debt of gratitude to two good friends. And there is something else you can do for me . . .' Katherine broke off as she saw Lewis approaching. 'We shall speak of this again another day.'

'Katherine, I was coming to find you.' Lewis's face was eager as he reached them. 'Mathew, you will excuse us, please.' He drew Katherine with him, as the secretary bowed and walked away.

'What is it? Have you news of Hades?'

'No. Something much more important! Mary Tudor is dead, and Elizabeth has been proclaimed queen.'

'Oh . . .' Katherine sighed as her hopes faded; then

she smiled, knowing how much the news meant to Lewis. 'It is the answer to your prayers. I'm glad, because it means you will be able to take your rightful place at Court.'

He squeezed her arm. 'And you, Katherine. Her Majesty has commanded us both to attend her as soon as possible. It has not escaped my notice that you are a beautiful woman now. You will be much admired at Court, and it is time a marriage was arranged for you.'

A chill entered Katherine's heart. 'A marriage? Oh, no, Lewis! I have no wish to marry. I shall stay at Dunline with you.'

He laughed. 'So you say now, but you would not thank me in a few years' time if I took you at your word. No, Katherine, we shall find a handsome husband for you at Queen Elizabeth's Court.'

She turned her face aside so that her brother should not see the tears in her eyes. Lewis could not know how much his teasing words had hurt her. He had no idea of her love for Hades, and even if he had guessed the truth, he would never agree to such an unsuitable marriage. Katherine realised now that it had always been a vain hope. Lewis liked Hades, but he would expect his only sister to marry according to her rank.

Katherine blinked rapidly, determined not to weep. Her only hope was that Lewis would allow her to remain unwed, for she knew she could never be happy as the wife of any man but Hades.

Life at Queen Elizabeth's Court was very gay in the weeks preceding her coronation, which was to take place on 15 January 1559. The Queen was still young, and happy to be free of the shadows which had haunted her since the cruel death of her mother. For on the day Anne Boleyn died, dishonoured and reviled, Elizabeth had ceased to be the spoiled pet of an adoring father, to become merely another unwanted daughter. The years which followed had been fraught with dangers for the princess, years in which she was to find herself a prisoner at the Tower and discover that faithful friends were few. To those who stood by her in the dark years, she was to prove most generous. The handsome Lord Robert Dudley, who had sojourned at the Tower while Elizabeth herself was confined there, was made Master of the Horse, and the Queen's old governess, Kat Ashly, was First Lady of the Bedchamber.

The celebrations were to be magnificent, for though Elizabeth knew how to be thrifty, she also knew when it was important to make a show. The people of England had welcomed her with open arms after Bloody Mary's death, and she knew that her people loved a fine spectacle. The palace each day was full of bustle and excitement as the preparations for the great day progressed.

The Queen loved to dance and ride out hunting with her ladies and gentlemen, delighting in the pastimes of music and sports. Plays, balls and jousting in the tiltyard were the order of the day, and Katherine found herself caught up in the lively atmosphere of the Court.

She had gathered round her a small court of admiring gallants of her own, who were always willing to escort her wherever she wished to go, so that she never lacked an escort when visiting the silk merchants to purchase a new gown. Lewis had shown himself mindful of the debt he owed her, showering her with costly presents of silks, laces and jewels, and she was as well dressed as any lady of the Court.

Katherine knew that her twin was proud of her, taking more pleasure in the compliments paid to her beauty than she. For though the various delights of the Court kept her from being bored, her heart was heavy. She would willingly have exchanged all her fine clothes and admiring gallants for a pair of salt-stained breeches and a smile from the man she loved.

The Queen had given Lewis a position in her household, including him often in the bevy of handsome young men she liked to have about her, though it was obvious that Lord Robert held a special place in her affections. Then, one day, she sent for Katherine, telling her in a private audience that she was to become a lady-in-waiting.

'I have heard you disobeyed my sister's royal command to make a marriage she approved of,' Queen Elizabeth said, looking at her sternly. 'Is this true?'

'Yes, Your Majesty. It was a marriage my father would not have approved, had he lived. Besides, Don Francisco was an evil man who held my brother prisoner for many months.'

The Queen smiled slightly. 'We cannot condone such reckless behaviour in one so young, but perhaps my sister's judgment was unwise in matters of marriage . . .'

Katherine thought she saw a sly amusement in Elizabeth's eyes. She felt that the Queen was secretly pleased with her for disobeying the late Queen's authority, though she might not say so openly. She was clearly in high good humour as she fingered a collar of large emeralds—emeralds as fine as those Hades had bought in the pirate's auction. In fact they were so similar that Katherine could have believed to be them the same, except that she knew it was impossible.

For several minutes the Queen questioned her about her adventures, her sharp mind probing and quick to understand much that was unspoken. She was very curious about life on board the pirate ship, and made

Katherine describe the battles at sea in detail.

'Would that I had been a man!' she cried, her eyes sparkling as Katherine finished her story. 'I have the heart and mind of a king, but I was born to be a queen . . .' Suddenly she smiled. 'We have decided to forgive you, Lady Katherine, and to show our pleasure in your safe return to our shores, we have interested ourselves on your behalf. A marriage has been arranged with the Marquis of Rothmere, which shall take place after our coronation. Then, in good time, you and your husband shall take your places at Court.'

Katherine's face went white. 'I do not know the Marquis, Your Majesty.'

The Queen's lips twitched but she did not smile. 'Methinks the gentleman has fallen in love with you from afar, and perhaps he is too shy to confess his devotion to you. No doubt he will do so when he returns from the country where he has lately been on matters of urgency.'

'But I do not . . .' Katherine swallowed hard, as she saw a flash of anger in the Queen's eyes. It was useless to resist Elizabeth's commands, for they would also be her brother's. 'I do not know how to thank you, Your Majesty.'

'Then do not try,' Queen Elizabeth replied, touching the emeralds about her neck with a secret smile. 'Go now, and send Lord Robert to me. You will find him waiting in the antechamber.'

'Yes, Your Majesty.'

Katherine curtsied and left the Queen's private chambers. Pausing only to pass on the royal message, she made her way hurriedly to the great hall where she knew she would find Lewis with the other courtiers. He was in conversation with Sir William Cecil, the Queen's Secretary of State, and she was forced to curb her impatience until they had finished.

Lewis was full of the tasks which had been placed upon him by the Secretary of State, and talked excitedly of the honour he felt at being singled out. So it was several minutes before Katherine could get him to listen to her news.

'So the Queen told you.' Lewis frowned. 'It was to have been a secret until Lord Rothmere comes.'

Katherine gasped. 'You knew! And you never breathed a word of it to me. Lewis, how could you?'

'Now, Katherine, don't look at me like that. There was good reason for the secrecy.'

'Yes! You knew I did not wish to marry. You might at least have warned me.'

'I thought it would please you.' Lewis seemed uncertain now. 'I know there was some quarrel between you and Hades, but you must see this is best for you.'

'Well, I do not see it,' Katherine snapped, her frustration making her want to scream. 'I shall never marry the Marquis—never!'

'You will do as the Queen bids you . . .' Lewis began, his own temper rising now. 'You've been allowed too much freedom, and you will learn to behave as befits a young woman of your rank. I will not have you disgrace us. Lord Rothmere comes soon, and I only hope he can control you . . .' Lewis found himself talking to empty air as she suddenly rushed away. 'Katherine, listen to me!'

She did not look back. Her head was aching, and her eyes stung with tears she was too proud to shed. How could Lewis be so cruel to her? He was as bad as their uncle—and she had believed that he loved her. It was heartless to force her to marry a man she had never met.

Reaching her own small room tucked away in a corner of the palace, Katherine gave way to her tears. It was not enough that she had lost the man she loved so desperately. Now they meant to force her to marry! In that moment she wished she had been born a man and free to choose for herself. Suddenly she sat up and wiped her tears. For many months she had lived as free as any man, so why should she let herself be pushed into wedlock, since she did not wish for it? There was one way of escape still open to her!

Running to her coffer, she took out the papers Mathew Sommers had given her a few weeks earlier. One was a bill of sale for the *Seabird*, the others were details of money deposited with a goldsmith in Cheapside—the last, a tiny scrap of paper with the name of a tavern written on it.

Before Katherine left the *Golden Eagle* to return to the castle, Jake had told her he intended to spend some time in England before putting to sea again, and he gave her the names of several inns where he might be found. Mathew had eventually traced him to the Three Dogs in Vauxhall a few days earlier.

Katherine gathered up the papers, the idea forming in her mind. Her ship was at this very moment in Portsmouth harbour, awaiting orders. If she could get word to Jake, she could meet him in Vauxhall and then go wherever she pleased. Jake might even know where she could contact Hades!

Somehow she must get a message to Jake, and she thought there was a young footman who would be only too eager to please her. Tomorrow she would go herself to the goldsmith and collect her money, and then she would meet Jake later in the evening.

CHAPTER TEN

IT WAS raining as Katherine slipped out of the palace, a dark cloak pulled up over her head. Tonight there was a grand ball at Whitehall and the rooms would be overflowing with noble families from all over England. No one would notice that she was missing, and by morning it would be too late. She would be on the road to Portsmouth and the freedom of the open sea.

Making her way through the privy gardens, she passed several members of the palace household going about their business, but they took little notice of her. If they saw her at all, they probably imagined she was keeping a lovers' tryst. When she reached the steps leading down to the river, it was already growing dusk.

Katherine peered anxiously into the gloom, hoping to spy a boatman waiting for a passenger to ferry across the river. At first she could see nothing, then a bulky figure loomed up out of the twilight, startling her.

'Row you across the river, mistress?'

'How much to the Three Dogs inn at Vauxhall?'

'Three silver shillings, mistress.'

'That's robbery!' Katherine said. 'I'll give you a shilling.'

'Two shillings, or I don't budge from here.' The man grinned, revealing a row of rotten teeth. 'There's a mist coming up. I doubt you'll find anyone else to take you.'

Katherine knew a moment of panic: she must get to Jake tonight! 'As you wish. I'll pay you half now, and half when we get there.'

'It's a bargain, mistress,' the man said, taking the coin she offered and helping her to step into the boat.

A fine mist was settling over the river, and the lights from the houses on the banks faded as the windows were shuttered and barred against the evil humours of the night. She shivered, pulling her cloak round her more tightly. It was early January and very cold. She thought a little wistfully of her room at the palace, and of the huge fire burning in the great hall. The flames of many candles and the press of people would combine to keep out the damp air. Almost she wished herself back among the lights and her friends, but then she thought of the empty life she must lead as the wife of a man she could never love, and her courage returned.

A picture of Jake's weatherbeaten face came into her mind, warming her. He would be waiting for her at the tavern. Fabius might be there, too. They would hire some horses and ride through the night to Portsmouth, and from there the *Seabird* would carry them wherever they wished to go.

In her heart, Katherine knew she wanted to find Hades. He might be angry with her at first, but she could bear his rages if only she could be with him again. Once she had spurned his offer to become his mistress, but now she would do anything to be in his arms again.

The ferry seemed to travel very slowly, the steady plop of the oars lulling her to a dreamlike state. So that when it ceased, and Katherine heard the scraping sound as the boat rouched against a flight of stone steps, she blinked at the boatman in surprise.

'That's a shilling you owe me, mistress.'

Hurriedly she took the coin from her purse and paid

him. 'Where will I find the Three Dogs?' she asked, peering anxiously into the darkness.

The man pointed to a shadowy building a little further along the bank. 'That's it over there. It ain't a place I'd let my daughter visit, but I suppose it does for whores and thieves.'

Ignoring his taunt, Katherine walked towards the building he had pointed out. Her skirts dragged in the mud, flapping uncomfortably against her ankles. Outside the inn, she paused to look at it, her heart sinking as she saw its seedy appearance. The boatman had been right, she thought, wishing she had arranged to meet Jake somewhere else. She had not dared to ask him to come to Whitehall lest by some mischance Lewis should happen to see him.

The footman she had employed had made no mention of the state of the inn when she enquired if he had delivered her letter safely, merely assuring her that all was well. 'Your friend said I was to tell you that he would be waiting. You are to ask the landlord to conduct you to a private room he has taken for your comfort,' he had said.

Jake was inside and expecting her; the knowledge gave Katherine the courage to open the door and go in. A rank stench of stale wine, sweat and rotting filth met her nostrils, bringing the vomit to her throat and making her pause on the threshold.

Her entry caused a little stir among the men and women already inside. Several pairs of eyes turned to look at her, and her heart beat faster as she heard the harsh whispers. Then silence fell, and she sensed their hostility. Though wearing her plainest gown, she was yet aware that the richness of its material was out of place in this hovel. She was not wearing any of her jewels, but everything about her shouted of wealth, and she saw a speculative gleam in some of the men's eyes. A shiver went through her. She had been unwise to come here alone!

A tall, heavily-built man with a hard face came towards her. 'You'll be the one, I reckon,' he said, jerking his head towards the stairs. 'You'll be her he's waiting for.'

'Yes,' Katherine agreed, anxious to leave this room of hostile eyes. 'Where do I go?'

'Top of the stairs, to your left.' The man leered at her. 'Mighty impatient he is, too!'

Katherine nodded her thanks. Going quickly to the foot of the stairs, she lifted her skirt to run up them, her heart racing. A flicker of light was showing beneath the door where rats had eaten part of it away, but as she lifted the latch and went in, the candle-flame was suddenly extinguished.

'Are you there, Jake?' she cried, alarmed.

'Catalina, I have been waiting for you . . .'

Katherine's blood turned to ice as she recognised the Don's voice and heard the sound of his laughter close by. She turned to leave, but found her way barred by a man's body. The light was restored and she looked up into the Spaniard's face, seeing the cruel triumph there. Then, even as she began to protest, she felt a blow on the back of her head and she knew nothing more.

Katherine moaned, her eyelids flickering as she stirred. Her head was aching, and she gave a little cry of pain as she opened her eyes. For a moment she was bewildered, her sight obscured by mist as she tried to focus on her surroundings. Where was she?

Now she could feel the motion of a ship beneath her, and as her eyes became adjusted to the gloom, she realised that she was in a cabin similar to the one she had occupied on the *Hispaniola*. All at once, memory returned, and she sat up in dismay. She was the Don's prisoner!

Jumping up from the bed, Katherine ran to the door and tugged at the latch. It refused to budge. She gave a little cry of despair. What a fool she had been to walk into the Don's trap. But how could she have guessed he would be waiting for her? And how had he learned of her plans to meet Jake?

She touched the back of her head; it was very sore, but there was no blood. Anger stirred in her as she thought of the man who had treated her so harshly. He might have killed her! She shuddered as she realised that perhaps the Don cared little whether she lived or died.

The sound of a key in the lock sent a shiver through her, and she stood tensely as the Don came in, carrying a lighted lanthorn. He stood looking at her pale face, a slight smile playing about his mouth. 'So you are awake, Catalina. I apologise for the manner of your abduction. My companion was afraid you might call for help, and exceeded his orders. I trust you were not badly hurt?'

'Please don't pretend you would care if the blow had killed me. You are a man without morals or conscience.'

The Don laughed softly, sending chills down her spine. 'How well you know me! But it would be a pity if you died too soon. It will afford me much pleasure to break your spirit. Besides, I have a score to settle with a friend of yours. The one sure way to bring him out of his hiding-place is to hold you captive, Catalina.'

'You want revenge on Hades!'

'How clever of you, my dear.' His eyes were twin points of ice. 'I have been unable to locate him, though I know his ship is still in port—but you were an easier target. And you made it so simple . . .' He smiled wolfishly. 'I was planning how best to lure you away from your devoted gallants, and then you delivered yourself into my hands.'

Katherine frowned. 'How could you have known I was to meet Jake? Unless . . .'

'It was the footman, of course. Did you never wonder why he was so eager to serve you? Or did you accept it as homage to your beauty? He was my spy, with orders to gain your confidence. He brought your message straight to me.'

Katherine pursed her lips. 'I have been foolish! But what have you done to Jake?'

'He left the inn some days ago. You were careless, my dear. You should have sent Mr Sommers to enquire, before trusting a stranger with such an important letter.'

It seemed that he knew everything about her. She turned her face aside, unwilling to see the gloating expression in his eyes. 'I may have acted unwisely, but you are mistaken if you believe that Hades will follow me.'

'You think not?' Don Francisco laughed wryly. 'If it is only for his pride's sake, he will come. Hades is a predictable animal. I sent a message to your brother, informing him that you are my prisoner, and offering to exchange you for Hades. Oh, yes! Hades will come.'

'My brother does not know where to find him.'

'No?' The Don's brows rose. 'Then that is unfortunate for you, Catalina.'

Katherine shrank away from him as he touched her cheek. Her head whirled and she swayed, catching at the bedpost to steady herself.

He frowned. 'You are faint, Catalina. We shall renew our conversation at another time. I want you to be fully aware of what is happening to you. Besides, I have work on deck if we are to reach the appointed meeting with

Captain Hades.' He sneered as he saw the fear in her eyes. 'Oh, yes, I have made sure our friend knows where to find *me*.'

Katherine shivered as she heard the menace in his voice, sitting down on the bed as he went out. The sound of the key being turned filled her with despair. Burying her face in her hands, she wept as she realised what she had done. Because of her, Hades would come after the Don, and they would fight. When she last saw him, nearly four months ago, he had not fully recovered from his unjuries, so how could he hope to fight the Don, and win?

Katherine closed her eyes, praying that Hades would not come after her, but she knew it was a vain hope. He must come, because he could not ignore such a challenge . . .

Suddenly the pattern of her thoughts was scattered as she heard the sound of running feet and shouting on deck. Then a terrific roar of cannon-fire shook the ship from bow to stern. Kneeling on the bed, she peered out of the window into the grey light of a winter's morning. A fine mist was swirling over the water, but between the intermittent patches she could just make out the dark shape of a ship. She could tell she was an English vessel by the cut of her jib and the sleeker lines. She was faster than the Spanish ship, and not so topheavy in the water.

Hades had come—but much sooner than the Don had expected! Somehow he must have discovered what had happened and set out in pursuit at once, surprising the Spaniard under cover of the mist.

Katherine watched as smoke belched from the *Golden Eagle*'s cannon, feeling the shudder which ran through the Spanish vessel as she was hit broadside on. The girl's heart lifted with pride, and she felt no fear. Hades had come as an avenger, refusing to bow to the Don's threats. He knew that she would prefer to die in the attack than live as the Don's prisoner.

'Sink him!' she yelled fiercely, knowing, that her words could not reach Hades, but filled with an exultant triumph. 'Kill the Don . . .'

So engrossed was she in watching the battle that she did not at first hear the door open. Then she laughed in the Don's face. 'Methinks your plans have gone awry, sir.'

'If I die, you'll die, too.'

Don Francisco's eyes were filled with an insane rage. He dived at her, trying to seize her wrist, but Katherine dodged past him. Running towards the open door, she was out of it and half-way up the wooden ladder before he caught her. Hampered by her long skirts, she could climb only slowly. She felt his hand clutch at her ankle, and she kicked out at him, scrambling through the hatch to the deck as he swore and let her go. But then he was behind her again, and as she paused to get her bearings, he grabbed her arm, dragging her with him to the mainmast.

He shouted orders at some of the sailors, and Katherine was seized by several pairs of hands as they surrounded her. A rope was thrown round her waist, binding her to the mast so that she could not escape.

The scene was one of utter confusion. The Spaniards had been taken by surprise, and everywhere men lay wounded among the wreckage. Others were trying to put out small fires which had started in a dozen different places, while on the gun-decks she could hear the shouting as the gunners struggled to reload those cannon which had not been smashed by Hades' broadside. But it was too late for retaliation. The *Golden Eagle* had closed in, and grappling-irons were being thrown across to hold the ships together. Katherine watched the pirates swarm abroad, wicked-looking cutlasses in their hands. The Spanish sailors left the fires to meet the new danger, fighting desperately against the tide of vengeful Englishmen.

She looked for Hades' commanding figure, and found him in the thick of the fighting, wielding his sword with all his old power and skill. She whispered his name as she saw him surrounded by the Spaniards, her heart filling with love and pride. Don Francisco had tried to cut him off from the others, knowing that his ship was burning around him, and caring only that his hated enemy should die.

Pressed back by six of the Don's men, Hades was forced to retreat. Katherine screamed as she saw burning canvas fall from aloft, but he leapt out of the way, and two of the Spaniards were cut off by the flames. Now another man had cut his way through to Hades' side, and Fabius' sword flashed out to take on a Spanish blade. The tide had turned as Hades dispatched one of his attackers, thrusting hard at another who saw he was outmatched and suddenly threw down his sword, begging for mercy. Seeing this, the last two Spaniards followed suit, abandoning their weapons as they found themselves hemmed in on all sides.

Absorbed in the fighting, Katherine was unaware that the Don was at her side. He cut through the ropes which bound her to the mast, seizing her wrist and dragging her towards the open hatch. Flames were shooting up from the deck below, and the smoke choked her, making her cough and splutter.

'Hades!' Don Francisco shouted. 'You think you've won! But you'll be too late to save her.'

Hades looked at them, realising what the Don meant to do, and that he was too far away to reach her in time.

'No!' he roared, desperation in his eyes. 'Katherine . . .'

Don Francisco laughed, his eyes glittering with insane hatred. 'Farewell, my lovely Catalina . . .'

Katherine screamed, struggling and fighting with all her strength as he dragged her to the edge of the hatch, striking out at him wildly as he pushed her forward. She felt herself falling, and her fingers clutched at his arm, pulling him down with her as she tried to save herself. They fell across the open hatch, their bodies suspended on the very brink momentarily as they both fought for a secure hold, the thick smoke swirling about them. Then she felt strong hands catch her ankles, and she was hauled roughly to safety even as the Don went slithering over into the smoke and flames.

Lying shivering on the deck, Katherine heard his screams as the fire engulfed him, and her head swam as the darkness threatened to close in on her. Then she opened her eyes to find Jake bending over her anxiously.

'You saved me,' she said, choking painfully as the smoke filled her lungs.

'Thank God I was near enough to reach you in time,' Jake said. 'He was looking at Hades, and didn't see me. Here's the Cap'n now.'

Then he was kneeling at her side, lifting her into his arms. 'Hades . . .' she whispered, tears sliding helplessly down her cheeks.

'Hold on to me, Kitty. We must get back to the *Golden Eagle* before the fire spreads to her.'

'I can walk,' she said, but he took no notice, his arms tightening about her.

All around them the pirates and Spaniards were retreating towards the *Golden Eagle*, driven back by the fierce flames and black smoke. They scrambled across the gangplank, helping each other in the common desire to escape death. But Katherine was aware only of the strong arms holding her and the nearness of two hearts beating as one.

Then they were across, and he set her down gently on the deck, looking at her soot-streaked face in concern. 'Can you stand, Kitty?'

The tenderness in his voice brought her close to tears. She smiled tremulously. 'Yes, I'm well enough. Save your ship!'

Hades nodded, calling to Jake to take care of her as he strode away, no sign of a limp to halt his progress now. It was a race against time to disengage the two vessels before the flames could leap across the narrow channel separating them. The grappling-hooks were thrown off, and English and Spanish sailors worked together to thrust away the burning hulk of the other vessel with long poles.

Gradually the distance widened as sails were hoisted and the wind began to move the ship. A burning spar fell on the deck of the *Golden Eagle* and was pitched into the sea by willing hands. The wind blew a shower of sparks aloft, starting several small fires, but these were swiftly dealt with. Now there was sea-room between the vessels, and a triumphant cheer went up from all sides.

Katherine watched with the others as the fire suddenly swept the whole deck of the Spanish ship, licking up the masts and catching the sails. Flames were shooting out of the gun-ports, and then a terrible explosion rent the vessel. As they stared in silent horror, she upended and slipped beneath the waves. No one left on board could possibly have survived.

An odd silence hung over the crew, and some of the Spaniards were on their knees in prayer. The death of a ship was an awesome sight, and everyone knew that only luck had kept them from going down with the galleon.

Jake was at Katherine's side. 'Come below now,

matey. You'll be best in Hades' cabin. There's a chill wind, and the mist looks as if it's thickening.'

'Yes, I'll be best below.'

She let him lead her away, feeling the weariness sweep over her. She was close to tears, shaken by the knowledge that her wilfulness had brought her friends close to disaster. Hades had come for her, but in doing so he had almost lost his ship and the lives of all his crew.

When they entered the cabin, Jake lit the lanthorn; dusk was coming early on this dull winter's day, and the flame was a welcome sight.

'Here, you'd better drink this,' he said, pouring her a tot of rum from a flask on the table. 'Come on, Kit. Swallow it down.'

Katherine gulped the fiery liquid obediently. 'It was my fault,' she said. 'If you'd all been killed, it would have been because of me.'

'Nay, lass, it was bound to happen one day. Hades and the Don were old enemies. It could not end until one or the other was dead.'

She stared at him, acknowledging the truth of what he said, but still feeling her guilt. 'It's over now.' She shivered, recalling the Don's terrible death.

'Ay, it's finished at last,' Jake said with a little frown. 'Now, perhaps, Hades can put the past behind him. Try to rest, lass. It will be a while before the Cap'n is free to come below.'

Katherine bit her lip. 'Can't I help you with the wounded?'

'Not this time! Cap'n's orders. He said you were to be took care of, and I'm not the man to disobey him.' Jake grinned at her.

Katherine's head was aching, and she did not feel like arguing. 'Before you go, Jake, there's something I'd like to give you.' She felt inside the bodice of her gown and took out a small packet. 'This is the bill of sale for the *Seabird*, a merchant ship in Portsmouth harbour. I shan't be wanting her again, and I would be pleased if you and Fabius would accept her as a gift from me.'

Jake hesitated, then reached out to take the packet from her, a suspicion of tears in his eyes. 'So you'd have us turn honest merchants, matey!' He grinned at her. 'I can't speak for Fabius, but an easier time would suit me very well. I'm getting too old for this life!'

He went out then rather quickly, and Katherine knew his emotion was choking him. She smiled, glad that she had been able to do something for her friends in return for all that they had done for her.

Katherine sat in Hades' chair to wait. The minutes crawled by with terrible slowness, dragging into weary hours, and still he did not come to her. At last she got up and walked over to the bed, lying down with a sigh, her face against his pillows, inhaling the remembered scent of him. She closed her eyes, unable to fight her weariness any longer.

It was light when she woke. The sun had pierced the mist, which was almost gone. She sat up blinking, then became aware that Hades was sitting at his table, watching her with a tenderness which set her heart racing like the wind.

'You were tired, Kitty.'

'Yes. I think it may have been the blow to the back of my head when the Don seized me. I did not wake for hours, and it gave me a bad headache, but it seems to have gone now.'

A spark of anger lit Hades' topaz eyes and he stood up, coming towards her. 'If he harmed you . . .'

'No. I'm better now. Truly I am,' Katherine smiled at him, her heart pounding wildly as she saw the warmth of his look. 'He is dead, Hades. It's all over.'

'Yes, it's ended at last.'

His voice sounded so strange that Katherine stared at him, wondering at the sadness in him. 'You hated him,' she said softly. 'Long before you met me, you hated him. Why?'

He frowned, and she saw the shadows of an old grief flicker in his eyes. 'When my father was young, he visited Spain to start a business venture. There he met Don Francisco, and they became partners. Their venture was a great success, making them both wealthy men. My father then took his leave of the Don to return to England, but on the day his ship was to have sailed he was arrested as a heretic and tortured by the Inquisition.'

'So that's why the Don thought he knew you!'

'Yes.' Hades smiled oddly. 'I wanted to tell him the truth then, and slit his throat, but I knew we had walked into a trap and I dared not arouse his suspicions. So I lied, and said he would not know my father's name.'

'It was my fault that you were drawn into the trap.'

'No. I meant to trap the Don myself, but my plans misfired. I had lived for nothing but revenge for years. You see, the Don had hoped to gain my father's share of their profits himself, but my father had other friends in Spain who worked for his release. He was eventually freed and allowed to board his ship.' Hades' eyes glittered with anger. 'But not before he had learned to hate the Spanish priests who tortured him in the name of God. He sailed back to England, married, and had a son. Then a Catholic queen came to the English throne . . .'

'Go on.' Katherine watched him as he faltered. 'Please tell me everything, my love.'

He leaned over to touch her face, the coldness fading

from his eyes. 'Bloody Mary was determined that all her subjects should become Catholics—or be burned for their heresy . . .' His voice grew harsh. 'My father vowed as he was tortured by the Inquisition that he would never recant. He was arrested on suspicion of plotting against Mary, and he died at the stake. I swore to avenge his death.'

'That's why you were so angry with me when you thought I was betrothed to Don Francisco's son . . .' she gasped, seeing the lines of pain in his face.

'You told me you were the ward of Queen Mary—the woman I hated above all others. She who had my father burned to death. I vowed always to remember what she had done, and I prayed for the day when Elizabeth would be queen. The night you were brought on board my ship, I had arranged a meeting with other Protestants who were working secretly to that end. Our fear had always been that Mary might seek to harm her sister and so prevent Elizabeth's succession to the throne.'

'You believed I was a Catholic, too . . .' Katherine stared at him, suddenly understanding much that had puzzled her. 'I was the ward of the Queen, so you thought I was of her faith, until you heard me talking with Lewis.'

'Yes. If I treated you harshly, Kitty, it was because of the bitterness in me that would not let me forget the vow I had made to avenge my father's murder. For murder it was. He hated Mary, but accepted her as England's rightful queen. He was innocent of the crimes for which he died.'

'Oh, Hades!' Katherine looked up at him, her eyes filled with tears. 'You didn't treat me harshly. It doesn't matter. I love you. I have loved you from the very first night when I came on board your ship. You stared at me so fiercely, and then I saw the laughter in your eyes.' She moved closer to him, her hand trembling on his arm. 'Take me with you, Hades. Let me be your woman? Please, I beg you . . .'

His eyes glowed with golden fire, his hand tracing the white line of her throat, making her tremble with the longing to be in his arms.

'Why did you run away this time, Kitty?'

'They meant to force me to a marriage I did not want. The Queen told me that a marriage had been arranged with the Marquis of Rothmere . . .'

'And did that displease you?' There was a strange note in his voice, which puzzled her.

'How can I marry anyone when my heart belongs to you?' Katherine cried. 'Don't you understand that I would rather die than live as the wife of another man?'

'Kitty, my love.' He drew him to her, his lips caressing hers with such tenderness that she thought she would swoon. 'But I am a pirate, not fit to kneel at your feet. You are the sister of an earl, and should marry according to your rank.'

She pulled away from him, her eyes blazing with anger. 'Oh, you foolish man! How many times must I tell you I will have you or no one as my husband?'

To her amazement, Hades began to laugh, throwing back his head to roar with mirth. 'Oh, Kitty, what a trial you will be to me! Did ever a man have a woman such as you to plague him?'

Katherine stared at him, her eyes widening. 'Then you mean you will marry me?'

He caught her up in his arms, hugging her to him. 'Oh, Kitty! My wicked, wanton Kitty! Why could you not wait in patience, as befits a young lady of quality? Had you been obedient to your brother's wishes—to say nothing of Her Majesty's commands!—Lord Rothmere would have come to claim his bride at the ball last night and you need never have suffered that blow to your head. Poor Lewis was so upset when he read your note—he thought the Queen had told you . . .'

'Had told me?' Katherine stared at him, suspicion dawning in her eyes. 'You mean you are . . . Oh, you demon! You let me think you had forgotten me all this time, and you had arranged it all with Lewis . . .'

Hades grinned, bending his knee to make her an elegant bow. 'Lord Rothmere, at your service, ma'am.'

'You loathsome . . .' she exploded. 'I thought you didn't want me.'

'Not want you?' he breathed. 'You are more precious to me than my life, sweet Kitty. It is I who am not fit to worship at your feet. I meant to banish Hades to his underworld kingdom and come to you as the Marquis of Rothmere, humbly to beg you to be my wife.'

Katherine stared at him, then she began to giggle. 'You—humble, my lord? I do not believe it.' She caught her breath as his eyes took fire. 'Nor do I wish for it, my dearest Hades.'

He took her hand, a smile playing about his mouth. 'Do you think you could learn to call me Alaric?'

'Alaric?'

'It is my name.'

'It will take a little time, but I shall try . . . Alaric.'

'Thank you.' Suddenly the laughter died from his eyes, and he went down on one knee before her. 'Will you honour me by becoming my wife, Lady Katherine?'

Katherine knew that tears of happiness were sliding down her cheeks, but she did not care. 'Oh Hades—Alaric—you know I shall!' She knelt swiftly beside him, so that their eyes met. 'You know I love you. Why did you not tell me the truth before?'

He stood, drawing her up with him, to stand with his arms about her. 'I asked Lewis to keep the secret months ago when I did not know whether I would ever regain my estate. Then, when Mary died, I sought an audience with Elizabeth . . .'

'Then those emeralds were the ones you bought on the island. So that was why you wanted them so badly!'

He smiled. 'Yes. I always planned to present them to Elizabeth when she became queen. I gave them to her when I asked for her pardon for my father. She has agreed to clear his name of the charge of treason.'

'God bless Her Majesty,' Katherine said, guessing how much it meant. 'So the Queen knew who you were? Yet she did not tell me.'

'Elizabeth loves to tease,' Alaric said. 'No doubt she thought Lewis would tell you, and he believed she had told you the whole . . .'

'Instead, I flew into a temper and ran away.' Katherine gazed up at him. 'You should beat me again.'

'Never!' His lips gently touched her forehead. 'Your happiness shall be my only concern from this day forth. I shall love and cherish you so tenderly that you will forget the Hades ever existed.'

Katherine lifted her sea-green eyes to his, their depths full of mystery. 'Oh no,' she whispered, her lips curving in a wicked smile that made his heart beat wildly. 'I shall never forget him—that handsome pirate captain who stole my heart. You see, though I may be Alaric's wife, I shall always be Hades' woman . . .'

A flame glowed in Alaric's eyes as his arms closed round her and he swept her up in a passionate embrace. Carrying her to the bed, he laid her down, his lips brushing hers with the promise of all that was to come.

'And you will always be my Kitty—the saucy minx who drove me mad for months on end,' he whispered, as his mouth came down to take possession of hers. 'My beautiful, hot-tempered, adorable Kitty . . .'

KING ST.

Set Three
BOOK 10

The Wedding

The Wedding
King Street: Readers Set Three - Book 10

Text: Iris Nunn
Editor: June Lewis

Published in 2014 by Gatehouse Media Limited

ISBN: 978-1-84231-135-6

British Library Cataloguing-in-Publication Data:
A catalogue record for this book is available from the British Library

Gwen is getting married.
It all happened like this:

As you know,
Gwen goes to college.
She studies computers.
She would like a job in an office
and she needs computer skills.

Gwen has a little boy, Harry,
from her first marriage.
She goes to college part-time
and Neeta from next door
looks after Harry.

One day at college
Gwen was in her class.
The tutor had to leave the class
and Gwen was stuck.

She just did not know what to do
and she started looking round
for the teacher.

On the other side of the room
was Eric, another student.
Eric had wanted to talk to Gwen
for a long time.
She looked really nice, he thought,
but she always rushed off
after classes.

In computer classes
the students don't talk to each other.
They just look at their screens.
But today Gwen was so desperate
she called out,
"Can anyone help me?
I'm really stuck!"

This was Eric's moment.
He was off and over to the other side of the room like lightning.

"Can I help?" he said.

And that's how it all started.

They went for a coffee break together.
They went for coffee breaks together
every day.

One day Eric said,
"Can I give you a lift home?"

Gwen was very grateful
because she had two long bus rides
to get home.

Now that she had more time
Gwen said, "Can I buy you lunch?"

So they had lunch together
in the college.

One day on arriving at her house,
Gwen said,
“Would you like to come in
and meet Harry?”

Eric and Harry hit it off straight away!
Eric really liked children
and Harry liked Eric.

To cut a long story short,
Eric and Gwen finally decided
to get married.

Eric has now got himself a job.
He has a good job with the council
on their computers.

Gwen is still going to college part-time
and Harry has started nursery.

After the ceremony,
they are going to have a reception
at the King's Arms.

The ceremony is going to be
at the registry office.
Gwen's dad is giving her away.

Eric's best friend,
Colin, is the best man
and there are bridesmaids.

There is Ros from number five -
she has always wanted
to be a bridesmaid
and is thrilled to bits.

And there are the twins,
Mandy and Pam,
from number sixteen.

At the King's Arms,
Sid and Brenda are rushing around
getting everything ready.

Steve is helping with the food
and Shane is helping with the drinks.

The cake has just arrived
and on the top is a COMPUTER!

"I hope they get the joke,"
says Sid.
"People can be funny
about these things."